Rave reviews for Gerald Brandt's *The Courier*:

"*The Courier* is lean and mean as Kris's rugged ride, ripping through plot and world-building at a relentless pace, which makes its quieter and more contemplative moments all the more striking, giving us just enough time to catch our breath before Kris has to hop on her bike again and get moving. Brandt has created a darkly gripping vision of the future, and we hope to explore the strata of San Angeles in many more novels to come."
—Jeff Somers, B&N Sci-Fi and Fantasy Blog

"A stunning debut: a fast-paced cyberpunky story of a future Los Angeles with a kick-ass heroine you'll never forget. A terrific book from a distinctive new voice."
—Robert Sawyer, Hugo Award-winning author of *Quantum Night*

"A motorcycle courier is caught up in a web of corporate espionage in this gritty near-future science fiction thriller. . . . Brandt's debut offers intriguing possibilities for later books in the series." —*Publishers Weekly*

"In fine cyberpunk tradition . . . for the right reader, *The Courier* may be just what the doctor ordered."
—Winnipeg Free Press

"Gerald Brandt tells an impossible-to-put-down tale and introduces us to an exciting heroine I'd love to see more of." —University City Review

"I wasn't quite expecting everything *The Courier* delivered and I enjoyed the journey." —The Book Pushers

"*The Courier* is a fast paced science fiction thriller, with a heroine you can really root for and a world you can't wait to to learn more about." —The Heroine Bookstore

THE COURIER
A SAN ANGELES NOVEL

GERALD BRANDT

DAW BOOKS, INC.
DONALD A. WOLLHEIM, FOUNDER
375 Hudson Street, New York, NY 10014

ELIZABETH R. WOLLHEIM
SHEILA E. GILBERT
PUBLISHERS
www.dawbooks.com

First paperback printing, November 2016
1 2 3 4 5 6 7 8 9

For Marnie, Jared, and Ryan

ACKNOWLEDGMENTS

I'd like to thank: Barb Galler-Smith for showing me that Kris had to be more human. The members of my writers group, Poverty of Writers: Sherry Peters, Evan Braun and Bev Geddes for the critiques, and especially Sherry for reading almost every incarnation of this novel cover-to-cover. Karen Dudley for seeing things I missed and generally making me a better writer. I'd also like to thank Robert J. Sawyer, who never fails to help new writers. Always pay it forward. Special thanks to my editor Sheila Gilbert and all the good people at DAW, and Sara Megibow, my agent at kt literary. And finally, thank-you to my family: Marnie, Jared, and Ryan. Boys, I'm sorry, but I still have to lock myself in my office to get the next books written. You can interrupt me any time.

one

THE TIRES OF the motorcycle chattered on the broken concrete of the road, breaking the quiet electric hum of the motor. Chips popped from under the smooth rubber, ricocheting off the boarded-up windows that lined the street, leaving small white explosions where they hit the gray, weathered wood. An old woman pushing a shopping cart full of empty cans and bottles glanced back at the barrage, ducking behind her cart. I slowed down.

The bike hit a patch of fine sand and grit and I stood on the foot pegs. The stuff was always falling from the ceiling on the lower levels. My stomach took a split-second free fall as the rear tire of the bike slipped out from under me. The tire was beyond bald, showing threads in some spots. I should have replaced it months ago, but money was tight. Shifting my weight, I pulled the balance point of the machine back and rode through the slide. The tires grabbed the road again and I twisted the accelerator to get more speed.

The city rose seven levels high. My little piece of it used to be Downtown Los Angeles; now it was just a small piece of a megalopolis that stretched from San Diego to San Francisco. They named the place San Angeles, with smaller wards named after the original cities it engulfed. The roads on Level 3 were pretty bad, and they only got worse on the way down to Level 1, or as I called it, Hell. I had never been above Level 5. It was my dream to see Level 6 or 7, but access was controlled, and I knew someone like me would never be allowed in.

I found a smooth patch of asphalt, and the almost constant chatter was replaced by the wind whistling through the gaps in my cheap helmet. I stood on the pegs again as the bike hit another broken section. The smooth center of the tires slid until what was left of the knobbed edges found a tenuous grip.

Other couriers kept their bikes lean and trim, with powerful motors and sticky rubber tires. When they had deliveries below Level 4, they would weave their bikes along the street, swerving around the potholes, cracks, and other vehicles.

I didn't give a shit. My bike was old and tough and could handle the road just fine. And so could I. Ride the damn thing and get from point A to point B as fast as I could, or as fast as the crappy rear tire would let me. Get the delivery done and get on to the next one. That's where the money was—the little I got, anyway.

My day had started out like every other one. The alarm clock went off at five a.m., a piercing whine that could make small children cry. I was a pretty light sleeper, but I had found the thing in a dumpster on Level 5, and beggars can't be choosers. I crawled out of bed into the cool room. It was always cool on Level 2; that's what you get for living five levels away from the sun. The Lee family, the people who rented me my room above the fish market, never turned on the heaters at night.

Most of the stuff in my tiny room was scavenged. My bed frame was an old door raised on cinder blocks. The chair, placed by the crates I used as a table, had had a short leg when I found it. Now it had four short ones, but it was stable. The only new things I owned were my motorcycle helmet and the jacket. The helmet was a courier standard, the cheapest I could get in plain black. It had the built-in comm unit and barely serviceable enhanced night vision, along with the standard stuff.

The jacket was another story. I still hadn't paid it off. The interest the store charged me was atrocious, but it was worth it.

The jacket produced power from air. The manual said something about absorbing local electromagnetic charges and storing them in its built-in batteries. I didn't care how the thing worked, as long as it kept my comm unit charged and gave the bike a bit of extra juice when it needed it. The jacket came with a Taser. The thing was tiny enough to hide in the small of my back, and the jacket kept it fully charged. I called it a Taser, but it was really a hybrid between a stun gun and an actual Taser. If I needed to use it in close quarters, the probes wouldn't fire and I could jab it into someone. The way I always thought of using it was as a full Taser, shooting fifty thousand volts into a person from eight meters away. The secret was in how hard you pushed the trigger. In theory, if I screwed up, the jacket would help protect me. I had never needed to use it, but other couriers had, and that was a good enough reason to have one. The jacket was snug and stiff, so it didn't flap in the wind when I rode, but it was bulky enough to hide the fact I was a girl.

Some jackass switched lanes right in front of me, and I hit the brakes. On any other day, I would have been hollering through the helmet and thumbing the horn, but today had been a good one. Dispatch had kept me on Levels 4 and 5. Cleaner air, better roads, a feeling of freedom created by the higher ceilings. A nice day to be on two wheels. For the first time in weeks, I'd had enough deliveries to pay the day's rent and be able to eat more than just rice. All I had to do was get the paperwork back to Dispatch and head home.

I was ahead of schedule, despite the long run Dispatch had sent me on. It was early enough for the Lees to still have the market open, which meant I would be able to get a hot shower, get some of the road dust off.

A good day.

LEVEL 2—TUESDAY, AUGUST 9, 2140 4:30 P.M.

Quincy leaned forward, staring into the eyes of the man across from him. Gorō Kadokawa, fifth son of Takeshi Kadokawa, was already dead. He just didn't know it yet. Quincy still saw anger in those eyes, still noticed the red flush high on Gorō's cheeks.

Gorō sat in his black mesh office chair, his shirt ripped open, buttons lying like wounded soldiers on the newly finished bamboo floor. Blood trickled from the small cuts Quincy had inflicted on the man's chest. Soon it would be time to escalate the process. Quincy could tell that Gorō still had too much pride, too much misplaced faith, to believe this could end badly.

Quincy raised the knife slowly, twisting it so the overhead lights flashed in the long curved blade, making Gorō struggle against the zip ties that held his arms and legs to the chair. He whimpered through the tape covering his mouth, twisting in the chair, almost as though he was trying to push himself through the back of it. Quincy pulled a corner of the tape away.

"Please . . . please no! I'll give you anything."

The knife moved closer.

"What do you want? Anything!"

The last word came out muffled as Quincy pushed the tape back into place and lowered the knife. He smiled.

It was all a ruse, he knew that. They all begged at first. Believing if they only said what he wanted to hear, they would be free to go on with their meaningless lives. They didn't actually start telling the truth until the reality set in. Quincy could always tell when that was: when the look in their eyes changed, when they stopped staring at the knife and started looking into his eyes. That was when Quincy worked best, increasing the pain and the blood bit by bit, until they would sell their own children just to make it all stop.

Gorō wasn't close to that yet—not quite. When he was, Quincy would start asking the important questions, see whether Gorō knew what was in the package or if he was just an unfortunate bystander.

Quincy looked over Gorō's shoulder, out the window at the external ceiling less than a meter above him. He hated being on Level 2. Hated the stale, stinking air. Hated the invisible weight of the levels above him, crushing him, waiting to collapse and destroy the life he had created for himself.

He drew in a deep breath. The scent of blood, tangy and coppery, calmed him, filling him with longing, building desire in his veins. It mingled with the smell of the newly painted office walls. He liked the smell of new paint. It always reminded him of a job well done.

Quincy raised the knife.

LEVEL 3—TUESDAY, AUGUST 9, 2140 5:17 P.M.

I rolled into the depot about fifteen minutes late, still thinking of a warm shower. A cop was parked just around the corner, waiting for a courier to zip out of the parking lot going too fast. He was there every day. Everyone knew it, but he never changed his pattern. One of the joys of working for the government, I guessed. The corporations would have run a tighter ship.

The building was a squat, ugly thing behind a strip mall. With its peeling gray paint and broken windows, it looked like it was about to fall apart at any second. Someone had spray painted *The World is Dyeing* in bright red on the side. I hoped so—the uniform gray of the lower levels was starting to get to me. I pulled in beside the only other bike there, a dirty blue hand-painted machine that was even older than mine. The motorcycle's owner came bolting out the door and jumped down the three concrete stairs just as I was done plugging my bike into the outlet.

"Yo, Kris, dude." He paused. "Dudette. You don't want to go in there."

Howie was a laid back "cool guy" who seemed to drift through life without any direction. His long, frizzy hair lay on his shoulders, still twisted and creased from the braid he kept it in while working. This was the most excited I'd seen him in a long time.

"What's up, Howie?" I asked.

"Dispatch has a late delivery. Get out while you can, man, I think she's looking for you."

"Damn." I kicked the tire of my bike in frustration. "I've got a hot shower calling my name and I gotta drop off my papers. You know how Dispatch is about her paperwork."

Howie grinned. "Oh, man, good luck."

A late delivery. Fucking great. And it figures Dispatch sent me on a long haul for the last run of the day. Sometimes I thought the bitch had it in for me, and shit like this reinforced the idea. Just soften me up with a day of smooth runs, and then wham! Nail me with a late delivery that will ruin my whole fucking day. I put my bike keys into my pocket, giving the golden figure on the key chain an extra rub for good luck. I grabbed the door handle, ready to barge in and tell her no. I hesitated. Maybe if I walked in quiet I could put the paperwork on top of the pile and get out before she saw me.

I pushed on the rusted steel door just enough to slip through and closed it softly behind me. The sound of Howie's bike winding up and leaving the parking lot came through the opening before the door latched.

The office was empty, always a bad sign, but pretty much what I expected. The old chairs and couches, covered in stains and crushed potato chips, seemed to smell even worse when the place was empty. Someone had brought in a plant a few weeks ago, probably trying to brighten it up. Now its brown leafless branches stuck out of the dry, cracked soil, looking deader than the building itself.

Dispatch's desk was hidden behind a half wall that cut the room in two. She wasn't sitting at it. She was probably prowling the halls looking for the last sucker. Maybe it was a bathroom break. Maybe the delivery wasn't urgent and could wait until tomorrow. Maybe Dispatch had a heart of gold. Yeah, right. Still, there was a chance I could get out of here without being caught.

I dropped my paperwork on top of the teetering stack and tiptoed back toward the door.

"Kris, girlie. Could you wait a minute?"

The voice of Dispatch stopped me in my tracks.

Her voice always confused me. It was soft and maybe a little high-pitched and breathy. If you didn't look, you would have pictured a tall blonde, probably not natural, makeup caked onto her face, a tight skirt riding high up long legs and a bra that pushed her boobs right up under her chin. Instead what you got was Dispatch. A huge, swarthy woman, her face cratered and creased by age and, most likely, too many nights buried in a bottle. She grew a mustache better than most guys I knew, and she had a weird growth just under her chin that sprouted long, thick black hairs. Most of the time you didn't have to look at her, though. Usually her face was buried in her comm unit, or staring at one of those pulp rags that talked about three-headed babies and how Elvis, whoever the hell he was, was still alive.

I turned back to face her, feeling the dank air in the room fill my lungs. Dispatch stood in the hall, almost touching both walls with her hips. I think the walls were light gray once. Surprise!

"Kris, I got a late call. Just a quick run. Could you do it for me, sweetie?"

"Look," I said, taking a step back, "I'd love to, but I've been riding hard all day. I want to get home."

"It's just a short run, a pickup on Level 4 and a delivery on Level 2. You can take the paperwork home with you, honey, and drop it on my desk in the morning."

I just stared at her. Having Dispatch let you take the paperwork home with you was like being plucked off the street and taught how to fly a shuttle to and from the Sat Cities. Shit like that didn't happen, especially where Dispatch was concerned. I really didn't want anything to do with this. I turned partway back to the door and paused, feeling her stare on the back of my head. The bike really needed a new rear tire. The extra cash would help.

"I can drop the paperwork off tomorrow?" I asked, turning back, still not believing her.

"That's right, honey. I'll look for it on my desk in the morning when I get in."

I stared at my boots, covered in road dust, and thought about it. Level 4 wasn't too bad of a pickup, depending on where it was, and Level 2 was home as long as the drop-off wasn't at the edge of my area. Not having to come back up after the delivery was a definite bonus.

Maybe it wouldn't be such a bad run after all. Rack up another delivery and get a little more cash in my pocket. A lukewarm shower would work once I got home. I was used to them.

"The pickup client is a tipper, sweetie. I saved the trip for you."

I looked at the door, then back at her sideways. *Honey* and *sweetie* weren't her usual choice of words. Why was Dispatch being so nice? She had never been nice to me before. In fact, she was barely civil to any of the female couriers. It creeped me out, and I thought of just heading home. But I needed that tire. One day it would slip again, or blow, and I would be in serious trouble.

Dispatch took a step forward, the smile leaving her face, replaced by a look of concern. "I know you need the money, Kris. Take this one, and I'll make sure you get more good runs, until things get better." She reached out and gently touched my arm before her look changed again, to the cold, calculating one I knew. "If you can't take the delivery, I'm not sure I'll have anything for you tomorrow, girlie."

I felt heat rush up my face. That bitch. I almost said the words out loud; instead I swallowed hard, forcing them back down my throat. It looked like I wasn't being given a choice after all. This was the Dispatch I knew. I waited until my voice would sound calmer before answering. "Yeah, okay."

"Thanks, sweetie." The smile came back. Dispatch walked down the hall toward me and stopped at the desk. She stretched her huge bulk over it, reaching for the papers. "Here's the paperwork. The clients are both waiting for you, so you shouldn't have any problems."

I grabbed the forms and turned back for the door, looking at the pickup and drop-off addresses.

Fuck! The pickup was out of my area, way north. The closest up-ramp was under construction. I would have to take a detour, adding time to the ride there.

This was going to be a shitty end to my day.

LEVEL 3—TUESDAY, AUGUST 9, 2140 5:35 P.M.

I tucked the paperwork into the carryall, unplugged my bike, and checked the charge. It should be enough to get the job done. I slipped the bike into gear and rode slowly out of the parking lot. The Ambients, bolted to the ceiling at regular intervals, would be starting to dim soon, casting the streets into an early evening gloom and making it harder to see the potholes. A fine mist covered my visor and I wiped it with my hand, leaving behind a greasy smear. It must be raining on Level 7, pretty hard too, to make it mist like this down here. By the time the water got down to Level 1 it would be almost toxic from the trip.

People that worked or lived on Level 1, which used to be open air and grass and trees, had the sense to stay out of any water that managed to drip its way down there.

Rumor had it the stuff could kill you in three days if it touched your skin. I used to live in that hellhole, so I knew different. I even got desperate enough to drink it once, when I ran away from home. I had peeled the moss off an old brick wall, hoping it would act like a filter, my hands shaking from hunger and thirst, and squeezed the lifesaving fluid from it. It must have worked; I'm still here. Maybe I just got lucky. It didn't matter. I was never going back there.

I rode the ramp up from Level 3 to Level 4, turning into the Italian sector. When the corporations began building the cities up, starting in the cores of Los Angeles and San Francisco, the richer people moved up with the levels, creating new pockets of societies. Huge chunks of Chinatown moved up and further east, leaving behind empty buildings and poorer people. The same happened to the Italians. Over time the separation of levels created different types of societies. The Level 4 Italians were stuck in the past, with their gold chains and flashy tight clothes . . . something you would never see in the Level 3 Italian section.

My helmet's heads-up display started glowing red on the road ahead. More construction. What the hell was going on here? Did the corporations suddenly have so much money that they wanted to spend it all? Christ. I looked at the map and took a quick turn down a side street, skipping the detour the other traffic was being forced to take. I smiled. These were my streets. The commuters would add an extra half hour to their drive. I added only ten minutes to my trip by racing down a back alley and cutting across a business promenade between two buildings. Driving the promenade was illegal, but only if you got caught. There were hardly any cops in this neighborhood, so I figured I'd be all right. At the lower levels, there may not have been cops, but there were cameras. Maybe they thought people were more civilized, less likely to break the law up here.

As soon as I entered the business center, the flickering neon ads and animated billboards started springing up. It was worse than Chinatown. The sides of the buildings became advertisements for clothes and watches and fast food, each one fighting to get more attention than the next. They kept most of the advertising where the money was.

I pulled up to the pickup address a few minutes later. The building cut through the Level 4 floor, dropping down through the thick concrete structure. A corporation supertower. Shit! I pulled off my helmet and turned off the bike, leaned over the railing that ran around the drop-off, and stared into the level below. A steady updraft, carrying the stench of the lower level, blew through my short brown hair. The building stopped on Level 3. I could have cut half an hour off my trip by staying down there. Building security would have let me ride the elevator up to get the delivery. I had another reason to hate Dispatch. She knew the pickup was out of my area. She should have told me it was a supertower with Level 3 access. Instead, she told me specifically it was a Level 4 pickup.

I jammed my helmet back on and dialed Dispatch on the comm unit to ask what the hell was up, but killed the connection before it finished. The chance of catching her at the office was slim to none. The hag was probably at home halfway through her first bottle of cheap Canadian wine. Forcing myself to calm down, I looked up, following the walls of the supertower as they punched through the ceiling to Level 5.

With the late delivery, and pressure from Dispatch, maybe this wasn't another fake package. Almost all of them were. The corporations used us couriers to move information they didn't dare put on the Net, where it could easily be intercepted. Then they bombarded the couriers with fake packages, so it was harder to know when real ones were being delivered. It didn't matter to me, as long as I got paid—and the tip Dispatch promised.

I started the bike up again and rode over one of the walkways connecting the tower to Level 4, pulling it right up to the front door, and plugged it into an empty socket. They were there if you knew where to look. This one was hidden behind a gigantic planter full of fake greenery. They probably ripped it out and put in a huge fucking fake tree there at Christmas. Gotta get juice to the damn lights and make everyone happy and cheerful. I hated Christmas. I shook my head. I could get arrested for theft—stealing electricity—just for plugging in, but most of the time, we couriers got away with it. I pulled my lid off again and slipped my arm through the visor, walking to the door with the paperwork in my hand.

LEVEL 4—TUESDAY, AUGUST 9, 2140 6:30 P.M.

The building had five brass-framed glass doors in the front. Upset by the lost time, I strode to the first one and pulled hard. My shoulder jerked tight and I felt a small pop before my fingers slipped off the door handle. Dammit! The door was locked. The bastards were supposed to be waiting for me. I gently checked the other doors before I leaned into the glass and cupped my hands around my eyes to stop the glare from the dimming Ambients and flickering electronic billboards. The damn security desk was empty. I took a step back and sucked in a deep breath, trying to let my anger go with the expelled air. It worked about as well as my last boyfriend.

I looked for the call button. Every big building had

one . . . some way to let security know you wanted in. I found it eventually. They put it so far away from the doors that you almost couldn't see it. At Christmas, it would be behind the fucking tree.

I pushed the button, bending my thumb backward with the pressure. Five times. No one responded. What the hell? Did the big corps send their security guys home at night?

I stuffed the paperwork into my back pocket and slipped on my lid. I could at least leave a message for Dispatch. That would cover my ass in the morning when she found out the delivery wasn't made. The computers would keep a record of my call, and maybe life wouldn't be as bad as it could be if I didn't try.

Dispatch answered right away. I felt the hairs on the back of my neck stand up, and a chill ran down my spine. This day was getting stranger by the minute.

"Hey, girlie, you finished the delivery?" Dispatch's voice sounded richer over the air than it did in person, losing some of its breathiness.

"Hell no. I just got to the pickup point. Why the hell didn't you tell me it had doors on Level 3? I could have been home already."

Dispatch's voice lost some of its softness. "Don't you take that tone with me, girlie. You think you're privileged, riding that machine around all day, making runs and flirting with all the clients? Fuck you. You're the one that's supposed to know the area, not me. Do your job."

At least ten thoughts pushed to the front of my brain, each one a worse idea than the other. I bit my tongue and waited a while—it was better than mouthing off to Dispatch. That would just make life more of a shit hole than it currently was.

I took another deep breath. "Yeah, sorry. Listen, the door is locked. I can't get in."

Dispatch's voice softened again. "You wait right there, girlie, and I'll get back to you."

I heard the connection close off.

As I waited for Dispatch, I could feel a low flame burning in my gut, and it was slowly building into a roaring fire. Who the hell did the bitch think she was anyway? This was Kris time, a fucking rare commodity. Twelve hours a day on the job didn't leave much for me. My whole night was so fucked up now, I may as well just sleep in the damn street and show up to work stinking. Hell, I would too, if it wouldn't mess up my almost nonexistent tips.

"Hey, girlie."

I looked at the time on the comm unit. Ten fucking minutes to see if someone was around. I pushed a "What!" through clenched teeth.

"Stand by the front door and flash your ID at the cameras, sweetie. The door will unlock and you can get in. The elevator will only stop at your floor, so no wandering around."

"Wandering around?" My voice rose a notch, the fire beginning to show. "Why the hell would I want to wander around? I want to get home and eat and take my goddamn shower."

"Don't take the Lord's name in vain, sweetie."

Fuck that. "Just make sure there is somebody at the end of the run to take the damn package."

"Such a tone from such a girlie. I try to do you a favor, and this is how you say thank you? We'll talk about your attitude tomorrow."

I heard a hard edge in Dispatch's voice, even over the comm unit. Shit, now I'd done it. Life would be a bitch at work for the next little while. What the hell, I might as well go in all the way. "Just make sure someone is there, okay?"

"Already done, sweetie, now get your tight little ass in gear."

The connection closed again.

Tight little ass? That was a new one. What the hell was her problem? I was the one out here waiting. And why the hell was she still at the office? I'd done a few late runs before, and she was never there. I always had to slip my paperwork in the door slot as well. Everything about this delivery felt wrong, and I didn't like it.

I walked back to the door and found the camera sitting in its upside-down black bubble. I pulled out my courier ID card and held it up, angled so the camera could pick it up easy. The door clicked and I pulled it open, holding it there with my foot while I put away my ID. Something didn't like that though, and a loud beeping started coming from the security panel just inside.

⬤➤➤➤

LEVEL 4—TUESDAY, AUGUST 9, 2140 6:47 P.M.

Old techno-fusion pop music played over the tinny sounding speakers in the elevator. I had heard the song before. Back when I first started couriering, some redhaired bimbo in a business suit had walked on the elevator, looked at me, and made a decision based on what she saw—I wasn't even worth noticing. She'd started singing to this shit, a quiet little whisper that turned into a full-belted song when I ignored her. I felt like imprinting the back of the bimbo's head on the package. Instead, I'd gotten off on the next floor and walked up the stairs. Life was too short to put up with crap like that. I've hated techno-fusion ever since. And elevators.

The elevator opened on a hallway that was even worse. Sure, the music had stopped, but that really didn't help things. These corporate buildings were pretty much all the same, and they didn't get any more corporate than this place. The stale air and the background hum of electronics made me feel trapped, like I was stuck in a maze with no way out.

The short hallway ended at a reception desk, light brown with frosted glass around its back half, kept nice and clean to make a good first impression. Just behind it was what everybody called "cubeville." Rows and rows of bland, gray-carpeted walls, topped with more of the frosted glass. None of it standing more than a meter and a half tall. Even *I* could see across the entire floor, the maze laid out before me, leading to the guy standing by a door in the far wall. He was waving his hand over his head. To couriers, anyone that spent their days locked in an office was a freak, and this freak was full on, with his three-piece suit and bright red tie.

There wasn't a receptionist, it was too late in the day for that, and the freak didn't come out to meet me. What the hell? I started walking toward him, picking a path between the carpeted cubicles.

With every step, my gut clenched tighter. Each breath felt harder to take. I moved to the outside wall and the pressure fell off a bit. Doors, all of them closed, dotted the wall every three meters or so, though it seemed they skipped a door in the corner. Maybe a bigger office or a private meeting room. Most of the doors had little removable nameplates on them. I shook my head. What a life, your identity diluted down to a removable nameplate.

By the time I rounded the corner to the back wall, the freak was in full gear. His face looked flushed and beads of sweat stuck to his forehead.

"I've been waiting forever. What, did you decide to walk all the way here? And why did you take the wall? The aisles are way faster."

Aww, hell. Why did he have to be an asshole as well as a freak? I took a deep breath and held my tongue for the second time in the last few minutes. There was no point in getting reported and having Dispatch even more upset with me. All this for a few extra bucks? I should have just gone home. I put on what I hoped was my sweetest smile.

"Sorry, sir. Bad traffic this time of day. Could I have the package, and I'll need your signature here?"

He grabbed the paper from my hand and started reading all of the fine print on the back. What the hell, hadn't he ever used a courier before?

"It's a standard courier form, sir." I was still trying to be sweet.

He ignored me. As he read, I looked behind him into the cramped office. It wasn't much bigger than the cubes, but I imagined it would be nice to be able to close the door and shut out the world for a while. He even had a window, not that there was much to see. I'd gone up twelve floors, which put me just underneath Level 5, right up against the ceiling. The undersides of these things weren't made to look pretty. All I could see was concrete, I-beams, and downward facing Ambients everywhere. All of it covered in years of grime. The billboards threw their light against the rough ceiling, scattering it in every direction. Personally, I would have closed the blinds.

I never thought about it much, but this close, the ceiling didn't look like it was strong enough to hold up the other levels. But then again, they were thick enough to have three or four stories of parking and machinery in them.

The freak noticed me looking into his office. He took a step closer, I matched it with a step back of my own, and he closed the door behind him. Private little fucker. He shoved the signed paper and the package, a simple manila envelope, into my hands and stared at me.

"Thank you, sir. The package should be there in under an hour."

"If you take as long to deliver it as you did to pick it up, I'll be lucky to have it there next week."

Forget freak. This guy was a fucktard right to the core. I turned without bothering to answer, and walked along the wall back to the reception desk and elevator. Thank god it was still waiting for me. I rode it back down to the Level 4 entrance and grabbed my bike. So much for him being a tipper.

Dispatch was really a deep down bitch.

LEVEL 4—TUESDAY, AUGUST 9, 2140 7:10 P.M.

The mist had finally stopped, but water still dripped from the ceiling, leaving a greasy wet layer on the ground. The roads would be slick for a while, until the sweepers could come in and clean things up a bit. If they came at all. Any kind of service was always intermittent, especially when you got down to the lower levels. I accelerated down the deserted streets of the Level 4 business section. Most of the freaks had gone home, and those still left behind were probably in for a long night of overtime.

With the lack of traffic, the ride down to the Level 3 ramps was almost pleasant. No shitheads on their way home to swerve in front of me, hoping to beat the courier to the gap between the slower cars. Level 3 would be busier, but mainly with foot traffic, which meant more cops hanging around. I'd have to ride slow. Level 3 was less of a Freak Central and more a small shops kind of place. People would be out doing whatever it was they did with all their cash, and there was always scum looking to prey on that. The ride to the Level 2 down-ramp wasn't too long, either.

When they engineered the levels, they scattered the various up- and down-ramps all across the city, adding more as Los Angeles grew and eventually connected with the southward growth of San Francisco. I was told Fresno and San Diego used to be separate cities. They were all just subdivisions now.

The engineers didn't want to keep the ramps all in one place—something about congestion and pollution and death tolls. To me it was a major pain in the ass if I had to move between levels quickly. I slowed down as I rode past one of the huge Transfer Elevators used to move people and emergency vehicles between levels. I twisted the throttle and kept on going. If I used it with the bike, I'd lose my courier license, and have a hefty fine I wouldn't be able to pay. No unofficial vehicles allowed.

I made it through Level 3 pretty quick and hit the Level 2 down-ramp. I was just coming around the last curve when the shitheads on their skateboards showed up. Dammit, things were just not going right. There must have been at least twenty of them, dressed in drab gray-and-green body armor that may have actually looked good at one time. The boarders walked in a staggered line across the entire ramp, their boards swinging from their hands in time with their steps.

Boarders would usually take a ramp and shut it down completely, forcing traffic to find another route or wait until they moved on. Eventually the cops would show up and move them out, making a couple of arrests if they could catch them. Cameras had been placed on every ramp, but it didn't take too long before the repair crews stopped coming out to fix them. This group was on their way up, walking to get the free ride back down.

As soon as they saw me, I cut to the edge where the

group was thinner; there weren't enough of them to stretch across the entire ramp. They preferred to walk right in the middle where they could stop all the bigger traffic.

Boarders and couriers had an unspoken rule, or maybe it was just boarders and motorcyclists. We never reported when they showed up, and in turn they would let us through. A group split off and started walking to the edge I was riding ... I wasn't sure it was going to work this time. Hell, no couriers worked this late at night. They probably thought I was out for a pleasure cruise. Right. On Level 2. Boarders weren't too smart.

By the time I got close, half the group had swarmed to the wall I was following. Like most of the lower-level ramps, the walls here had crumbled, and the loose dust and gravel mixed with the rainwater created a slippery mess. The bike lost traction and I pulled it back in line.

I got about three meters from them before I cranked on the throttle. I leaned left, aiming the bike for the gap left by the boarders that had moved over to block me. The back end of the bike slipped out on me again and I slammed my foot to the ground to keep it balanced. The knobs on the tires grabbed in the loose gravel, shooting the bike toward the opening.

One of the boarders swung for my head with his skateboard. I ducked and leaned away from him, holding the bike upright. The skateboard missed me by a couple of centimeters. Too close. I twisted the throttle more and forced the bike into a quick slide. The rear tire jerked back into line from the impact against the boarder's legs, a good solid hit, and I raced past the group. The boarder would be all right. The bastards wore so much body armor, I doubted the idiot had gotten more than a light bruising.

Too bad.

LEVEL 2—TUESDAY, AUGUST 9, 2140 7:55 P.M.

The building on Level 2 looked pretty much like all the others. A grimy gray block. It went up five stories, connecting directly to the ceiling above it. Its only distinctive feature was a yellow neon sign, still bright and clean as though it had been installed yesterday: Innotek, with some sort of swooshy thing under the name and a shuttle flying up and away. It looked like the swoosh was supposed to be the shuttle's exhaust. I could see someone in a uniform standing just inside the door as I rode up to the building. Security. At least something was going right.

The bullshit client and the close call with the boarders had left me with a hollow feeling in the pit of my stomach, like I had lost control of the bike and was just waiting for the bone-jarring impact. Feeling on edge, I rode up on the sidewalk and parked the bike parallel to the building just outside of the light coming from the front doors. I locked the bike up and walked back into the light, holding up my ID and the package.

The security guard took one look at me and grinned, showing a perfect set of white teeth. Some jerk that liked to think he could get the young girls. He let me in and radioed up to the office. His uniform looked like it had just come out of the wrapper, crease lines and all. It seemed Innotek was the new kid on the block, trying to look good for the fuckers on Level 4. He put his hand low on my back, pushing me to the elevator. I shuddered and walked faster.

The elevators were all Level 2: old and creaking, feeling like they were going to collapse and kill anyone inside. Man-made coffins. I really hated small, enclosed spaces. The thing finally stopped on the fifth floor and the old doors rattled open.

The hallway smelled of new paint with some sort of earthy metallic undertone. The smell clung to the back of my throat and I felt my gut clench. I stepped off the elevator and listened to the door close behind me, followed by the rattle of it returning to the first floor.

I looked at the package. Room 540. The arrows on the wall told me to turn left. I passed the exit leading to the stairs and turned the corner; 530, 532 . . . glued-on numbers on closed doors. The metallic smell got stronger. I raised my hand to my nose. What the hell were these guys working on anyway? Whatever it was, they should invest in some air fresheners. 540 was next. I shoved the package into my lid and slipped my arm through the visor, freeing my hands for the paperwork.

The door was open a crack, so I pushed it the rest of the way and stepped over the threshold, pulling out the paperwork for the signature. The smell hit me full force, sweet and coppery, grabbing at the back of my throat with a million tiny claws. I froze midstride, rooted to the floor as my brain tried to process what my eyes were seeing. The image burned into my retinas.

There was a man in a suit, or it looked like a suit anyway, laying on the floor only a couple of steps away. He had been split open from his groin to the base of his throat, and everything that should have been inside of him was on the ground. Standing by the suit was another man in plastic painter coveralls. His arms and chest were covered in blood, and strands of it still dripped off him into a puddle on the floor. He held a knife in his hand, long and curved with a serrated edge on the inside. It looked eager to cut again.

I stopped breathing.

He looked up, staring at my face with dark, bright eyes. He stepped over the body toward me.

I stumbled backward into the hallway. Some part of my brain still worked, telling me to put something between us. I reached for the office door and grabbed it. My fingers almost caught as it slammed shut. I ran down the hall. Back toward the elevator. I pressed the button and heard the creaking start below me. Fuck, the elevator had gone back down.

Stairs. I had passed stairs. I scurried back to the door and slammed full speed into the bar. The door flew open. The damn thing nearly smacked me in the face when the compressor arm stopped the door from slamming into the wall. I stumbled down the stairs, taking four or five at a time, grabbing onto the handrail to swing around the corners. Snatching the first floor door handle at full speed, I yanked it open, ignoring the feeling of my shoulder popping again.

Security was still in the same place, standing by the front doors as though his life depended on it. Maybe it did. The image of the suit five floors above crept back into my mind. Security turned his back on the front doors and walked toward me, a concerned look on his face.

I had trouble catching my breath, gasping out the words.

"The ... guy ... the guy on ... the fifth floor ..." I couldn't get the words out fast enough. "Dead ... killed by ..."

The guard reached out and grabbed me, spinning me around and slamming me face first against the wall. He moved in close, almost wrapping his body around mine.

"So, you met Quincy, eh? I'm surprised you got away, he's usually much better than that."

He spun me around again, pinning me back with a

forearm against my throat, looking straight at me. I clawed at his arm, still fighting to get my breath back. His other hand reached under my jacket, groping.

He leaned close and whispered in my ear. "We got a few minutes before you can meet him again."

Memories washed over me: *the dirty white undershirt, the smell of alcohol and pizza, the tearing sound my shirt made when he ripped it off me.*

My stomach heaved, pushing bile into my throat. I swallowed, the acid burning on its way back down. Anger and shame took over from the fear. I wasn't some damn thirteen-year-old girl anymore. I jerked my knee up and found the sweet spot, feeling his balls crush under the force.

His breath hissed out, and his eyes widened in pain. He fell back. I was running for the front door before he had even fallen to the ground.

My hand shook as I thumbed the lock on the bike. My vision blurred. I wiped my eyes with the sleeve of my jacket and jumped on, my arm still stuck through the lid's visor with the package jammed in it. I couldn't suck in a full breath. The keys fell from my hand, the gold figurine on the chain glinting in the light from the building's sign as it bounced on the sidewalk. I lean over and swooped them up, jamming the key into the ignition. In my mirror I saw Quincy storm through the door. I gunned it, squealing the tire as I left the sidewalk and turned onto the street. He was holding something in his hand, pointing it at me. A gun? I swerved across the road and turned the corner.

TWO

D EVON MCBRIDE REMEMBERED the day, over a decade ago, when they moved him into this bland office between Levels 6 and 7. There were no windows, just a CFL floor lamp and a small LED light on his desk. Two of the walls were lined with bookcases, each filled to maximum capacity, the shelves bowed under the weight of books and file folders, looking as though they would collapse at any minute.

Most of the books had titles like *Cryptographic Systems* and *High Speed Wired and Wireless Communication Protocols*. Books were old-fashioned now, but to him they added a comforting smell to the room.

A large desk sat in the corner opposite the bookshelves. On the corner of the desk itself stood two wide flat-panel displays, each as thin as a sheet of glass. Beside the screens was Devon's pride and joy, a ten-centimeter glossy black cube with a single blue light on the front. The cube contained more computing power than some of the smaller terrestrial corporations had at their disposal.

The cube was obviously the most expensive item in the room, and the only one without a thin layer of dust on it. A single piece of comfort wedged itself between the left side of the desk and one wall of bookshelves: an old chair made out of curved plastic that rocked a bit when you sat in it, covered in books.

People like Devon were the reason couriers still existed. Just about every piece of information that went over the Net eventually went through his cube. Disparate hardware and software components tapped into the Net, collecting and resending the data they monitored. Occasionally, some of the components would be discovered, and a small portion of traffic would be lost for a period of time. If they were lucky, they already had a redundant system in place, and the data flow would continue on as normal. His little black box would flag the compromised device as lost, and enter a ticket for replacement.

Devon liked redundant systems. All data was important data, and once lost it was almost impossible to find.

The displays on his desk gave off a faint glow in the office's dim light, washing Devon's pasty face in an unhealthy blue shimmer. The right display showed columns of data, automatically sorted by his system into order of importance. The algorithm that sorted the data was his baby, the result of years of tweaking code and watching information flow across his screens. His algorithms were so tight that half the data was sorted before the decryption engines had completed their jobs. The left display varied with whatever he was working on. Right now, it showed lines of undecipherable code in multiple windows.

Devon flicked his ponytail across his chin, a habit he had unconsciously formed when he was in deep concentration mode. He was working late today. The Massachusetts Institute of Technology had discovered a flaw in the latest rolling 8192-bit Kolinski encryption algorithms, and he wanted to be sure his systems were able to exploit it.

Beside him on the table was a small red and white checked tablecloth topped by a bowl of split pea soup and an egg salad sandwich, both made and packed by his mom for dinner. The soup had gone cold and a crinkled green skin had formed on top. Devon sat hunched over his keyboard, his long legs stretched out under the desk, typing at a furious pace.

Movement and a change of colors on the right display drew him up from his deep concentration. The data in the table had shifted. Normally, the first couple of rows were fairly stationary, holding a few items of interest specified by the assistant director, stuff like corporate Black Ops team movements or the amount of activity from specific data centers. Of course, there were always a couple of extra items placed in there by Devon himself, just a little something to help him make better investment decisions. But now the rows were different. The computer had automatically inserted a new item and was slowly sorting it to the top of the list.

Devon touched the screen and flicked the new item to the left display. It ballooned into a full-size window, obscuring the latest code modifications he'd been working on, and started to fill with more detailed data. Displayed in red were the four items that had caught the computer's attention.

1. A SoCal corporate hand scanner had just been activated inside a new Innotek office.

2. The last time that scanner had been used, it had been in the hands of a SoCal Black Ops agent.

3. The scanner, according to the accelerometers and GPS info, was pointing away from the building.

4. The data being read belonged to a courier, long after normal business hours.

New digs being scanned by the competition was to be expected, nothing there to flag. What was interesting was that the scanner was Black Ops, and it was aiming away from the new office space, though that needed to be taken with a grain of salt. The GPS repeaters on Level 2 and below were notoriously flaky. It still wasn't a standard scan.

Why would a Black Ops guy make the effort to get into a competitor's closed office building and then scan something outside of it? The fact that a courier was being scanned meant that SoCal figured this one was carrying valid info, something ninety-nine percent of them didn't, and whatever was being carried was too important to send over the Net. The data was flagged at 7:58 p.m., late for a courier to be running. Four minor points the cube thought added up to something weird going on.

Devon touched the data line about the courier. Another window popped open and displayed a snapshot. The status indicator showed the system was still working on obtaining the courier's information. That was always a problem with redundant and looped-back data paths all coming from places that didn't want to release their data . . . not all the information arrived at the same time.

The picture of the courier showed him racing away. It looked like a small kid on a big bike. The courier's helmet was still on his arm, which seemed strange. Devon zoomed in on the helmet. It was an old model, definitely well used, but the cube told him it had built-in access to the Net for road and traffic conditions, as well as communication and minimal night vision enhancement. Too bad he wasn't wearing it; the computer would have been able to backtrack the data feed and find the courier's current location.

Devon looked closer. Inside the helmet was a standard letter-sized envelope. It didn't look too thick, but then again, who said it had to be holding paper? The envelope itself was upside down, obscuring the sender's and receiver's addresses. He moved the zoom to the courier. No chance of an ID from there, all the camera got was the back of the courier's head. The bike plates were completely covered by the sand and dust being thrown up by the rear tire. He knew the cube was already processing the image to try and clear it up.

Devon tagged the information and sent it to the director. Not that he'd be there right now anyway, not this late at night.

With his concentration broken, Devon decided to call it a night. The computer picked a random exit and assigned him an entrance for the morning. Devon saved his work, packed up his cold supper, and stood, stretching the kinks from his joints. The computer noticed his departure and locked the door behind him. It wouldn't open again until his thermal and other signatures combined to create the key.

LEVEL 2—TUESDAY, AUGUST 9, 2140 8:20 P.M.

I raced to the next corner, barely slowing down to take the sweeping turn. The lean on the bike was almost to the point where the foot pegs were scraping on the ground. For the first time, I swore at my choice of knobby-edged tires as they slowly lost their grip on the concrete and started sliding out from under me. I finished the corner and pulled the bike back upright before the skid became uncontrollable. The bike lifted its front wheel off the ground in response to the harsh twist I gave the accelerator.

How could I have missed the obvious signs? Since when did a goddamn security guard, especially on Level 2, have a clean and pressed uniform to wear? The guys guarding most of the front doors were just hired fucking help. No way they would spend a chunk of their paycheck on shit like that. Were there more of them outside the building? Were they watching me now? My heart started pounding harder. Each shadow became a hidden person, a hand reaching out to grab me. As I sped down the street, the Ambients dimmed to their nighttime levels, and the shadows deepened to murky black pools of fear.

I let up on the throttle and took another corner at a slightly more controllable speed. The thing to do now was to get as far away as fast as possible, but not so fast that they could tell where I was just by the surprised look on people's faces. I decided on one more high-speed turn before forcing myself to slow down to the speed limit, but I still took as many corners and double-backs as I could to find out if anyone was following me.

What I really wanted to do was pull over and put on

my helmet. Then I'd be able to ride with no lights and monitor some of the emergency frequencies to see if these guys had the cops on their side or not. Everything was so corrupted by the corporations, you just never knew. But I was still scared, and there was no way I was stopping just yet. Not until I had more distance between me and the bloody corpse.

After twenty more minutes of riding and transferring from street to street, doubling back and getting to the same spot by a different route, I felt the noose around my neck start to loosen a little. No way someone could have followed me through all of that, not even another courier, and we knew our streets. I took a deep, shaky breath and pulled the bike into a crowded 24-hour Super Store parking lot, turning off the motor, watching and waiting for a few minutes longer before the noose disappeared.

The parking lot had its own lamps, and even with the dimmed Ambients, it was bathed in a glory of light. I tossed around the idea of hiding down a side street or back alley, safe in the shadows, but something told me to stay where the light and the people were. The place wasn't so packed I wouldn't be able to see anyone approaching, but it felt public enough that you would have to feel pretty sure about yourself to attack someone here.

I sat and watched for about five minutes before taking the package out of the helmet and stashing it in my jacket. I put the lid on and dropped the visor, pulling up the artificially enhanced traffic flow. I moved off the standard courier band and started to monitor the police frequency. The police band was borderline illegal, but I didn't know of a courier without it. All of it, the traffic, the people, the comm band, was the same standard shit. No news about a speeding motorcycle, no news about a murder in the district I had just tried to deliver to. Nothing to differentiate this night from any other.

It made me feel uneasy again. I fired up the bike, watching the battery levels stabilize. I was just about out. It was time to get home. Normally the bike lasted the entire day, as long as I plugged in at some customer sites, and it was always fully charged by morning. Today had been extra long, and I'd used a fair amount of power getting away from the last delivery.

I eased the bike back into traffic and began the slow ride home. I went on autopilot as I navigated the traffic with the help of the visor, and began to go over the events that just occurred.

The security guard brought back memories I thought I had put away forever.

LEVEL 1 & 2—THREE YEARS AGO

Life was hard after Mom and Dad died. They were coming back home after work later than usual, following the path of least resistance to our little apartment on the edge of Chinatown. The police said they got mugged by a street gang looking for cash or drugs. Dad tried to be the hero, protecting Mom as best he could. They were both beaten for his efforts, until there was nothing left to hit. The cops came and took me from my home that night. A week before Christmas.

I was thirteen.

I ride past the old apartment a lot, but I never look at it, never stop. As the cops dragged me out, I grabbed for something, anything, that was theirs. Something to help me remember them. I got Mom's favorite ornament from the Christmas tree by the front door. A real tree they grew in a pot, reusing it every year. The ornament I grabbed was one she got from her mom, passed down from mother to daughter for generations. It was a solid figurine, arms clasped to its chest, holding what looked like a sword, painted entirely gold. Mom called him Oscar, though no one could remember why. I just grabbed for what I could, and got that. I didn't consider myself lucky.

It took them a few days to find my aunt on my dad's side, and a few more after that before Auntie and Uncle agreed to take me in. I spent most of the time crying, thrown into a halfway house, huddled in the bottom bunk of a bed that stank like unwashed bodies. When my Auntie picked me up and saw my puffy, bloodshot eyes, she told me the time to cry was over. They took me to their Level 1 apartment and stuck me in a tiny back room, expecting me to get to and from my new school on my own. I'd never been to Level 1 before, and I wished I was anywhere else. Auntie and Uncle worked at the sewage treatment plant. It seemed everyone on Level 1 worked at some treatment plant or another, making things better for the levels above them. Auntie worked the day shift and Uncle worked evenings. I think being apart so much was the only thing that kept their marriage together.

I cried some the first week there, and got a smack in the head for it. I learned then to keep it all inside.

I was too young to work legally, but I managed to bring in some cash by cleaning rooms at the old folks' home down the street. It was a place full of cranky old women who bitched and complained about everything and men who leered at me every time I bent over to pick something off the floor. The smell of old people still makes me sick to my stomach. I kept as much of the money as I could, hiding it from my aunt.

Uncle Stan was strange. He was tall and thin, and all his bones stuck out at weird angles, making him look like a broken mannequin that had been glued back together by a small child. He always had a bottle in front of him, when he wasn't sleeping or working. When he got drunk, he got mean, and I quickly learned to stay out of his way.

It started happening just before my fourteenth birthday.

The first time, he accidentally walked in on me while I was taking a bath. He apologized really quick and left, but I saw him take a furtive look at me in the mirror before closing the door. I caught him looking a lot more after that, but never when my aunt was home.

The second time was in the bathroom again. The door didn't have a lock on it, and I started making sure to be in there only when Auntie was home. She went out for groceries, and he walked right in on me, his eyes red and bloodshot from too much booze. He just stood there and stared. I remember trying to cover myself up, reaching for a towel to pull over me. Then he just turned and left, went into his bedroom and closed the door. I got up out of the tub and closed the bathroom door before drying off and getting dressed. When Auntie got home, I got in trouble for the wet bathroom floor.

After that, he got braver. He would help me with my homework, always managing to touch me when he did, his thigh on my shoulder, his arm on the front of my shirt when he pointed stuff out to me. I tried to talk to Auntie about it, tried to convince her what Uncle Stan was doing, how he made me feel when she wasn't home. But she just called me a slut and pushed me out of the room.

The next time he did something, it was a cold and dark Saturday. The Ambients had failed that morning, and the work crews hadn't arrived to fix them up yet. Uncle Stan cracked open his bottle about five minutes after Auntie left. I stayed in my room pretty much all the time now, the homework I used to do at the kitchen table spread out on my bed instead.

He just walked right into my bedroom, not bothering to knock on the door. I sat up, the pen still gripped in my hand. He took the pen away from me and shoved my hand into his pants. I just sat there, scared and confused. I was fourteen, I knew what was in my hand, knew what was happening. I felt the fear creep up my spine and settle in the back of my brain, cold and hard like the steel fence around the schoolyard. I remember the strong reek of alcohol, and my homework had been corporate history— the First Corporate War in 2074, big corporations fighting amongst themselves to control more of the world. It's strange how memories associate themselves with events.

When he was done, he pushed my hand away and zipped up his pants. His words were slurred almost beyond recognition, but the threat was as clear as could be. He stumbled from my room, leaving me to throw away the destroyed homework and to start again.

I took the memories and locked them away with the tears.

Two months later, I ran away. I waited until Uncle Stan was passed out on the couch, packed all the clothes I could fit into my school bag, and walked out the door, more scared than I'd ever been. Before I left, I wrote a note to Auntie and hid it in the box of pads in the medicine cabinet. Uncle Stan would never go anywhere near them. Then I found every bottle in the apartment and poured them down the drain.

Getting Uncle Stan's wallet was the scariest part, but it gave me a bit of a head start once I was out of there. I'd grabbed the sharpest knife in the kitchen and held it while my other hand reached into his pocket. He was so drunk, he never even noticed.

I hadn't been back since.

Being fourteen and alone on Level 1 wasn't safe, but I was scared the police on Level 2 would find me and take me back to him, so I stayed. I spent the first few nights hiding under piles of rubble and garbage, shivering from either the cold or fear, when the gangs got too close to me. When the money I'd earned and stole ran out, I scavenged for food, eventually resorting to licking out whatever was left in the bottom of empty cans I found, when the hunger took control of who I was.

By the time I found my hole, I was ready to do almost anything to eat. I'd crawled into a depression in the debris of a collapsed building, part of me wanting to hide for the night, part of me looking for a place to die.

Under the trash at the bottom was a deep hole. I squirmed into it. The hole turned into a tunnel so tight I wasn't sure I would have fit if I'd had any food in me. It eventually opened up, dropping me into the subbasement of the collapsed building. I don't know how long I crawled through the blackness; I don't know what kept me going, or how many times I woke up, pulling myself from the edge of insanity. I'd like to think my mom and dad helped guide me to the storage lockers. Some of the doors had been busted open by the force of the collapsing building. Inside, I found bottled water and tins of fish in oil. I ate and drank until I threw up before passing out.

I'd found a place where I could survive.

LEVEL 2—TUESDAY, AUGUST 9, 2140 8:20 P.M.

"What do you mean, got away?"

Quincy pulled the comm unit away from his ear and sighed. Sure, Jeremy was his boss, but sometimes he didn't seem too smart. "I scanned her and the bike." He already knew who the courier was, but past experience had taught him to never give away all his secrets.

"Send me the information," Jeremy said.

"Already on its way."

"Good. Gather a team and get ready for my call. I want that package back."

"Yes, sir."

Quincy closed the connection and watched the corner the courier had disappeared around, a small smile on his face, before turning back toward the Innotek building.

Paul still lay on the floor, slowly rocking back and forth with his hands on his crotch. It looked like he was breathing again, so he'd probably be all right. Too bad. The asshole screwed up, and should pay for it. He walked into the building and lifted Paul to his feet.

"You let her get away."

Paul's breath still came in short gasps. "Me? You're the idiot that let her get into the stairwell."

Quincy let go of Paul, dropping him back down to the floor. It was true; he had given her the opportunity to get away, hoping for the added thrill of the chase. He figured he'd corner her by the elevator, but she was faster than he thought she would be.

No matter. It was Paul's job to stop anyone from entering or leaving the building. And Paul fucked up.

He looked down at Paul and smiled again, placing his heel on Paul's outstretched fingers. "If you ever talk to me like that again, you'll join our friend upstairs." He twisted his heel, feeling the knuckles pop like ripe grapes. He could almost hear the sharp crunching of bones through Paul's screams.

Quincy stepped back, still looking down at Paul. "Take care of your hand while I get a team together.

We're going after her. We've got her ID number, we'll be able to track her. It's only a matter of time."

LEVEL 2—TUESDAY, AUGUST 9, 2140 9:00 P.M.

The distant flickering neon glow of Chinatown, a pool of multicolored light in the Ambient-induced night, pulled me from my memories. The lights shone bright enough to reflect off the coarse Level 2 ceiling, bringing a sense of normality back to me, the feeling of being home and the world being right.

Well, as right as it had ever been.

I pulled my bike over just on the edge of the neon stream. I opened my visor and took a deep breath. The familiar sounds and smells of Chinatown washed over me in a warm wave, shutting the memories, both old and new, back in the locked box. Back to where I could at least pretend things were normal. My breathing slowed and I edged the bike back into traffic. Level 2 Chinatown. Home. I'd moved here as soon as I could scrape up enough cash, back to the neighborhood I'd lived in with my parents.

The markets were beginning to shut down around me for the night. Owners hosed down the sidewalk in front of their businesses, using too much water, pushing the day's debris into the sewer system, and from there to the treatment plants on Level 1. The neon never quit, but the flow of people moving from point A to point B crept deeper into their known world, away from potential outsiders. Chinatown closed down from the outside in.

I snapped the visor back down, shutting out Chinatown. Shit. With all the crap I had been through tonight, I forgot to contact Dispatch about the package. Hell, no one would be there, but the computers would log my attempt. That, combined with a bit of luck, and I might not get docked a couple days of pay. Taking packages home was breaking one of the cardinal rules. I connected to the Net and sent off a message to Dispatch telling her there was no one at the delivery site to accept the package, and I wasn't riding all the way back to a locked building to try to drop the thing off either. I would leave the package on Dispatch's desk in the morning, and another courier could deliver it.

I didn't mention the gutted man or the too-well-dressed security guard, the amount of blood, or how the man's insides glistened and steamed on the floor. None of that needed to be said. If someone found out I was there, they might try to get me to testify or something, and that was getting way too involved. The thought of the tortured man having a family entered my head. Was his wife keeping his supper warm? Did he have kids waiting to be tucked into bed? It didn't matter ... I couldn't let it. Corporate killings were nasty stuff. And they never seemed to end well for the witnesses. I was suddenly glad I didn't see a cop while I was racing away.

The bike's motor cut out. Damn. The battery couldn't last the ten more blocks till home? One more thing to mess up my night. I glanced around, feeling helpless without the ability to take off at any time. I noticed my hands still shook as I unzipped the charge cord from my jacket and plugged it into the bike. A few minutes later, the bike had just under one quarter charge and the jacket was empty. I pulled away from the curb as soon as the cord was packed away.

My stomach grumbled as I idled the bike down the street, looking for an opening in the foot traffic so I could pull it up onto the sidewalk. I didn't think I was hungry. The thought of food actually made me feel nauseous, but I hadn't had anything since breakfast—I glanced at the time on my visor—over twelve hours ago. I knew I had to eat something before my body shut down. I didn't have anything at home, so ordering out it was. It would bite into the budget, but what the hell.

The chance of getting a shower tonight had gone completely out the window. Rule number one for the Lees was "no running water after nine o'clock." It was their way of dealing with the water shortages. Maybe trying to make up for the excess they used on the fish.

The people separated for a second, and I pulled in, parking my bike as close to the big window as possible. I always liked to keep an eye on it. Then I locked the bike and walked around the corner and into my favorite delivery joint, Northern Dragon Chinese Cuisine. The place was a hole in the wall. One table with a couple of plastic chairs, a short counter, and plenty of woks on the stoves behind it. The sign outside had been broken for years; if you came here, it was because you already knew it existed. I liked it because the owner, Kai, refused to use MSG. The crap gave me migraines. Kai had known my parents before they died, but we never talked about that.

I paused just outside the door, rubbing my shoulder under the jacket, trying to put a happier look on my face. The shoulder didn't feel too damaged, nothing a bit of rest wouldn't heal. I pulled the door open with my left arm. "Hey, Kai, how's the night going?" I thought I sounded pretty good. Normal, at least.

The old man behind the counter looked up, a sudden smile making the crow's feet around his eyes deepen into crevasses.

"Kris. Long time no, eh? You don't come in here much anymore. Old Kai thought you had found another place to eat."

I put my helmet on the counter and grinned, no longer trying to fake it. The old man always cheered me up. He was at least a tenth-generation local and still had an accent. His mannerisms and dress all spoke of the old country. Where he learned how to do that was anyone's guess . . . maybe he actually went back for a visit one time. More likely, he watched one too many old kung fu movies. Level 2 people didn't have the money to travel.

"You know I wouldn't go anywhere else. You've got the best ginger chicken this side of Level 7."

"You know I do! Now, what can old Kai get for you?"

"Whatever is hot and ready. I'm tired and I just want to go to bed."

Kai's face lost its smile and he leaned in close. "You work too hard. You need to learn to relax and go out once in a while. My grandson is about your age. You two should go out on a date."

"I'm already seeing someone." The lie felt wrong when I said it to him. I'd had boyfriends, of course. The last one got me into being a courier, even giving me my first bike. I replaced the bike at the same time I dumped him.

"Better than my grandson? I don't think so. You come here tomorrow at supper and take a look at him. You'll like what you see, I promise."

A small chuckle bubbled from my chest. "I might just do that."

"Good." The smile came back. "Now, you sit and I bring out your food."

"I don't really have—"

"No excuses! You sit and relax and eat a good meal." He gave me a gentle push to the table.

What the hell. There was nothing much to do at home anyway, except sleep. Last time Kai had insisted I stay, he had joined me at the table. The food and the company had combined to make a memorable evening. I sat down and picked up a pen lying on the table, twirling it between my fingers as I waited. The sound of something hitting hot oil came from over the counter and my mouth started watering.

Kai's talk of boyfriends made me think of Jake. He was the last in a string of bad guys. Older guys. Back when I thought I couldn't get by without someone, a man, to help me. In some ways, he was the worst. In others, the best. When he wasn't in a drug-induced rage, his guilt came through. He taught me how to ride, and when I turned sixteen, gave me a motorcycle and walked me into Internuncio. Dispatch gave me a job that day, delivering crap until I passed my security check. When I found out the bike was stolen, I got rid of it as fast as I could, selling it for enough money to pay for my current one. My current bike was older, but solid and legal.

Kai brought over plates of food, and we both dug in. By the time I left, with extra food in a takeaway container and a promise to not stay away so long next time, my mood had lifted. The night air had cooled, a byproduct of the Ambients being turned down. I shivered in the sudden change of temperature and zipped my jacket up right to my neck. Kai's place was always warm. The package, still shoved down the front of my jacket, crinkled as I walked to my bike.

I unlocked the bike and started the motor. The ride home was short. The pedestrian traffic had slowed down, and I made a clean merge onto the street. Most of the bums and druggies had already found their little cubbyholes for the night, and those that weren't able to just lay on the sidewalk in front of the local businesses. A young boy was just settling down for the night, pulling garbage over his legs to keep warm. I stopped and gave him my leftovers before continuing home.

I pulled the bike up to the Lee Fish Market, just outside the alley the trucks used to deliver fish, and chained it up for the night against the steel barriers guarding the front windows and doors. The bike's own locking mechanism was great for quick stops to complete deliveries, but for overnight, nothing beat a titanium and nanotube composite chain and lock. I plugged it into the socket hidden below the window ledge, the only one that actually worked. A small concession from the Lees.

The food in my stomach was making me sleepy, and I rubbed my eyes before slipping the helmet over my arm. I walked to the side service entrance in the alley, thinking of my warm bed. The sound of tires chirping on the street made me stop and look over my shoulder. A white van pulled up and stopped across from the Fish Market entrance.

LEVEL 2—TUESDAY, AUGUST 9, 2140 11:00 P.M.

Two men vaulted out of the van and ran toward the closed front doors of the Fish Market. I ducked into the darker shadows near the wall, breathing hard against the cold, wet concrete. Even the persistent neon glow of Chinatown didn't reach here. They hadn't seen me, they hadn't seen me, they . . . I repeated the words, a constant litany trying to convince myself, trying to make them true. I recognized one of the men as the butcher from the delivery site.

I felt my hands start shaking again, and the food in my gut had turned into rock. It was a face I wasn't ever going to forget. His complexion was lighter than I remembered, and he had cleaned off the spattered blood, but the narrow face matched, with its well-groomed mustache, the nose that looked like it had been broken once too often. And the eyes. Dark as Level 1 during a blackout. They glittered with an intensity that scared the bejesus out of me. I could still feel them boring into me.

His name popped into my head—Quincy.

I crept backward through the shadows to the side entrance.

Christ, once they found the front door locked, they were bound to try and come around the back way. There weren't too many places to hide. Two soft voices came from just around the corner.

"Hey, let's see that image. This looks like her bike. She's here."

"You head down that way, I'll wait here and check if the other guys have seen her."

I crouched lower in the shadows and slid behind two green dumpsters used to hold the Fish Market's cast off garbage. A huge rat ran between my feet into the alley, dragging its fleshy tail through years of built up fish guts, scales, and oil, scared by the intruder into its domain.

I understood it.

The dumpsters were standard issue refuse containers, pretty much like any others you find around the city. Their huge metal lids squealed in anger every time they were opened or closed. I moved deeper behind the bins until I came to the gap between two of them. I slid between the bins, jumping to catch the top edge, and maneuvered my feet onto a small ledge. Another rat scurried out from under the dumpster.

Light flashed into the alley, moving quickly from the entrance to the bins where I hid. The flashlight shone behind the dumpsters, a quick check before moving back to the shadowed side door of the market. I heard the handle being twisted and shaken.

"The door is locked." The voice was soft, trying to keep

up the pretense of being secretive. The asshole was traipsing around a dark alley with a flashlight. Who did he think he was fooling? "I'll move further down the back."

A quiet hiss of electronic static was the only answer I could hear.

The stench from the rotting fish in the dumpster was making me gag. I took a deep breath through my mouth and held it, coating my tongue in a slimy glaze of oily fish residue that permeated the air.

The flashlight shone behind the dumpsters again. A slower, more lingering examination than had been given before. I thought of dropping to the ground and sliding back behind the bins when the flashlight moved off and pointed down the alley. If he looked in between the bins, I was toast. Fear froze me to my spot. I pulled myself closer in instead, trying to reduce my silhouette.

And then I remembered. I had a damn Taser! I'd forgotten about it again, but it had been sitting in the small of my back since the day I bought the jacket. Would it still be charged after draining the coat into the motorcycle's batteries? Carefully, slowly, I moved one hand off the lip of the dumpster. My weight shifted, and my right foot popped off its tenuous toehold. My body pivoted, gravity forcing it toward the wall of the market. I grasped for the top of the dumpster again, stopping my slow fall. Blood pounded in my veins, blocking the sound from the alley. I balanced on one foot and tried again, forcing my torso to stay where it was. I wiped my hand on my pants and reached behind to grab the Taser, each movement as slow as I could make it. The sound of the coarse jacket material slipping against itself was a loud thrumming in my ears. How could he not hear me? My hand wrapped around the Taser's handle, ready to rip it off the Velcro holding it in place.

"I think I heard something further in. I'm gonna go check it out." More static hiss was the only response.

The flashlight, followed by the outline of a pudgy looking man, continued past the bins, moving farther into the alley. As soon as the light passed by the second bin, I started breathing again. Dropping silently to the ground, I waited, watching the light recede down the alley before leaving my hiding spot. I half crept, half ran along the edge of the building, looking over my shoulder at every step. The flashlight was still making its way down the alley. I kept my hand wrapped around the Taser, afraid to pull it off and make any noise.

Suddenly, the flickering neon light coming from the alley's entrance dimmed. I stumbled and looked up. The alley entrance was blocked by a figure. Momentum carried me forward, and I slammed into the man's chest before I could stop.

"Well, it's nice to see you again." His voice was as smooth as the Level 5 concrete, and just as hard. "Where is the package?"

I squinted up at the silhouette. A scream rose into my throat. Black eyes stared back at me.

He clapped his hand over my mouth, partially covering my nose with his giant paw. "I don't think that would be a good idea just now, do you?" His hand pushed tighter against my face, blocking the air.

The scream died in my chest. I tried to jerk out of his grasp. His grip loosened and he slammed me up against the side of the Fish Market. The impact knocked the breath out of me. I sucked in a huge breath through my open mouth, forcing air through Quincy's fingers. It tasted like soap. The back of my head scraped the rough exterior of the building and he stepped in closer, pressing his arm against my throat, his body against mine, pinning me to the wall. This couldn't be happening. I closed my eyes, pushing tears down my cheeks.

"You are a fighter then, eh? Good!" Quincy leaned down and whispered into my ear. "I like fighters. They make my job so much more . . . entertaining."

He reached into his pocket for his comm unit. Holding it to his mouth, he thumbed the key. "I've got the girl."

"Team Two, roger."

"Team Three, roger."

I tightened my grip on the Taser. Using the comm unit had distracted him, and he had released a slight amount of the pressure holding me against the wall. It was the only chance I would get. I yanked, pulling the Taser away from its Velcro holding. It came off surprisingly easy, and I almost dropped it. The tearing sound of the Velcro was muffled through the jacket and the concrete wall. I plunged the Taser against his stomach, jabbing as hard as I could. Quincy looked down and took a small step back, a smile spreading across his narrow face.

"I was right, you are a fighter!"

The bastard actually sounded happy.

Quincy spasmed when I pressed the trigger, shooting 50,000 volts of pulsing electricity into his body. He stumbled back, still on his feet. His grin had turned ghastly, his lips pulled tightly over his teeth.

I stepped forward and pressed the Taser into his stomach again. This time, his body convulsed and dropped to the ground, twitching even after I'd stopped the retaliatory attack.

I noticed my hands had stopped shaking. I still felt like someone had hollowed out my insides . . . like the gutted man on the floor. But I was back in control. I had given myself another chance.

I bolted around the corner onto the front street. Back

into the meager pedestrian traffic that had either ig-nored, or not seen, what was happening in the alley. I ran for my bike, struggling to get the keys out of my pocket. Cold panic swelled in my chest, filling the hole inside me, slowly creeping out to my hands and feet. I tripped and fell to the ground, the keys flying out of my hand, past the bike. My helmet crashed to the concrete, scraping the back. I scrambled toward the locked-up machine. A fig-ure emerged from the alley on the other side of the Fish Market and turned toward me. I froze, terror mixing with the panic. I knew I wouldn't be able to get the chain off in time.

Forcing myself to my feet, I ran toward the white van parked across the street. Maybe they had left it empty. Maybe it was still running. Maybe it could get me out of here.

The driver's door opened and a man got out. I angled back, racing to the alley across the street instead. He was closer. His left hand was wrapped in a bandage, and he ran with a definite limp. Even with that, I knew I wasn't going to make it. When he was three meters away, I cut back toward the van. It had to be empty. God, please make it empty!

I waved my Taser at him, and he slowed down just enough to give me time to pull open the driver's door and jump in.

The engine was powered up. I had the van moving before the door was closed. I could see the driver in the mirror. He had fled back to the sidewalk. His comm unit was pressed to his mouth. Chances were they had the damn van tracked, but it was still the fastest way out of this place. I would get rid of it the first chance I got. But first I had to make it out of here. I pulled into a narrow Chinatown side street and disappeared from the main strip.

The truck itself had no comm device and no nav units. It looked like a throwaway vehicle. Something that could be used to do just about anything and not worry about having it traced back to you.

I raced out of the narrow street and onto a secondary, heading for a Level 3 up-ramp. I stood on the accelerator, weaving around the slower traffic on the almost empty streets. If the truck was monitored, I had to dump it before they caught up with me. If they had motorcycles, I was already fucked.

THREE

DEVON TURNED HIS comm unit on as he reached Level 6. The signal didn't make it up to his office, so there was no point in having it powered on in there. It beeped before he even had a chance to slip it back into his pocket.

A single message showed on his screen. He touched it with his finger and held the unit up to his ear.

"Hi, Bro, how's it going. Could you do me a favor and follow up on that gift for Mom? Call me when you get the chance. See ya."

Devon didn't have a brother; the only family he had left was his mother. He let the cool night breeze, man-made on Level 6, wash over his face before he turned and began to retrace his steps back to the office. It was dangerous using the same route twice, but the computer-generated entrance for tomorrow was on Level 7, and he didn't have time to get there.

The phone message had originated from the assistant director. It was a code they had agreed on long ago. If a call came in from his brother, he was to get to his office and contact the assistant director as soon as possible. The rest of the message was just garbage, used to cover their tracks by filling the message with random junk. If the call was too short or too long, the corporate computers would probably flag it. According to Devon, the average comm message was 7.73 seconds long. Any message left in that range, plus or minus half a second, would most likely be lost in the noise. But not to his systems. The noise is what they fed on, finding tidbits of information all over the Net and piecing them together into a coherent structure.

Devon retraced his steps and entered the maintenance corridors between Levels 6 and 7. A meter from his office door, he heard the quiet sliding and clicking of the locks, and metal sheeting rose to expose the entrance. His body's signature had been read when he was thirty meters from the room, and it was confirmed every three meters after that. Any major deviations would have kept the room locked and the sheet metal covering the entrance, making it look like the rest of the machinery and ductwork in the area. The same would have happened if there had been any other people within the thirty-meter radius.

Devon closed the door behind him and heard the faint rattle of the metal dropping down to conceal the door again.

He sat down at his desk and the displays. They'd powered up when he entered the room and showed the usual data. The high priority column now had the courier issue displayed in bright red. Devon picked up the hardwired phone.

"Devon," he said.

"Mr. McBride. Sorry for asking you back so late." The voice on the other end didn't pause. The typical empty reply was not only not necessary, it was unwanted. "I need more information on the courier situation. What do you have for me?"

"I'm checking now, sir." Devon flicked the courier item to his other display and read the information. "I have some secondary and tertiary information coming in. The system flagged it with an eighty percent probability rate of pertaining to the courier, sir."

"Yes."

"I also have some primary information on the courier. His name, sorry, her name is Kris Ballard, age sixteen, though her birthday is next month. A meter and a half tall, brown hair, brown eyes. She's been a courier for Internuncio Limited for about a year. Internuncio has access up to and including Level 5. They had Level 6 quite a few years back, but lost it due to the inappropriate behavior of one of their couriers. Do you want me to follow up on that, sir?"

"Not yet, what else do we have?"

Devon read the information on the screen. "She lives in Level 2 Chinatown, on top of a fish market, she's been there about six months. Secondary information shows SoCal Black Ops operatives in the area. Local monitoring indicates some sort of altercation in an alley near the market, with possible Taser usage."

"Local monitoring? We have an operative in the area?"

"Sorry, sir, no. Local monitoring in this case indicates comm traffic and verbal pickups placed by ACE representatives," said Devon.

"Continue."

"Secondary data also indicates a white vehicle being driven by a young girl leaving the area at high speed."

"Do you have an ID on the vehicle?"

The van line item was plain black text, indicating the computer had no information on it. "No, sir, I'm unable to track it."

"What about the girl?"

"The system's getting that information now, sir. Some of the government databases have been resecured, and it's taking time to get the information we need."

"Then how did we get her other information so fast?"

"Vehicle Registrations, sir. A low priority system that hasn't been converted yet."

"Get on it. I don't think we have the time, Mr. Mc-Bride."

"Yes, sir."

The line shut down. Devon hung up the phone and allocated more of the computer's resources to tracking and finding out about Kris Ballard.

LEVEL 3—TUESDAY, AUGUST 9, 2140 11:35 P.M.

I sped down the street to the Level 3 ramp, squealing the tires on the way up, and stopped just at the top. A small group of boarders lounged near the exit, either waiting for more of their friends to arrive before they rode the ramp down, or the last group to leave before the end of the day. I opened the van's door and jumped out, leaving the keys, and moved to stand in the glow of the headlights.

"Hey, guys, who wants a van?" I shouted. I figured if the van was traced, the boarders could have it. If they were caught, they wouldn't know anything, except for where they got the damn thing, and Quincy would let them go.

The boarders stopped talking, looked up at me, and started walking closer. I moved, placing the body of the van between me and the oncoming boarders. Once I couldn't see them anymore, I darted toward the nearest building and ducked into a shadowed doorway. I heard the van's side door open and rattle shut again in its tracks, and the tires squealed on the concrete as it sped away. My knees buckled underneath me, and I slid to ground, my back pressed into the darkness. I waited, the steel bars of the door pushing through my jacket into my back, struggling to breathe. I'd been holding my breath, waiting for the boarders to take the bait. Now that they were gone, it was time for me to move again. I pushed against the bars, rising to my feet, and left the meager protection of the doorway to head back to Level 2.

Lights flashed up the ramp wall, followed by the sound of a racing motor. I sprinted back to the doorway I'd just abandoned, wishing it was deeper in the shadows. The vehicle stopped on the ramp just shy of the Level 3 exit before moving closer. A plain white van. It was quickly followed by another. The two vans sped off, following the route taken by the one I had handed off to the boarders.

Why the hell had the vans stopped midramp? Did they let someone off, someone to watch for any returning traffic? Did they somehow know I'd ditched the van and was planning on heading back down? Shit, what the hell was going on? All I knew was if there was someone on the ramp, I had to move. Now. My hand went into my pocket, fishing for Oscar, before I remembered. He'd been with me a long time . . . the only thing I had to remind me of what I'd lost. Now even that was gone.

I put my helmet on. Habit had kept it on my arm during the wild drive here. I dropped the visor and began to scan the area. The real-time traffic data was useless, so I turned that off, but kept the comm tuned into the police bands and used the lid's visual enhancers to look into the dark places. If the guys following me had one of these, I was fucked. Hell, they probably had infrared scanners. My stomach churned as the fear, temporarily pushed away by adrenaline, twisted its tentacles into my gut. I felt more exposed than ever. The best my helmet could do was to use the available light to look for potential road hazards; it wasn't designed to be used as a night vision system.

Keeping my helmet on, I moved farther away from the ramp. There was no way I was going to use that one again. Walking to the next down-ramp late at night wasn't my idea of a good time, but I didn't know what else to do. I had to get back to somewhere I knew, somewhere I could hide. Only one place came to mind, and I shuddered at the thought.

The next down-ramp was about fifteen kilometers away, which meant a little over a couple of hours before I got there, longer if I stuck to the shadows. The good news was it was an express, skipping Level 2 entirely, and it dropped me right on the edge of my old Level 1 neighborhood. I took the Taser out of my jacket and checked its charge. Empty. Maybe if I held it, it might give anyone second thoughts.

The sound of another vehicle coming up the ramp forced me into an alley. I watched from behind a pile of stinking garbage as a blue hatchback zipped down the street. I must have kneeled in the alley for close to half an hour, alternating between being convinced Quincy was waiting for me to move and knowing he was nowhere near.

When I finally left the alley, I headed away from the path the vans had taken. I skulked through the shadows, dashing across the open spaces to the next dark pool, where I stood still, looking around to see if I had been spotted. The only sound I heard was my own footsteps echoing down the empty alleys and streets. The first time my jacket scraped against the side of a building, I jumped, thinking someone was creeping up behind me. Thoughts of the night's events kept rolling through my head, the pieces falling into place where they could. The more I tried to figure out what happened, the deeper a cold shaft of fear jabbed into my brain. I went over it one more time.

Okay, Dispatch gives me a late delivery, no big deal. The pickup is a pain in the ass, but again, no big deal. The drop-off was totally fucked. How did you even do that to a man? Wasn't there bone and shit in there to stop that? The image of Quincy's face thrust into my head. I was sure I'd never seen him before, and I was usually pretty good with faces. Was I just in the wrong place at the wrong time? No, no, that couldn't be it. Quincy had asked where the package was. They were there to get the package. It could have been any courier, they didn't give a shit that it was me. Did they? If they didn't care, then how did they track me back to my place? Dispatch wouldn't give that information to a client. Besides, no one was at the depot this late at night, so what the fuck?

Wait a sec. When I left the drop-off, Quincy had come running out of the building and pointed something at me. I thought maybe it was a gun, but there were no shots. What if it had been a comm unit?

Somehow, the idea didn't comfort me.

If the guy had butchered someone, run down five flights of stairs, and had the intelligence to not shoot at a moving motorcycle, but to grab a picture instead . . . That definitely sounded like a pro, not some hack job trying to grab an unknown package. These guys—Quincy— knew what was in the package. And when it was going to be delivered. How the crap did they do that? Then again, if they could figure out where I live from a snapshot of my bike, they might be able to track courier logs as well.

The thought sent a shiver up my back.

That meant big money. And big money meant the corporations. I was royally fucked. I had to get rid of the package, and let them know I didn't have it anymore. If they had feeds into the courier system, then in theory all I had to do was return the package to Dispatch and disappear for a while. But then would the next courier get hit? Would it be Howie? I didn't want others to die because of me.

At the top of the express ramp to Level 1, I'd made up my mind. First, I needed a place to hole up for the rest of the night. Not that there was much left of it. I checked the time on my helmet. Christ, the walk here took almost twice as long as it should have. Tomorrow, I would return the package to Dispatch and give a full and detailed account of what happened. They wouldn't send another courier after that, and I'd disappear while everyone figured out what to do. Find a place to stay for a couple of weeks. My hand reached into my pocket again, searching for Oscar, wanting to hold him for luck. I stopped before sliding my hand in too deep, mad at myself for not remembering. And being so weak.

I crept down the ramp, sticking close to the walls, and entered Level 1.

LEVEL 3—TUESDAY, AUGUST 9, 2140 11:45 P.M.

Quincy's comm unit rang just as he was reaching for it. The van in front of him was riddled with holes. A couple of the kids had made it out, and their bodies lay a short distance from the van, facedown in pools of blood, multiple bullet holes in their backs.

One big fucking mess. No girl, no package, and one big fucking mess.

Quincy knew without looking who was on the other end of the connection. He sighed and raised the unit to his ear.

"Hello."

"You keep making mistakes." Jeremy's voice was calm and conversational, never a good sign when something had gone wrong.

"Yes, sir."

"We've tracked her, and think we know where she's going."

Quincy's grip tightened on the phone. "Just let me know where."

"Not this time. Three mistakes in one night is more than enough, don't you think? I've sent Abby."

"I want this one." Quincy could feel the blood rising up his face. He hid the anger he felt from his voice.

"Clean up your last mess, we'll talk tomorrow."

The connection dropped and Quincy squeezed the comm unit tighter until he felt the plastic start to flex. He turned to the guy that had taken the first shot and started the slaughter on the street.

"Clean this up, before you end up just like them."

Quincy turned, his heel leaving a clean circle in the dust and sand on the road, and stalked back to his vehicle.

LEVEL 1—WEDNESDAY, AUGUST 10, 2140 5:00 A.M.

As soon as I hit the rubble-strewn street, I veered off to the side and crouched behind a massive concrete barrier protecting the ramp's walls. The air clung to my skin, oily and thick. I scanned the surrounding area, lingering on the darker shadows and places where someone could be hiding, using my helmet to try and pierce the deep gloom. There weren't any flashy billboards or ads here. No one on Level 1 could afford what they were trying to sell.

This late at night, or early in the morning, I guess, only the desperate and the insane entered Level 1. Which had its good and bad points. The good point was that no one really expected it to happen. Even if the local gangs had posted someone to watch the ramps, chances were they would be half asleep and not paying attention. The bad point was that, well, you had to be desperate or insane. I was a lot of both.

I let out a long slow breath, one I didn't even realize I was holding. It looked like luck was finally on my side. My lid's enhanced vision picked glints of light off of broken glass and the rough edges on the busted brick walls, but no movement, no sign of anyone watching the ramp's exit.

Revulsion crawled up my back as I scanned the area. Christ, to think I had lived in this hellhole for almost a year and a half. Just the smell of it made me want to throw up. A putrid mixture of stale air, garbage, and god knows what else. Why anyone would willingly stay down here was beyond me. If I could get out, anyone could.

At least it would be a good place to hide out for tonight.

It had been a long time since I'd been down to Level 1. Once I made it out, I vowed I would never come back. Now I was being forced here, back into my hole to hide. I could almost feel the hands on my shoulders, pushing me back, pushing me into this man-made hell. The low ceiling, only fifteen meters above my head, didn't help the feeling of oppression.

The Ambients started to rise, reducing the shadows lying close to the ground. I checked the time again. Five in the fucking morning. I'd spent so much time hiding instead of walking, it had taken me over five hours to get here—I'd been moving around the whole damn night. And I never did get my shower. No chance of that for a while.

If I remembered correctly, my old hiding spot was down to the left. If no one had found it yet, I could slip in and maybe grab a couple of hours of sleep before heading up to the depot. That would be a hell of a walk as well. At least during the day I wouldn't have to hide in the shadows.

I moved off to the left as the Ambients continued their slow climb to daylight strength. I walked past the decrepit buildings, their empty windows staring at me, the lost child returned home. Time, vandals, or old earthquakes had destroyed them. Sometimes all three. I ducked low, below any open windows, and dashed past doorways and streets to the relative safety of the walls again. The opposite of what I'd done on Level 3. Down here, doors could lead to places I didn't even want to imagine. The Taser's smooth surface felt slick in my grip. I wiped my hand on my pants, trying to stay calm and alert.

The ramp had exited on South Central Avenue, right by the Santa Monica Freeway. They seemed to put the Level ramps between the old freeway on-ramps. I followed South Central, staying close to the buildings converted from warehouses to apartments, before most of them became abandoned. I stopped a few blocks from the ramp and crouched behind a rusted hunk of old car that sat in front of a building shaped like an old ship. I couldn't tell if the bottom of the wall had once been painted black, or if it was just the Level 1 filth that made it look that way. I waited a few minutes, watching for any signs of someone following me, before continuing on.

When Central took a slight jog to the left, I turned down 6th, entering the area I only knew as Skid Row. In the distance I could see what was left of old Downtown, what my history classes had told me were once majestic towers of glass and steel, truncated at the fifth floor, squashed between the earth and the man-made ceiling. I kept on walking, counting the blocks until I reached seven. Last time I'd been here, a beat-up sign had told me the street name. The sign was gone, and my memory served the name up for me. San Julian Street. I turned left again.

My Auntie's apartment was only about fifteen blocks away from here, fifteen blocks and a lifetime. I had never been back, and never wanted to go back. That life was gone. Hell, I didn't want to go back to my hole, either, but I couldn't think of anywhere else to go right now. I would never be desperate enough to go back to Auntie's though.

Exhaustion pushed at the edges of my brain, threatening to shut it down completely. I needed to sleep before I ended up just keeling over wherever I happened to be. Dredging up past history wasn't getting me someplace safe.

The block had obviously become more used than when I lived here, or survived here. Paths wandered amongst the broken brick and twisted metal, which looked like it had been sorted into salvageable and non-salvageable piles. The rumors said the whole block had been destroyed by the earthquakes in 2118, but that couldn't have been true. There had been enough issues by then that SoCal had come down and rebuilt the infrastructure to handle the occasional quake and the extra load of Levels 6 and 7. These days, when one hit, the retrofitted mass dampers took care of every-thing. The most damage you'd get would be the broken glass I'd seen earlier, or maybe a displaced brick or two. Then again, maybe this stuff had collapsed before then.

People always wondered why the corporations had bothered to fix the old buildings. Why not just let them collapse? But I figured I knew. Every society needed the downtrodden, the poor, the homeless. It made the richer people feel good about themselves when they gave money or time, made them feel like they were giving back somehow. None of it really seemed to work. In-stead, life went on for anyone living down here. A life filled with drugs and hate and disease. I wished I was anywhere but back here.

The northern corner of the lot still looked unused. At least I hoped it was. Lying under the layered garbage and crushed bricks was an entrance into the old basement of the building that had once stood here. An entrance that, at least a couple of years ago, only I had known about. The access itself was a tight squeeze, as though it was made for a small kid. I hoped I could still wriggle through the openings and tight tunnels created by the collapsed structure.

Sudden motion caught my eye, and I twisted to face it. Something slammed into my chest. I jerked backward, stumbling over the rough ground. My heel caught on some loose rubble and I fell on my back, laying stunned, staring at the mottled gray ceiling and Ambients through a layer of fog and flashing points of light floating above me. I moved my arm across my chest and struggled to sit up. Two thin wires lay across the ground, embedded in the front of my jacket and leading to a pile of garbage about six meters away.

The pile moved.

LEVEL 1—WEDNESDAY, AUGUST 10, 2140 5:40 A.M.

Awareness struggled to rise through the thick fog in my head. As it began to clear, I realized what had happened. The wires were from a Taser. I flexed my hand, looking for the Taser I had held only moments ago. It was gone.

Unless things had changed over the last two years, Tasers were not the weapon of choice for the Level 1 gangs. Baseball bats and knives were more their style. Maybe the assholes in the white van knew where I was heading, but how?

My reaction to the Taser wasn't what I'd expected either. I had felt some surge of power, and my chest felt bruised, but where was the pain? I'd seen firsthand what a Taser could do when I hit Quincy. I moved my arm again, searching in the dirt for my own Taser.

Footsteps approached from the pile of garbage, accompanied by the sounds of scraping bricks and the hollow clang of empty cans banging. Someone knelt down beside me, and I lashed out with my feet instinctively, using all the strength I could gather from my prone position. I felt contact. The figure grunted and fell, sprawling on his back. I stood and ripped the Taser hooks from my jacket before sprinting deeper into the piles of rubble.

I slid to a stop and threw myself behind a large mound. My heart pounded in my chest, a sharp pulsating roar that filled my ears. The only other sound I could hear was the sharp intake of my breathing. Nothing from the lot surrounding me. The Ambients continued to raise the level of light, and I knew my chances of slipping away unnoticed in the dark were falling. I forced my arms to move, pushing myself up to my knees, ignoring the small rocks and glass grinding under them, and peeked over the pile. I scanned the area, looking for the man that had attacked me. The lot was empty. Where the hell did he go?

My Taser was back where I had first fallen. Even though I knew it was empty, its loss made me feel exposed, naked. I rubbed my palms on my thighs and looked down at them. A glint of light shone from my wrist. The indicator on my jacket's cuff. The damn thing was fully charged! It must have absorbed the major hit from the Taser. I was lucky it didn't blow out the jacket in the process.

I looked back out at my fallen Taser. Come on, where was the bastard?

"Are you looking for me?" The voice was clean and crisp with a slight lilting accent.

I spun around. The man in front of me was huge. From my crouched position, he looked at least two meters tall. His clothes were made out of the garbage he'd been hiding in. Thin shavings of bricks, rusted cans, gravel, and wire were attached to his pants and jacket. His bald head was painted in blotches of gray and brown to match. The glasses on his face looked weird, almost as though they held some sort of tech. Probably infrared night enhancers. Shit. He had probably seen me coming before I even entered the lot.

I dropped my shoulders in defeat, lowering my head and staring at his boots. In the same motion, I pushed off the pile behind me toward him, hoping to drive my head into his gut and make a run for it.

He sidestepped with the agility of a cat and grabbed onto the collar of my jacket, jerking me off my feet and flat onto my back. My breath blew out in a giant rush, and I lay there, my mouth flapping helplessly, trying to suck in a fresh breath.

He grabbed the front of my jacket and picked me up

with one arm, throwing me against the pile of rubble I had just been hiding behind. My lungs released, and the disgusting air of Level 1 filled them like a sweet nectar. I wrapped my hand around a broken brick and swung without thinking about what I was doing. The man jerked back, but the brick hit, pulling the glasses off his face. Blood poured from his nose, dripping down his chin and staining the metal on his chest.

"You fucking bitch!"

He jabbed me hard in the chest and followed up with a sharp slap, spinning me around. I felt my nose rupture, and blood spilled across my face. I collapsed onto my hands and knees, the ground spinning beneath me, threatening to give way at any moment. The helmet slid down my arm to my wrist. I felt him grab my shoulders as the spinning slowed. He twisted me around, slamming me against a partially standing brick wall.

I almost laughed. This was the same wall I had ripped moss off of, sucking the water out of the green spongy growth, when I had run away from home. It was going to end almost where it had all started. I raised my hands to protect my face, curling my arms around my head.

"They only said I had to deliver you, they didn't say you still had to be pretty."

Through my protective cover, I saw him pull his hand back and curl his fingers into a tight fist. His lips stretched into a grin underneath the blood.

A single thought pulsed through the fear: the jacket.

FOUR

I COULD FEEL THE adrenaline course through me, making my skin prickle, and a sharp thrill settled in my gut. The damn jacket was charged.

My attacker raised his fist, swinging it at my head. I fought the reflex to duck and jumped toward him instead, hitting the switch in the collar of my jacket at the same time.

As I leaped forward, the direction of his blow changed, lowering to catch me as if I was ducking away. The two moves combined perfectly, as though we had choreographed and practiced them beforehand. His fist hit my chest in a blinding flash of light when the jacket's stored charge released at the point of contact. I stumbled, falling to my knees. He flew backward, arcing through the air, and landed a few steps away from me with a dull thud. Electricity sparked across the wires attached to his clothes and his body twitched in silence.

Sharp pain lanced through my chest and I hunched over, pressing my hands against my heart, sucking in air through my clenched teeth. *Please don't let it be a broken rib.*

I crawled to the nearest scrapheap on my knees and one hand, using it to pull myself to my feet. Every muscle in my body complained. It felt like every joint was twisted, and every bone scraped against another one. My brain wasn't working at full speed. I teetered to my feet, not knowing what to do next.

I don't know how long I stayed there, breathing through my mouth, wobbling, crying. My bloody nose dripped slowly, mixing with the dirt between my feet. My hand wrapped around a length of rusted wire as I pulled myself from the black hole I was circling. When was the last time I'd slept? At least twenty-four hours ago.

The man still lay on the ground twitching and moaning. I hobbled over to him and tied his arms and legs together as tight as I could. With each twist of the wire, I could feel the knot loosen in my stomach. Anger rose in its place. I turned when I heard a growl, before realizing the sound, guttural and fierce, came from me. I twisted the wire tighter.

I grabbed the back of his collar and dragged him closer to the wall, using my anger for strength, leaning him against the old brick before checking to see if he had any weapons on him. I found a small handgun and several magazines of bullets, as well as his Taser, emptied of all power, and a short knife in a sheath tucked into one of his socks.

The gun felt weird. It was light and definitely not made of metal. I shoved the gun and bullets into my pocket, throwing the spent Taser away. When I turned back, the man's eyes were on me. I couldn't tell if I saw anger or admiration in them.

Either way, it was time to get some answers. I slid the knife from its sheath. It was made from a single piece of metal. The blade was short and black and vicious, thin and sharp, almost surgical looking. Two fine curving hooks, facing backward to the holder's hand, sat a few centimeters from the guard. If it went in far enough, pulling it out would create a lot of damage.

Images of Quincy, his hands covered in blood, standing over the body of the gutted man, flashed through my mind. I almost threw the knife away, a wave of revulsion pulsing through me. But I hesitated. This guy had just tried to beat the crap out of me. Whatever I did, he deserved. It didn't sound convincing, even when I said it to myself. I held the knife loosely in my hand and crouched in front of my attacker.

"Who are you?" My voice sounded gravelly and low. I sucked my tongue, forcing some spit into my mouth, and swallowed.

The man gave me a sullen look before dropping his gaze to the ground between us. He didn't look at the knife in my hand.

"I'm not in the mood to fuck around, asshole. Who are you?"

Silence.

I moved the knife to the man's groin and hesitated again before poking the tip of the sharp blade into the material. He shuddered and tried to slide closer to the wall.

"Last chance, asshole." I slid the knife deeper into the material. "Who are you?"

The look in the man's eyes had turned to pure terror.

"Frank. Frank Bow—"

"Do you work for Quincy?"

Confusion washed over his face. "I don't know a Quincy. Please . . . please move the knife away."

"Who do you work for?"

"I . . . I don't know."

I pushed the knife a bit deeper and saw a small stain of blood appear on Frank's pants.

"Honest, I don't know." His voice had gone up an octave, and the accent became more pronounced. "I'm telling you the truth. I was . . . I was contacted on the Net and told to come here and wait for you."

"Who contacted you? How did they know to send you here?"

"I don't know." Frank stilled a sudden twitch. "I never do. I just get told where to go and where to pick up the money." The words came out of his mouth almost faster than he could say them.

"You said you had to deliver me. To where?"

"I was supposed to give you to another guy on Level 5, near the McConnell Park up-ramp."

"Why?"

"I don't know."

I twisted the blade slightly.

"I don't know. I told you . . . I just get told what job to do and where to get my money."

I paused, thinking. "How were you going to get me there?"

"I have a car, two blocks north."

"I didn't find any keys on you."

"The ignition and lock are code-activated."

"What's the code?"

Frank stared at me. "I can't get out of here without my car."

"Who says you're going to get out of here anyway?" I wiggled the knife without pushing it any deeper. "What's the fucking code?"

Frank's face turned white and the code poured from him. "14159."

I sat back on my heels and pulled the knife away, cleaning the blade tip on Frank's thigh before standing.

"You've got to let me go. If you leave me here I'm dead meat."

I looked down at him. Let him go? Hell, the bastard just admitted he was going to abduct me and give me to someone he didn't even know. They could have been planning to kill me for all he cared. Why the fuck should I worry what happened to this shithead? I took a step away.

"Please." The urgency and panic in his voice were clear.

Damn, damn, damn. Why couldn't I just leave him? After what he had done, was planning to do, to me. It was my right to leave him here, to let the Level 1 scum take care of him. I wiped the drying blood from my nose and turned to leave again before giving in to the silent argument in my head.

I crouched in front of him. "Lean forward."

Frank leaned until his chest was almost lying on his outstretched legs. I cut the wires holding his arms and took two quick steps back.

"If you try to follow me, remember I have your gun."

Frank stared at me, rubbing his wrists. Blood seeped from the fine cuts left by the wires. I know I had tied the wire tight, but I didn't think I'd tied them tight enough to cut. The bastard had been trying to get loose the entire time we had been talking.

A sharp crack cut through the silent air and I felt a burn on my neck. Frank flew back into the wall, a small black hole magically appearing in his forehead, and slid into a slouch. Where the back of his head scraped against the wall, blood and bone intermixed with gray stuff smeared on the rough brick, mixing with the already wet moss.

I spun and dived behind another pile. A second crack and I saw a cloud of dust and rock chips flying up from the brick beside Frank's body. Right where I had just been standing.

LEVEL 1—WEDNESDAY, AUGUST 10, 2140 6:12 A.M.

I pulled my hand away from my neck. It was smeared in blood. Was it from my nose, or my neck? A wave of nausea swept through me and I leaned my head against the pile of garbage. I tried to push the feeling aside. Someone was shooting at me, trying to kill me. Who the fuck was this guy? Not a friend of Frank's, unless hitting him had been an accident. I looked back at his crumpled body.

From where I'd been standing and where he had been shot, the shooter had to have been near or in the building directly across the lot, in the Madison Hotel. Probably somewhere above ground level so he could get a better view. I placed my back to the heap of garbage, looking for a way out of this mess.

The ground in front of me was strewn with rubble from the collapsed building. The next structure big enough to hide behind was a little over a meter away. If I crawled on my stomach, I might be able to reach it without being seen. It was a big if though. What if I was wrong about the location of the shooter? I'd be a nice, slow-moving target, that's what. I could feel the tears coming again, blurring my vision. I wiped them away roughly with the back of my hand. This wasn't the time.

Three meters to the right was one of the entryways

into my old basement hideout. This one was just a low depression in the ground that turned into a tight tunnel under the concrete floor. The tunnel dropped into an elevator shaft, and if I hung from the lip and swung, I would land on a tiny ledge and be able to squeeze through the partially open doors. Or I could miss and fall to the bottom of the shaft. I had never used the entrance when I lived here. The thought of using it now made me shiver.

One slip and I would end up lying in who knows how many meters of cold, filthy water. I guess I was a pragmatist, though. Or an idiot . . . Years ago I had placed candles and matches just inside the elevator doors, just in case.

All of that was pointless if I couldn't get there. Would the shooter expect me to run through open ground? Even from here, the entrance hole looked like nothing. From the hotel, it couldn't be seen at all. Once I wiggled under the concrete, I'd be safe from bullets at least.

Before I could talk myself out of it, I held my breath and launched, running to the depression and sliding to the ground, lying as flat as I could. No shots rang out. Maybe I'd taken him by surprise after all.

The opening under the floor was still there, but it was a lot smaller than I remembered. Christ, I wasn't even sure I would fit. Keeping my head low, I snaked toward the small dark hole, pushing my motorcycle helmet ahead of me. When I reached it, the helmet fit, with enough room on the sides for my shoulders. Or so I hoped. I pushed the air out of my lungs, praying it made me smaller.

A first for me.

My head followed the helmet. When my shoulders hit the outer edge, the hole became pitch black. Once I almost stopped, too scared to move forward. The thought of the gunman kept me going. I pushed the helmet farther in, grabbing at the walls with my hands, looking for something to grab onto. I dug my toes in, willing my shoulders past the constricting entrance. I popped through and scrambled a few centimeters before I got stuck again. I felt the package in my pocket crinkle. Twisting, I pulled it through and wiggled in deeper.

Suddenly, brick and chips of concrete exploded around my calves, followed by the muffled crack of a rifle. Fuck! I pulled and pushed myself deeper into the hole, my mind an icy wall of panic. Slivers of pain cracked through the ice, and I started kicking with my heels. Loose chunks of corroded concrete and dirt fell from the ceiling, partially closing the entrance to the tunnel. If I couldn't get into the basement from here, I'd be trapped. But maybe the fucker with the gun couldn't get in either.

Now in complete darkness, I slithered forward as fast as I could, grabbing the helmet and pushing it ahead of me. The tunnel widened and I stopped. My breath was coming in quick, short gasps, each inhale spreading a dull ache through my chest where Frank hit me. I could feel sweat pooling in the small of my back.

Keep moving, keep moving, keep moving.

I repeated my new mantra over and over again until I started squirming forward. I barely crawled a meter more when my helmet and hands felt nothing but air. My breath whooshed out of me. I jerked backward and froze again.

I lay as still as I could, fighting the sensation of falling headfirst into the gaping maw of the pit. I wasn't sure how long I stayed there, struggling to get my racing heart under control. Once I could feel the unmoving earth beneath me again, I slid forward and peered over the edge.

Rocks and debris, pushed ahead while I crawled, fell into the shaft, creating echoing splashes when they hit the water below. I only saw more of the same blackness. Staring at where the elevator door should have been, directly under me, I thought I saw a faint outline. When I looked closer, it disappeared from view, like a ghost hiding in the dark, waiting for its prey.

I couldn't lie here forever. Eventually whoever was shooting at me would make his way down. There was only the loose rubble I'd managed to kick from the ceiling between me and a bullet. It wasn't enough. I braced myself against the tunnel walls and began the process of bringing my feet around. Only my height saved me from getting permanently stuck, and I thanked whoever was responsible for making me short.

Another first.

The pain from my calf faded into a dull throb as I twisted and crunched my body into shapes even a contortionist would be proud of. Finally, still lying on my stomach, I slid my helmet onto my arm and lowered my legs and hips over the abyss.

My kicking feet found nothing but hard concrete walls. Shit, where the hell was the door? I lowered myself farther, catching the edge on the bottom of my ribcage. I didn't know if they still hurt; all I could feel was terror pulsating through me. My feet still felt only cement. Shifting further, my jacket slipped, and a scream tore from my gut.

I hung on the brink from my armpits, my hands grasping uselessly at the dirt floor. My legs dangled into the depths. Small rocks fell silently, until they hit the dank water below. I kicked my feet again, hearing the dull ring of metal. Slowly, I swung my legs to the left and right, looking for the opening I remembered.

There! Oh thank god. How far up the door was I? How far below me was the ledge? I struggled to remember the height of the elevator door, the width of the opening and the size of the ledge. The memories of my fourteen-year-old self came fragmented and incomplete.

I heard rocks being moved from the tunnel entrance, and a shaft of light struck the ceiling partway up. It was now or never. I moved the helmet past the edge, my fingers finding purchase on the dirt. I slid down some more, until I was hanging from the lip. My hurt shoulder strained, but held up under my weight. I hung from my fingers, completely committed, my feet searched for the opening again. I knew I didn't have the strength to climb back out. My left foot banged against the door, a loud metallic thud, and my right swung into open air. Moving my foot sideways, I found the edge of the door and hooked it with my heel and knee, pulling my body closer to the wall. I felt dirt slide under the fingers of my left hand, turning to sludge as it mixed with drying blood from my neck, and it popped off the edge.

I dangled above the darkness, held my breath and let go.

LEVEL 1—WEDNESDAY, AUGUST 10, 2140 6:17 A.M.

Instead of dropping straight down, I began a slow-motion fall backward. My fingernails scraped the shaft wall as it moved out of my reach. I could feel the inky blackness reach up to grab me . . . to pluck me off the wall and discard my carcass in a watery grave. I pulled at the edge of the open door with my leg, jerking my body in closer. The tips of my fingers felt the cold metal and I leaned in, scrabbling for purchase as the door slid past.

My right foot impacted the floor just outside the door. The dull pain in my calf blossomed into a white-hot sear. My leg collapsed under me. I felt the edge of the door, and I grabbed, fingers sliding between the metal and the crumbling rubber door guard, cutting into my skin. I tightened my grip around the sharp metal lip and pulled. My helmet slipped off my arm and splashed into the dark water below.

I slammed onto the ledge with my hip and stopped, hugging the door with every ounce of strength I had left. Somehow, I'd managed to get both legs into the hallway and a firm grip on the door. My entire body vibrated, threatening to loose me from my tenuous perch. I pressed my forehead to the cold metal, fighting the exhaustion and nausea that threatened to overwhelm me. My legs twitched uncontrollably. I sat there, stunned and unable to move, until light burst in from the tunnel above. I commanded my body into motion, forcing it to obey, and scrambled for the hallway.

The hall was as dark as the elevator shaft. I groped along the floor, looking for the candle and matches I had placed there years ago. If they were gone, I was fucked. Trying to move around in this place in the dark was going to get me lost and dead from starvation.

The candle, wrapped in plastic and covered in dust and bits of fallen concrete, was exactly where I had put it. I grabbed the package and slid on my butt, backing away from the elevator door. My hands shook as I unwrapped the plastic. When I struck the match, it went out almost right away from the violent spasms of my hand. I struck another one and lowered the flickering flame to the candle's wick. The hallway came into view, revealing the familiar blue-green walls, the paint cracked and peeling. I stood, using the wall for support. It felt slick and damp. I wasn't sure if it was the wall or from the cuts on my fingers. The candle flame shrunk to a small blue glow. Moving my hand from the wall, I cupped my fingers around the feeble flame, casting the hall in front of me into shadow. The flame grew again, and I limped forward.

If my candle was still here, there was a pretty good chance no one had been in my basement since I had left. That meant my old cubbyhole would still be there, just an old mattress shoved against the wall and a tattered blanket.

I took a step onto my hurt leg and almost cried out in pain. I lowered the candle to the floor and rolled up my pant leg. It didn't look as bad as I thought it would. As bad as it felt. There were no bullet holes or visible bones, just the beginning of what promised to be a hell of a bruise and small cuts that covered the entire back of my calf. I still wasn't sure about my ribs. I straightened up and winced as I walked, adding my hip and cut hand to the growing list of pains.

The route to my old home came back to me as I walked, even after all this time, each corner and hallway recognizable in the flickering light of the candle. The old tenant storerooms were just ahead, and tucked in amongst them, my cubbyhole. What I had once called home.

The room was a lot smaller than I remembered it. There was barely enough room to sit and sleep. The bed, too short for even me, was covered in a thick layer of dust and fine gravel, and probably a whole ton of mouse shit, but right now it was the best thing I'd seen in a long time. Maybe if I shook out the tattered blankets, I could lie down for just a few minutes. I barely had the blankets moved when I fell on top of them, my body forcing me to do what my brain said I shouldn't.

LEVEL 1—WEDNESDAY, AUGUST 10, 2140 11:00 A.M.

I sat up, hands scrabbling for my face. A scream pounded my ears. I grabbed something small and furry, throwing it as far from me as I could. The room was pitch black.

Where was I?

I couldn't see anything.

Panic grabbed me and squeezed tight. I leaped to my feet, pain stabbing my leg, and fell back down. A cloud of dust rose around me and I coughed until tears fell from my eyes.

The pain woke me up completely, and I remembered where I was. The basement. My candle must have burned down to nothing, leaving the room in a cold cover of darkness. I crawled onto my knees, blindly reaching for more candles and matches on the small box I had once used as a bedside table.

I felt the matches and struck one. The remaining candles had been gnawed down to nubbins of wax scattered on the box. Pain seared through my fingertips and the burned out match fell to the floor. I pulled another match from the box, ready to strike it, before common sense kicked in. Walking down here in the dark was suicide. Better to save the matches for when I needed them. I counted the matches in the dark. Five left.

I stood and groaned. Every piece of me hurt, from my calf up to my head. Even brushing off the bits of dirt that clung to me brought a wave of protest from my muscles. I stretched and felt the dry blood on my neck crack.

How long had I slept? If the candle was burned down, it had to have been at least a couple of hours. My helmet would have told me, if I hadn't lost it. What if those bastards found a way in and were waiting for me? At least if they had light, I'd be able to see them.

The guy who tried to grab me this morning. What was his name? Frank. He said he had left his car a couple of streets north of here. I doubted it was still in one piece — the gangs took whatever they wanted. They didn't usually work during the day though. If the car *was* there, I could grab it and get out of Level 1. It obviously wasn't safe here anymore. But then what? Run? I'd decided long ago I would never run again.

It was becoming a hard decision to live up to.

I could feel the anger building in my gut, familiar and scary at the same time. For now, I reveled in it, feeding it all the shit I'd been through since yesterday. The anger grew, pushing the aches and pains away. Enough of this fucking running and almost getting killed every step of the way. I needed to turn the tables on these guys, needed to find out who they were and why they were coming after me. I laughed quietly. It *sounded* so simple. And stupid.

I took a step forward, stubbing my toe on the box. My hands reached out ahead of me, looking for the doorway to my room. My eyes played tricks on me in the dark, showing me the outline of the doorway until I turned my head and it disappeared. The doorframe brushed my shoulder as I went through it, and I turned right, stretching my left hand out to reach for the wall, but finding only air. I took a step left and my fingers smashed into concrete, sending a spasm of pain through my cut fingers and up to my elbow. I had found the wall.

I stood there, getting my breathing back under control, and mapped my way forward. Once I found the exit, I'd have to turn right again. Somewhere in that hallway was a pile of rubble I'd created long ago, full of broken glass and sharp steel. I couldn't remember exactly where it was. After that was a tee, and I had to turn left. No wait, right, I had to go right. Left would get me to the stairs leading to the lower basement. I shook my head. I hadn't realized how much navigation relied on being able to see. I set off, clutching the matches in my hand.

By the time I reached the tee, I was down to three matches. I struck one and held it up to the wall. A faded black arrow on the wall pointed left, to the sub-basement.

I turned right and walked until the match burned down to my fingers.

I was heading to one of my emergency exits. When you were a young girl, hell, just a girl, on Level 1, you had to have an escape route. More than one. A lifetime ago, I'd snuck into an adjoining building and made one.

In the exploration of my hiding spot, I'd found a connection between the two basements. Just a busted pipe running between them, big enough for me to crawl through. The other side had a grate covering the pipe. I'd tried to move it, but it had held fast. When I snuck into the other building, I replaced all the screws holding the grate in place with smaller ones. They held the grate up, but made it loose enough to come off with some effort. That's what I hoped anyway. Some days, I just lay in the pipe, listening to people doing their laundry, wondering if my life would ever be that simple again. For a while, it was.

The walk to the pipe used to take me a couple of minutes. Today it seemed to take forever. I'd run out of matches, and the pitch black reached into my brain. I saw lights in the distance, darker shadows shifted and hid in every corner. My heart thudded in my chest, hammering in my ears. I held my breath until spots flitted in front my eyes.

One of the distant lights refused to go out, getting brighter as I walked toward it. I focused on it, watching the dim glow slowly take shape, becoming a faded circle in the darkness. The pipe.

I crawled headfirst into the pipe with a sigh of relief. When I reached the grate, I grabbed it with both hands and pushed. The grate didn't budge. A surge of dread rushed through me.

I leaned back and threw my weight against it. Nothing happened. Blood rushed to my head and my chest suddenly felt hollow. This had to work, it was my only way out. I was out of matches.

I leaned back and lunged again and again. Each time, the panic rose higher in my chest. Then the grate popped off, its weight almost pulling me from the pipe onto the floor. I lowered it the rest of the way and crawled through the opening into the weak fluorescent light shining through a partially open door. I lay on the floor, breathing deep, staring at the light.

Before I left, I refastened the grate. I couldn't find one of the screws, but it held in place anyway.

You never knew when you would need one of your old haunts.

From there it was an easy walk up the stairs to the exit on South San Pedro Street. When I stepped outside, the Ambients were still bright, so maybe I hadn't slept more than a few hours. My stomach grumbled, but I wasn't starving. My last meal had been at old Kai's last night.

I found the car at the corner of San Pedro and Fifth. The car was, surprisingly, still in one piece. Someone had tried to smash the windows—busted rocks lay on the hood and I could see tiny marks on the windshield and side windows. A shattered baseball bat lay near the front tire. This wasn't an ordinary car. I moved to the driver's door and entered the code. The lock opened immediately and the car started. I jumped in and slammed the door closed just before another rock exploded on the glass. I ignored it, adjusted the seat to my height, and drove to the distant up-ramp.

LEVEL 2—WEDNESDAY, AUGUST 10, 2140 11:40 A.M.

Once I reached Level 2, I went on autopilot. I knew these streets. The taller ceilings helped lift my spirits. When they first started building the cities up, they'd kept

the levels low, whether they didn't trust their construction or they just wanted us to feel contained. Level 2 had
twenty-one-meter ceilings, and Level 3 went right up to
twenty-seven meters.

Turning the tables on these guys was a noble idea, but
not a very well thought out one. The few hours of sleep
I'd managed to get and the fresher air on Level 2 helped
to recover some of my senses. Whoever I was running
away from were professionals. This wasn't just a gang
member trying to earn points. This was a planned and
concerted effort to get me and my package.

The last thought stopped me short and pulled me
from my reverie. My package? What the hell was that
about? The thing was, it wasn't my package at all. I was
just a fucking courier. Why kill the messenger? Because
I'd seen the murder or because I still had the package?

I was really beginning to miss my helmet. I could have
contacted Dispatch and told her I was coming in with
the delivery. I paused midthought. No, wait. Hadn't I
done that already? The previous day was just a blur.

I fingered the gun in my jacket pocket. Its cool, hard
surface scared me, but at the same time, it was strangely
comforting. I didn't even know how to shoot the damn
thing. What if I had to use it, and found out I couldn't?
A picture of Frank's head, exploded and smeared
against the wall behind him popped into my brain, and
I jerked my hand out of my pocket. A Taser was one
thing, but if I pulled out the gun, I had better be willing
to face the consequences of using it. I wasn't sure if I
could.

Something in the car beeped.

It sounded like a comm signal. A surge of panic skit-
tered up my spine and I felt the hairs on the back of my
neck stand on end. Oh man, was the car being tracked?
Tears threatened to push their way to the surface again

and I blinked to keep them away. *Get a grip, girl, pull over and see if there's a comm unit in the damn car.*

Just ahead was a twenty-four-hour Super Store. I giggled. It came out as a high-pitched bubble of almost uncontrollable laughter. This was the same fucking Super Store I had pulled into yesterday, just before my entire fucking life collapsed. I pulled into the lot and found a spot buried in amongst the other cars. I figured it would be tougher for the sniper to get me here. If he was still around somewhere.

I sat in the quiet of the car waiting for another beep. It never came. If there was a comm unit in here, where would it be? The most obvious place to look would be the glove box. Why the hell they called it that was a mystery to me. Did anyone actually keep gloves in there? I popped it open and hit the jackpot on the first try.

Inside the glove box was a sleek new comm unit, all black and chrome and shiny. It didn't have any corporate logos on it, not even a brand. The unit fit into the palm of my hand and turned on automatically. Sure enough, a message had come in. I stared at the blinking message indicator before placing the unit on the seat beside me. Tucked into the back of the glove box was a plain white envelope. I pulled it out, opened it, and gasped. It was filled with cash, and lots of it. I shoved the envelope into my jacket without counting, looking out the windows to make sure no one had seen it.

I searched the rest of the car the best I could without opening the doors. The way the glass had stopped bricks, I felt a lot safer inside it than out. I didn't want to lose that feeling. Everything else in the car was clean. Almost factory clean. There wasn't even a stray candy wrapper under the damn seat. Going through it made me realize how gross I felt and looked.

I stared at the comm unit's flashing indicator before

picking it up. It was locked, asking for the pass code before it let me do anything. I tried the same number I used to unlock the car. I couldn't believe it worked. I read the message.

Please advise on status of current assignment.

That was it. No signature, no how do you do. The phone had only one other message, dated yesterday. I selected it and froze, my breath caught in my throat.

Displayed on the screen was my picture. It took me a second to place it before I realized it came from my courier license photo. Below the picture were some stats like hair and eye color, height, and a description of my motorcycle.

What I read below that caused me to hold my breath again.

Known places of presence.

It listed most of my regular hangouts, including Kai's restaurant. But it also had my aunt's apartment and the old address of my basement hiding place on Level 1. How the fuck did anyone know about that?

The last line said *Confirm Delivery to Level 5 McConnell Park.*

I slammed the comm unit into an inside pocket of my jacket, started the car, and continued on to the depot. Back to plan one: lose the package.

FIVE

LEVEL 6—WEDNESDAY, AUGUST 10, 2140 9:00 A.M.

DEVON WOKE TO the enticing smell of frying bacon and eggs. Thick blue curtains kept his room dark, but he could see a faint outline of light around them. He had gotten home pretty late last night, spending most of it completing the Kolinski flaw exploitation. Not all the government databases used 8192 Kolinski, of course. It had taken them three years just to agree to talk about changing their database protection systems, never mind implementing it. The corporations were usually faster. He had just needed something to do while the computer scanned and tagged all the relevant data about the courier and shipped it upstream to the assistant director.

Hell, he didn't even need to be there for that. But if the AD called back, Devon wanted to be there to answer the hard line. It wasn't because of the potential career advancement, since there was none; it was just what he felt compelled to do.

He got out of bed, put on his slippers and housecoat, and checked his comm unit for any messages before he headed downstairs to the kitchen.

"And how is my boy this morning?" Devon's mother turned from the stove with a look of concern on her broad face.

"Great, Ma. Did you sleep good?"

"Who can sleep when their son doesn't come home, eh? He doesn't even call to tell his momma where he is. When did you come home last night, eh?" She looked at him sideways, hope in her eyes. "Was it a date?"

Devon winced. Damn he forgot to call. "No, Ma. I had to work late. A special project came up."

"Work. Work is all you do. A young boy like you should be outside, looking at the girls. Not playing with your silly computers."

Devon smiled. It was the same thing every time he worked late. "I wouldn't call thirty a young boy any-more, Ma."

"You are younger than me, no? You be nice to your momma, or I start calling you my little baby again." She turned back to the stove, but not before he saw the smile on her face.

He hadn't been her little baby in a long time, but she liked to tease him about it anyway. It was part of the pattern that made his life, and the "silly computers" he played with had gotten them this house on Level 6.

They could've gotten something on Level 7, but that would have freaked out his mom too much. A lifetime of living under a concrete ceiling could do that. Plus it would have added a new level of scrutiny to his daily affairs, scrutiny from the wrong people. Devon watched his mother's back.

What if he was caught? If he ever did disappear, she'd be taken care of. Well taken care of. Devon had made sure of that, and made sure that ACE wasn't involved in it.

Devon's mom put a plate of bacon and over-easy eggs in front of him, and he dug in with gusto. She sat down and ate her toast and yogurt, glancing through the morning paper. It was an expensive habit. He figured the only reason she subscribed to it was to keep her hands busy turning pages. You could get better news from a comm unit.

<hr />

LEVEL 3—WEDNESDAY, AUGUST 10, 2140 11:00 A.M.

The comm unit in Quincy's pocket vibrated. He took it out, glanced at the caller's ID, and suppressed a chuckle. It was Jeremy, and if he was calling this soon after passing the problem off to Abby, it probably meant she had messed up. He answered the call.

"Quincy here," he said.

"Get to the Internuncio depot."

"And do what?" Quincy watched the steady flow of couriers entering and exiting the building. He had been sitting outside Internuncio most of the morning, hoping Kris would show up.

"I want this problem gone, Quincy. All of it. I don't want to have a single byte of data, a scrap of paper, left in existence that shows a package was ever picked up or delivered."

"I'll get a team together," Quincy said, "and we'll get in tonight and clean up."

"Tonight is not soon enough."

Quincy paused, keeping his voice level. "What do you mean?"

"I mean tonight is not soon enough. How much clearer do I need to make it?"

"It won't be clean."

"Just get the job done."

The connection went dead. Quincy looked through his windshield at the Internuncio sign on the building outside and sighed. There was no way Kris would show up here after this.

He'd also be losing a contact that had taken him a lot of work to cultivate. This one had been harder than most to crack. Though she'd started in the right place—with a deep void in her life, a void that needed true human contact to fill—her natural distrust had been the tough part. In the end, all he'd had to do to entrench himself in her life was hold her hand. But getting there had been quite the challenge. From that point, it was a simple step for him to convince her to *help* one of the couriers that was down on their luck, one with no family and few friends. There was a big heart under her ugly exterior. It was just luck for Quincy that the choice turned out to be a young girl.

Quincy had also known Abby wouldn't get the job done. She just hadn't had her "special prep" time. Hadn't had the time to "discover the spirit" of her target. Quincy rolled his eyes, sighed again, and opened the door. He had everything he needed in the trunk. Always be prepared.

Quincy popped the trunk, grabbed a black briefcase, briefly checked its contents, and started toward the building. His heart started beating faster, pushing adrenaline through his system. The sound of car tires on the pavement behind him made him look back. He increased his pace. Corporate fleet vehicles. Lots of them. Life had just gotten more interesting.

He made it inside the building before the cars had a chance to park. He stopped at the counter and cleared his throat.

Dispatch looked up from her work, a smile spreading across her face. "Hi, Quincy."

———

LEVEL 6—WEDNESDAY, AUGUST 10, 2140 11:00 A.M.

Devon sat in the assistant director's office, with its over-stuffed leather chairs, a huge fake mahogany desk, a se-ries of worn Turkish rugs covering the floor, and an absolutely awful view. The AD's corner windows were just below the concrete ceiling separating Level 6 from Level 7. Twentieth floor and the lowest rent in the build-ing. At least the ceiling was painted blue. An office that even a small corporate executive would shun, which is exactly why it had been allocated to Nigel Wood.

The company Nigel worked for didn't want, or need, expensive offices showing the world how much money they had. In fact, the less the corporations knew about them, the better. Nigel told anyone that would listen to him that if he could have had his way, his office, along with everybody else's, would be down on Level 4.

The size, however, was a necessity. Some of the higher-level meetings that took place here had upward of fif-teen people in attendance, most of them standing. Today's meeting consisted of only Nigel and Devon.

The sign on Nigel's office door read GeoTech Envi-ronmental Research. In reality, Nigel worked for the same people Devon did, ACE, the underground Anti-Corporation Enterprise. Most people thought of ACE as a small group of subversives that spray-painted slogans on corporate billboards and tagged their buildings with rude drawings. And that was just the way ACE wanted it. In reality, ACE had two arms. One fought the corporations, trying their best to play the corporate game of espionage and backstabbing. The other fought the corporations on a different front. As long as the corporations were making money, they didn't care how they were destroying the planet. ACE made the old-fashioned Greenpeace look like a bunch of kids at a petting zoo.

Devon watched Nigel pace back and forth across the rugs, wearing the heavily used path deeper into the worn fibers. Nigel was a short, fat, disgusting man. His face was constantly red from the exertion of moving his weight from point A to point B. Beads of sweat were already appearing on his forehead, and Devon knew he would eventually pull a soiled rag from his pocket and mop at it. When he spoke, it sounded like his mouth was full of marbles.

"Where are we at, Devon? What's this situation all about?"

"As you know, sir—"

"Don't tell me what I know," Nigel interrupted. "Give me the new details."

"Yes, sir." Devon closed his eyes, recalling the latest information. "The package apparently originated from SoCal offices, Earthside, on Level 4. The delivery was to Innotek, a small, recently incorporated firm. The systems are still looking for any potential links to the Big Three, but it looks like some records have been inadvertently lost along the way."

"Which means one of the Big Three had their hand in the pie."

"It would seem like it."

"Can we rule out SoCal?"

"I don't think we can rule out any of them, sir. SoCal could have been sending a packet to itself, testing its internal systems and staff."

"Has your system ruled them out?"

"Not yet, it's still giving them a five percent chance."

"Based on what?"

"I don't know. I can have a report sent to you over the hard line when I get back to the office."

Nigel waved his pudgy hand, dismissing the idea. "Let the system work on it a bit longer first. What else do we have?"

"From the timing of events, it looks like the SoCal Black Ops guys showed up at the delivery site before the courier. A cleanup crew was dispatched later that same evening, though no reports of missing people have been issued. More specifically, no one known to be employed in the building or living in a ten-kilometer radius. We're scanning a wider area now and trying to find a potential victim."

"How close are we to finding out what happened in there?"

"Not very. The building had been newly renovated and several of our taps were removed in the process. The building was, still is, a black hole in our network."

"Damn. How long has it been that way?"

"Three weeks, sir."

"Damn."

"Yes, sir. Crews are waiting for an opportunity to get back in," Devon continued. "Shortly after the courier arrived, we have a snapshot of her leaving. It was the snapshot and subsequent communication on a known Black Ops device that tipped us off to their presence."

"Any chance of the device having been compromised?"

"Not that we know of, sir. The device is still in use, and

seems to be feeding location information back to So-Cal."

"Location information? On who?"

"The courier, sir."

"The courier?" Nigel made his way back to his paper-strewn desk and started fishing through documents. He grabbed one and started reading it. "You're telling me a sixteen-year-old girl is managing to avoid a Black Ops team?"

"We're not sure of that. It could be they're just following her, keeping tabs on where she goes."

Nigel looked at Devon and raised his eyebrows. "We've worked together a long time, Devon, I know there's a 'but' in there somewhere."

"Yes, there is. Either the information coming from the unit is being delayed on purpose, or she really is managing to stay ahead of them."

Nigel scanned the document in his hand again, his gaze resting on her image. "Is there any chance she's been trained?"

"Not that we can tell. None of the telltale signs are visible. No lost records, no altered timelines. Nothing we can see."

"Has she been altering or turning off her tracker?"

"Again, not that we can tell. We have had blackout situations, but always where we expect them. The systems just aren't catching any anomalies."

"Keep looking into it. Find out if we can nab her for ourselves or if someone's already done that."

"Yes, sir."

"What else have you got?"

"We have an actual body. A known freelancer dead on Level 1."

"And this relates how?"

"Kris—the courier—entered Level 1 late last night.

All we know for sure is that she turned north off the ramp. The body was found north of the ramp in an empty lot, the back of his head blasted off. A team was sent in and discovered at least one definite bullet impact point that looked new. From the angle, it could have been a sniper on the building across the lot. The computer gives it an eighty-two percent possibility of being related."

"Any sign of the girl?"

"Nothing since she went down the ramp."

"Okay. What about the package? What's in there that SoCal wants so badly?"

"We couldn't even begin to guess, sir. We can't even figure out if the SoCal Black Ops team knew which package they wanted to track, or if they just got caught doing something they shouldn't have and want to eliminate the loose ends. If they knew the package, they probably have someone inside Internuncio, the courier company."

"So basically we know the players, and nothing else."

"Right."

Nigel kept the paper in his hand and moved back behind his desk. "I want the girl and the package. Have the system run a position predictor on her. I'll get a team ready for the grab."

Devon stood and walked to the door.

"Time is of the essence here, Devon. If the girl dies and the package ends up back at SoCal, we could be losing a tremendous opportunity."

"Yes, sir."

SIX

I WAS HALFWAY TO the depot before I decided to call Dispatch. The last call I made was a little light on details, and I sure as hell didn't feel like hanging over Dispatch's counter having everyone hear how I'd almost gotten myself killed. They'd have some pretty wild guesses just by looking at me, though.

I grabbed the black and chrome comm unit, connected to the voice system, and placed a call to Dispatch. The display flashed red and the unit beeped twice. I looked at the screen.

Connection is not encrypted, continue?

My heart skipped a beat and my stomach flipped. The car suddenly felt confining. Another reminder of the strangeness I was trying to escape. I hesitated before pressing the okay button. Dispatch answered on the first ring.

"Yeah, Internuncio."

"Dispatch, this is Kris."

There was a sharp intake of breath from the other end of the connection.

"Where the hell are you, girlie?"

"I'm on my way in. Listen, last night's package—"

"This place has been crawling with corporate types all morning," Dispatch interrupted. "Girlie, what happened to the damn delivery?"

I could feel the anger that had been churning in my gut since yesterday spill to the surface. I'd had just about enough. To hell with the job, and the bitch behind the counter. "If you shut the fuck up for a minute, I could tell you." My voice rose until the last words were yelled into the comm unit.

Dispatch's tone changed immediately. "What's wrong, Kris?"

Was that concern I heard in her voice? It sure as hell sounded like it. Maybe I should have tried yelling at her months ago.

My anger dissipated like a popped balloon and the story of what happened last night poured out of me, leaving me feeling empty and tired. I rubbed my eyes with my fingers. What felt like an entire lifetime wrapped up into several sentences. When I was finished, all I heard was silence from the other end of the connection. "You still there, Dispatch?"

"Yeah. Yeah, I'm still here. Give me a sec."

"Look, whatever. I'm almost there. I'm coming in and dropping off the package."

"No."

"What?"

"No. Kris, this place is crawling. If you walk in here, you may never be seen again."

"What the hell are you talking about?"

"These corporates, they can make you just disappear, like you never even existed."

"You read too much garbage. I want to be rid of this damn package."

"Look, girlie." The hard edge had come back into Dispatch's voice. "I've got a coffee break coming. Why don't you meet me outside in say . . . five minutes? I'll walk out the parking lot door and meet you in the back lane."

"I'll be there in fifteen. As long as my name's off the paperwork."

"It already is, girlie. Be careful." Dispatch closed the connection.

What the hell did she mean by that? No way Dispatch ever did your job for you. Sure, she did sound worried, but taking your name off paperwork was something she just didn't do. Maybe Dispatch actually did have a heart, it just took a boatload of shit to bring it to the surface.

I parked the stolen car a couple of blocks from the depot and walked the rest of the way. My life had had enough fuckups recently, I wanted to make sure I had some sort of getaway planned, and the car was the best one I had. I started out limping, stretching my calf and hip. By the time I got there the pain had lessened and I was moving almost normally.

Walking to the back lane almost felt like coming home. With each step, my feet felt lighter and my pace increased. Soon I'd be rid of the damn package, and things—life—could get back to normal. The cop car wasn't parked in its spot yet, it was still too early in the day for him.

The back lane was between Internuncio and a strip mall of small business owners, dreaming of making it big.

I couldn't figure it out. What was the point of starting your own business? If you managed to do anything right, one of the corporations would notice and either buy you outright, or set up shop beside you with better prices and service . . . for a while. Either way you were out on your ass and trying to start over. As far as I was concerned, it was better to just collect a paycheck and save as much as you could for the leaner times.

The parking lot was almost full, with only a couple of bikes parked outside. Howie's was easy to see, with its hideous blue paint. The other vehicles were all large, dark cars with numbers stenciled on the back. Some even had those stupid "How am I driving" stickers with comm link numbers on them. Corporate cars, and the numbers and stickers made them all out to be low-level people. No way anyone higher up the corporate ladder would be caught dead driving around in one of those things. My gut clenched and I almost tripped over my own feet. Something wasn't right.

I hunkered down in the shadow behind the back wall of the strip mall and waited, watching the parking lot and back door. It smelled as though someone had used this spot as a toilet not too long ago. Despite the stench, I felt myself nodding off, exhaustion sweeping over me, and almost fell asleep before the door opened.

My heart jumped into my throat and my first thought was to run, but my feet felt like they were bolted to the concrete and my legs refused to move. What the hell was *he* doing here? Quincy walked through the rear employees' entrance and into the bright Ambients. He paused, his slim fingers putting his sunglasses on before stepping aside to hold the door open for the next person.

Dispatch walked through next, shielding her eyes from the light, and scanned the parking lot.

I decided my feet knew what the hell they were doing.

I stayed down, dropping to all fours, looking for a better place to hide. Keeping one of the corporate cars between us, I crawled across the back lane to the parking lot. Closer to Quincy, but at least with something more than shadows to hide me. I stopped behind the corner of the car and peered through its windows. Quincy and Dispatch were talking and moving closer to the back lane, scanning the lot as though they were looking for something. Looking for me. What the fuck was going on? Quincy glanced at his watch and sped up, stepping in front of Dispatch. I ducked, banging my head on the side of the car. He must have seen me. My hands felt clammy and I wiped them on my pant legs.

They were halfway across the parking lot when the world seemed to end.

A burst of light pushed into my eyes, followed by a tide of heat that felt like it would melt the skin off my face. I flinched and ducked as a rush of hot wind surged over the car. The window I had been looking through shattered, spreading its crystallized safety glass across the back lane and into my hair. The car rocked on its suspension, springs squealing in protest. Flaming pieces of wood and shattered chunks of concrete fell to the ground around me. I crawled under the still-shaking car. My window on the world, limited by the twenty-centimeter gap between the bottom of the car and the parking lot asphalt, was a direct view into hell.

Smoldering debris fell from the sky. Anything that was remotely combustible—paper, carpet, clothing— was being consumed by flames. The onslaught of wind had stopped, at least this close to the ground, but I could still feel a wash of heat from the depot. I was enveloped in a blanket of silence. It was as though I was watching a vid with the sound off. Something fell in front of the car and rolled partially underneath. It looked like the charred remains of a human hand. I closed my eyes and turned away.

The deafening silence turned into a tinny, high-pitched whine in my ears. Sound slowly came back. Car alarms rang and lights flashed throughout the parking lot, occasionally looking and sounding as though they were a tightly orchestrated band synced to perfection before losing control and filling the air with loud, random noise. I crawled out from under the car and stood, holding on to it for support, and looked toward the depot. Two of the outer walls were left partially standing, deformed parodies of what they had once been, now twisted and black with soot. Smoke and fire poured from the hole in the ground, quickly filling the enclosed space of Level 3 with a thick acrid cloud. Car lights flashed through the thickening gloom, eerily lighting the fine dust and grit that was starting to settle to the ground.

I didn't hear any cries for help. There was no way anyone had made it out of there alive. My body felt numb, and the feeling slowly slid its tendrils into my brain.

The first emergency crews arrived. Quick-response air drones, no more than thirty centimeters across, darted through the thick black smoke only to hover over something on the ground before resuming their flight. I covered my nose and mouth with the crook of my arm and moved farther away from the destruction and death around me. One of the drones—a police identification unit, I thought—followed me out of the cloud and hovered over me when I stopped to suck in a breath of fresher air. Even out here, the fine dust created by the explosion made the pavement feel gritty.

The drone left me, meeting up with a second drone coming out of the dark cloud about three meters away, following another stumbling figure. I watched as Quincy staggered and fell to his knees, tears streaming down his face, leaving a trail of clean white skin in their wake. He looked up at me and grinned.

The slower ground response units began arriving, stopping just outside the ever-expanding smoke cloud. The numbness snapped as piercing fear grabbed control of me. I took several hasty steps back, merging with the still-growing cloud. As Quincy disappeared from view, I saw him lurch to his feet and pull his phone from his pocket, quickly typing on the screen. The drones left him, heading into the smoke. I covered my mouth with my sleeve again and ran down the back lane to a side street.

By the time I reached the car, the smoke was already being sucked into the air purifiers. They had been switched to high, and the loud thrum of fan blades pulsed through my head, making me feel detached from the world. I unlocked the car door, opened it, and drove slowly away.

LEVEL 3—WEDNESDAY, AUGUST 10, 2140 12:35 P.M.

Several blocks away, the humming of the fans faded, re-placed by a waterfall of emotions. Every fiber of my being was hit by the rushing cascade. I stopped the car in the middle of the street, crying in great heaving breaths. I kept going back to Howie's hand-painted blue bike, parked just outside the doors.

Only the sound of more emergency vehicles racing past, their sirens blaring, pulled me from the edge. I put the car back into drive and continued to the closest up-ramp, my vision still blurred by tears.

Quincy had grinned when he came out of the smoke, his white teeth and tear streaks deforming his face into a mask of pure evil. Why the grin? What the fuck was that all about? Was Quincy the one who had set the bomb, or was someone else responsible? And why the hell had Quincy and Dispatch left the building together? Dispatch had definitely been looking for me across the parking lot, but what about Quincy? Were they working together? If that was the case, then it couldn't have been coincidence that I'd gotten the last delivery. Could it? I remember the day going really well until the second-to-last run, when Dispatch had sent me on a long trek. Had it been planned that I got the last "emergency" package of the day? Was I just a disposable item that wouldn't be missed?

The questions kept coming, pummeling my already tired brain until they blurred into a single mass of doubt. I'd only had about five hours of sleep in the last thirty-two, and the effects were starting to show. I couldn't think straight anymore. Every question seemed to bring up another one, another problem, another layer of disbelief. Why me?

A car pulled in front of me and braked hard. Adrenaline coursed through my veins. Quincy? Before I had a chance to react, it accelerated and passed the car ahead of it.

I still had the package. I pulled the crinkled envelope from the inside pocket of my jacket and threw it on the seat beside me. What the hell was in there that would make murder a viable option and cause me this kind of shit? Not just me and the guy at the delivery site either—everyone at the depot. Howie. He had never done anything wrong to anyone.

I grabbed the envelope and stuck the corner between my teeth, biting down on the paper. I gave it a tug. The corner pulled out of my mouth and I flung the envelope back onto the seat beside me.

Fuck! If I really knew what was in it, nothing would

stop the bastards from killing me. Just knowing I had the package seemed a good enough reason to them. As long as the damn thing was sealed, I figured I still had a chance. Quincy was still around, and still trying to get the envelope. What if I just gave it to him? Would he let me walk away? I saw the gutted man lying on the floor in his office again, and the grin Quincy had given me at the depot. I didn't think so.

So that meant I had to go above him, which was easier said than done. I had no idea who his bosses were. The only lead I had was from Frank, and I didn't think it was related to Quincy at all. I fished the comm unit out from under the envelope and read through the messages one more time.

What if I responded to the message? Would the person on the other end really want the package, or did they, as Frank had hinted, want me? If it was just me, why? Nothing I had ever done had prepared me for any of this shit. Hell, I didn't even watch mysteries on the fucking vids.

I could have dumped the package already. Quincy was right there. All I had to do was throw it at him. Stupid! I was so fucking stupid. I'd had my out, and I'd missed it. I almost turned the car around.

I drew in a deep breath and held it until my lungs threatened to burst. It was decision time, and the only one I could see to follow through on was the lead from Frank. I pulled the car to the side of the road and reread the last message, ready to send a response.

What tactic should I take? Was Frank the kind of guy who set the date and time for any meetings, or did he bend to the wishes of his masters? My uneducated guess figured him for a leader, not a follower. Sure, he worked for other people, but mostly on his own terms. That was the impression I got. Okay then, I would play it that way.

I keyed in a response for the last message: *Assignment complete. McConnell Park drop-off at three p.m.* I hesitated over the send button. What if this was wrong? What if it didn't work?

My finger touched the screen.

seven

DEVON SAT IN his office watching the displays blur in front of his eyes. He leaned back in his chair and rubbed his stiff shoulders and neck. Things just weren't adding up, and it was starting to take its toll on him. His shirt itched where it touched his skin, and even the faint hum of the computer was irritating.

It was obvious that SoCal had sent the package. It had originated from one of their offices after all. After that it had gone to Innotek where, go figure, SoCal Black Ops had been waiting for it.

There was some piece of the puzzle still missing, something that tied all of this together into a neat little package. Devon liked neat little packages, and he made sure that his world fit into those boundaries. His software made sure everything fit into those boundaries as well, but now it was doing anything but.

The amount of ancillary information collected around the courier and the package was staggering. Everything from a recorded interference by some skateboarders, to when the streets the courier had taken were last cleaned of garbage. And yet the systems couldn't find a thread, couldn't see how all the events tied together. That was a first. The only thing the system continued to do was track the courier—and by doing so, the package. Even that wasn't working too well . . . she kept dropping off the map.

The last report that came in was from a real-time feed. The building the courier operated out of had been utterly destroyed. The investigators would be picking through the rubble for weeks trying to figure out what had happened. The corporations were being quiet about the whole thing, considering that they'd had more people there in the last two hours than they had in the last decade.

Police drones had scanned Kris and another male survivor just outside of the billowing cloud of smoke. The only anomaly there was that a second drone was required to rescan the man. The first drone had gotten nothing but garbage. That could have been interference from the explosion, or the man could have modified his tracker ID. Devon had the computer searching for more information.

He ran his hands through his hair. Who was he trying to fool? The system had already started checking into the anomaly before he told it to. That's why they had the stupid thing. Some days, Devon wondered why he was even there.

The computer beeped and opened up a display window. Devon leaned forward and focused on the text. Damn, the anomaly was the same Black Ops agent who had scanned Kris's motorcycle at the failed drop-off point. No identification on who yet, just that it was the same ID number. SoCal really wanted whatever was in the package. The timing of the explosion couldn't have been better, for Kris's sake. If she had walked into the depot, she would never have walked out.

The computer popped open another window. It had just made a new connection between the disparate pieces of data. Apparently, the dead man on Level 1 had used a fairly high-end encrypted comm unit. That very same unit had just been used only a few blocks away from the bombed building. The chances of that being a coincidence bordered on zero percent. Kris must have grabbed the comm unit before she took off. It took another ten minutes for the system to crack the message and find out who it had been sent to.

Devon picked up the hard line and called the AD.

"Yes."

"Sir, the courier has just contacted someone using an encrypted comm unit."

"Yes."

"She's requested a meeting at 3:00 p.m. today at McConnell Park on Level 5. It may be that she's trying to dump the package."

"Who with?"

"It looks like IBC," Devon answered.

"Thank you."

"Are we going to do anything?"

"We have the situation under control. Keep me posted on any changes."

"Yes, sir."

The line disconnected.

Devon held on to the landline for a while before slowly lowering it back onto his desk. He looked around his office, safe in the knowledge that no one knew it existed. Safe knowing that if anyone came within a hundred meters of the place, he would be warned and could monitor the situation. All he did was hand out information. And here was a sixteen-year-old girl who had been through more in the last two days than he could ever imagine. And she kept on going. Kept moving no matter what the corporations threw at her. She was an anomaly. Something that didn't fit into the boxes he liked so much. The courier's tracker ID popped on the screen at his request, and he instructed the computer to continually update her position. A new window opened, displaying a map with a pulsing blue dot.

Devon watched the list on the right display. A line filtered to the top. Nigel Wood had assigned one of his teams to retrieve the courier. Devon smiled as the courier's box began to take form.

Another line pushed to the top of the list, and Devon's smiled disappeared as quickly as it had formed. The computer had identified the man emerging from the explosion.

Devon's life had just become more complicated. He left his office to make a call.

LEVEL 5—WEDNESDAY, AUGUST 10, 2140 2:45 P.M.

McConnell Park lay at the base of an up-ramp leading to Level 6. It was a medium-sized grassy area with a gravel path that wove its way around the perimeter between stands of sickly oak trees. A pond, which according to the sign had once held ducks and geese, filled the southern corner. The water looked like the trees, gray and bland, covered in the general dust and grime of a big city. I stopped briefly, using the fetid water to clean my face and hands. The liquid burned as it hit my neck and the cuts on my fingers, but I felt cleaner. The northwestern section held various monuments, men holding swords or guns high in the air, riding horses.

I remembered reading somewhere the significance of the horses in these statues. It was something like, if the horse was on its rear legs only, the person on the horse had died in battle, if the horse had at least a front and a rear leg on the ground, the person was just famous. Or some crap like that. Really, who cared anyways?

All I cared about right now was that I could see most of the park and stay hidden behind one of the statues. The one I was behind still had a plaque on it, the writing obscured by years of grime. I crouched near the base, the horse on its rear legs only reaching upward to the ceiling.

Level 5 always felt so open to me . . . a feeling I didn't enjoy. Levels 4 and 5 were about thirty-seven meters tall, almost twice the height of the twenty-one meter ceilings I'd grown used to on Level 2. Never having been on Levels 6 or 7, I had no idea how high up they might go. Being in the open space without my motorcycle or helmet made my heart race, pounding in my chest, and I slowed my breathing to try and calm it down. It seemed to work.

I could see why the park had been picked as a meeting place. The traffic heading up to Level 6 was all stop and go, waiting to be cleared through security before entering the rarefied communities and businesses. All of the drivers would be too concerned with their own business to be watching what happened in the park. Still, if something did happen, they were close enough to see just about everything. Three o'clock in the afternoon made sense, too. The trail through the park had a few mothers pushing baby carriages and a jogger or two, but other than that privacy was pretty much guaranteed.

The security at the up-ramp wasn't the government-run police either, it was corporate. For all I knew, they could have been paid to ignore anything that happened here anyway.

From my vantage point, I could see a couple of guys dead center, just north of the pond. They both wore short gray jackets and slacks, and they were the only people in the park who didn't look like they were just passing through. I pulled the comm unit free of my jacket and sent a single word.

North.

A few seconds later, the tall one with what looked like a freakishly huge comb-over pulled out his comm unit and read a message. He put the comm unit back in his pocket and walked to the gravel path, turning north when he reached it. The path would take him right past me. I watched him for a while before turning my attention to the other man. He had left the park and was heading around the south side of the pond. I ignored him.

I turned my attention back to the man with the comb-over. He followed the path until he was into the memorial statues. With each step, my uncertainty increased. For the tenth time today, my fingers reached for the golden figure of Oscar in my pocket. For the tenth time, I jerked them back.

I still wasn't sure this was the right thing to do. But did I really have any choice?

When he passed me, I stepped out behind him and pressed Frank's gun into his back. He stiffened for a second, and then continued his slow walk down the path. I followed close behind. He smelled faintly of coconut hand cream.

"We found Frank," he said.

I didn't falter. "Over to the bench."

Comb-over left the path and sat down slowly on the bench. He still hadn't looked at who might be pointing a gun at him, though if he had any kind of intelligence he would have guessed by my voice. I stayed on my feet behind the bench, the gun now pointed at the back of his head.

"You did quite the job on him," he said.

"I didn't do anything. Your sniper got him by mistake."

"Ahhh. We thought it might have been a sniper, probably on the building across the lot. Not one of ours though."

Not one of theirs? Who the hell had it been then? Quincy, or the people he worked for? Maybe. Maybe Frank had enemies, and it had nothing to do with me. That didn't explain my close escape in the elevator shaft, though.

"Explain," I said.

"Frank's job was to bring you here, to us, so we could talk to you."

I took a quick look around, shifting from one foot to the other. "Us?"

"Oh, yes, us. Of course, I'll be the only one you'll talk to, but there are several of my people around. I'd say right now you have about five or six weapons pointed at you. And unlike that sniper on Level 1, they almost never miss their target."

My back began to tingle, and I moved slightly to be in line with the statue behind me. Coming here was starting to feel like a mistake, but it was too late to turn back now. I tried to act brave. "And you expect me to believe you?"

"Of course. Here, let me help you, let me prove I'm telling the truth. Monica, would you please show us your weapon and then leave the park?"

I glanced around and caught a glimpse of reflected

Ambients on metal. One of the mothers pushing a baby carriage on the path raised a rifle out of the carriage, caressed the barrel, and placed it back quickly, covering it with a blanket. She turned her carriage around and took the shortest route to the perimeter of the park.

"Now, you may as well put the gun away. If you do pull the trigger, you will never leave the park alive."

I hesitated. He may have been lying, and the woman with the baby carriage was the only one in the park with them. Then again, there was the man he'd been standing with earlier. I put the pistol inside my jacket, keeping it in my grip, and moved around the bench, sitting as far from comb-over as I could get. The hidden gun pointed at his chest.

"What do you want from me?" I asked.

"Why don't we introduce ourselves first? You are, of course, Kris Ballard, the sixteen-year-old runaway with the curious ability to stay alive. I am Michael Fletcher. I work for IBC."

IBC, the International Business Cooperative, was one of the three major corporations that pretty much ran the country. Most of the rumors on the last election had said the president was just a puppet, bought and paid for by IBC despite what the people wanted. Which was exactly why I'd decided I was never going to vote. What was the point when the corporations basically fought amongst themselves to place a figurehead in the Oval Office?

Time to get to the point. "And why would IBC send someone to kidnap me and bring me here?"

"Kidnap? Oh dear, *kidnap* is such a harsh word. All we wanted was an opportunity to talk to you. Frank was supposed to be your escort to make sure you arrived safely."

"Yeah, right." This guy was an idiot if he thought I believed that.

Michael turned to look at me. "You are the reason we sent Frank. Or is it the 'escort' part you don't believe?" The bastard was actually smirking now.

My grip tightened on the gun. "Listen, Mikey." I felt a minor victory when Michael's smile vanished. Apparently he didn't like being called Mikey. His mother probably called him that, if the asshole even had a mother. "Everyone seems to want the package. I just happen to be the one carrying it, which is a job I don't want anymore."

"Ahh, yes, the package. I find it almost as interesting that you still have it as I do that you're still around to *tell* me you have it." He fixed his gaze on the stunted oak at the edge of the park. "Have you opened it to find out what all of this is about?"

A coldness sunk into my core. He had no idea how close I'd gotten to doing exactly that. "You're kidding me, right? If I open the package, I'm pretty much dead. If I can get rid of the damn thing while it's still sealed, I may be able to walk out of this alive."

"You really don't understand then, do you?" He looked at me as though I was some sort of freak. "You really are an anomaly. Fascinating."

I jumped to my feet. I'd had enough bullshit to last a fucking lifetime. It was time to find out if this guy was going to play ball. "I'll find someone else to give the package to."

"If you take one more step, it will be your last one."

He was a fucking asshole, but at least my bluff had worked. I slowly sat back down. "Just as long as you know—Mikey. If I feel any of this turning sour, you're not making it out of here either."

Michael shrugged nonchalantly. "Those are the risks I took when I accepted the job. The risks we all accepted."

"I didn't accept any of this bullshit. All I want is out."

"Out, or safety? Those are two entirely different things, you know."

I looked at him out of the corner of my eye. "What do you mean?"

"Let me fill you in on a few of the details first. Where did you pick up the package?"

I wasn't about to give this guy any information. "You tell me."

"If you insist." Michael sighed and continued. "You picked up the package at a SoCal Level 4 office. Pretty much a run-of-the-mill pickup, though maybe a bit late in the day. That, apparently, was planned. Emily—I believe you all just call her Dispatch—specifically picked you as the courier of choice for this trip."

"Fucking bitch."

"Hmmm, yes. I don't think she knew all the details, really. Just that this was an important package and needed a speedy and guaranteed delivery. The fact that she pulled you into it was probably meant to be a compliment.

"As I was saying, you picked up at SoCal and dropped off at Innotek. Innotek is a new subsidiary of Kadokawa, and a very quiet one. So, two of the largest corporations in the world are exchanging data. Not an interesting piece of information on its own. What makes it interesting is the presence of the SoCal Black Ops team when you made your delivery. Did you know that the president of Innotek, what was his name ... Gorō, I believe, has not been seen since that night? That's a very odd thing, considering how monitored our society really is." He shook his head. "But I'm straying off topic. Now why would SoCal have a team at the pickup point?"

Michael looked at me as though waiting for an answer.

"How the fuck should I know? I just deliver the packages."

"Think, Ms. Ballard. You haven't stayed alive this long by turning off your brain."

I mulled it over, playing along. "Maybe the package contains information SoCal doesn't want known?"

"Doesn't want known ... perhaps. How about should not exist? Now what information could SoCal have that should not exist? Interesting, don't you think?"

"No." But my mind was working at about two hundred kilometers per hour. SoCal was one of the biggest, if not *the* biggest, corporations in the world. They owned most of San Angeles, and maintained at least four of the massive Sat Cities sitting in geosynchronous orbit. That's pretty much where my memories from school left me.

"Now what if I told you the Black Ops team was Meridian, pretending they were SoCal? The problem is that we don't know. Kadokawa may know. To them, the package may only have contained proof of something. And now, Ms. Ballard, to the point. You have the package—"

"And you want it."

"If you interrupt me again, Ms. Ballard, I shall be forced to walk away."

For the first time in this meeting, a sense of calm came over me. "I call bullshit." There was no way he would go to all the trouble of getting me to just walk away.

Michael gave me another appraising look. "Hmmm, yes. Well, as you most succinctly stated, IBC wants to see the package."

"I don't have it. I gave it to Dispatch this morning."

"Do you think me a fool, Ms. Ballard? Do you truly believe we wouldn't know if you had the package or not? Your ... Dispatch does not have the package, and of course she never will. The package is still in your possession. If it was not, you would not have come to this meeting."

"Fuck you."

"Hmmm, yes . . . right. I think you are a bit young for my taste, though I find your haircut somewhat appealing, but thank you for the offer." He paused, staring off into the distance. "Perhaps I should make myself clearer. My job here is to verify that the package is in your hands, which, as I just stated, is clearly the fact. Still, I would like to see it. If I didn't, my employers may be a tad upset."

This guy thought he had all the answers. I shifted in my seat. "I left it in the car."

"And where is the car?"

"Two blocks from here, beside a little service shop."

"You should have informed us of this earlier." He tilted his head, moving his mouth closer to his collar. "Find and cover the vehicle."

Several people turned and left the park. Some of them, I hadn't even seen before they moved.

"Now, let's walk to the car, while I tell you about your part of the plan."

"My part of the plan?" What was this bullshit? "I'll tell you my part. I get the package and give it to you. End of story."

"Ahh . . . not quite. My specialty does not lie in that particular area. My instructions are to have you complete your job."

"My job?"

"Yes. You are to deliver the package to the new president of Innotek. I believe he is already ensconced in his predecessor's office."

"I already tried that. It damn near got me killed." If this guy thought I was going back, he was crazy. I almost laughed out loud to cover up the fear I was sure was written all over my face.

"You will, of course, have the protection of the IBC for this delivery."

"That didn't help Frank much, did it?"

"Frank may have been an error. He preferred to work alone, and in this case, his preference was also his downfall."

"And if I refuse?"

"Refuse? My dear girl, that is entirely out of the question. Meridian has traced you to the park already, and I'm told your friend is with them. I'm afraid I don't know his name."

"Quincy?" I did another quick scan of the park, my stomach clenched into a tight knot.

"Ahh, Quincy. I've had the opportunity to hear his name several times. He can be most . . . enthusiastic with his knife."

"You've got that fucking right."

"Hmmm, yes. I will ask you not to swear, Ms. Ballard. It is unbecoming of a young woman."

"Fuck you."

"Hmmm, yes . . . right." He stood and waved toward the pond with his hand. "I believe we should leave the park rather quickly. Perhaps it would be best if we went this way?"

"The car's over here," I said, moving off in the opposite direction.

"That may be the case, Ms. Ballard, but so is your friend Quincy. If you are so anxious to meet him, then by all means . . ."

I scanned the park. I couldn't see Quincy, but that didn't mean anything. My legs felt weak and breathing became difficult. Mikey seemed to be the lesser of two evils.

"I think I'll stick with you for a while."

"Of course. This way, please." Michael grabbed my arm and started pulling me over the grass to the edge of the park. "Quickly, please." Speaking into his collar again, he said, "Delay them."

I took a quick look over my shoulder, allowing myself to be pulled along. A jogger had just stepped off the path, obviously not looking where he was going, and ran headlong into two people wearing business suits, one of them tall and thin. I couldn't tell if it was Quincy or not. All three people ended up on the ground, strewn across the gravel path.

Before I knew it, I was being dragged into a small restaurant and pushed out the back door. Michael walked me briskly down the back lane before he slowed and let go of my arm.

"I think perhaps we cut that one a bit close, wouldn't you agree?"

"The jogger, he—"

"Yes, one of ours. We should consider ourselves lucky he was at the right place at the right time. Now, where did you say the car was again?"

EIGHT

THE VIEW FROM the boardroom was magnificent. It never failed to amaze Jeremy when he walked through the door. The entire back wall opened to a massive high-resolution viewport showing a blue-green Earth sitting stationary beneath them. A storm system was developing over Bermuda, heading northwest by the look of it. The view was, of course, only an image on a screen. Developing and maintaining a real viewport the size of the wall would not only be hugely expensive, but also highly dangerous. A small piece of space debris hitting the center of a viewport that large would be catastrophic.

Jeremy Adams turned and looked at the other members of the cabinet. Most of them, like Jeremy himself, were getting on in years. None of them had been around for the last Corporate War. Neither had he. But after this meeting, they would be around for the next one.

The men and women around the table had broken into small groups, talking earnestly amongst themselves. Even a newcomer here would be able to see the dividing lines in the power structure. Yang, his tallow-colored face appearing calm despite the surprise meeting, had the largest group. His dark brown eyes darted from the door to the president's chair. His control of the budget committee always garnered a large following, with Fredericks and her manpower cronies ranking second. Jeremy himself was in charge of the defense portfolio, a position that had become less popular with the passing of the last Corporate Wars into memory.

The noise settled down to a quiet murmur as the president walked into the room. He was the youngest president in the history of Meridian, and he had proven to be one of its best. In a room full of dark suits and ties, he looked too casual in a beige sweater and slacks. Still, he emitted an aura of control.

Jeremy had handpicked Jonathon Hemshire for this position. He had watched the young lad grow into a position of great responsibility, and had been his tutor every step of the way. It was his tutoring that had led to this day.

The president moved amongst the groups, never staying too long with one or the other, courting each group in turn. The president had the responsibilities of the entire corporation on his shoulders. Every decision was ultimately his to make. Yet without the support of the people in this room, his power would be only in name. Jeremy watched the ease with which Jonathon mingled and extricated himself from every group, a skill that had come naturally to the young man.

The president reached his chair, placing his strong hands on the back of it. "If we may begin . . ."

The groups broke up as each person went to their assigned seat. Two secretaries moved to place coffee and tea on the table before moving discreetly to the walls. The president's own secretary, normally seated just behind him, also moved to the dark mahogany wall and spoke quietly to the two already standing there. All three walked to the door and closed it behind them.

Jeremy watched the event unfold and smiled inwardly. He had taught his student well. The president could have easily made sure there was no one in the room except the current cabinet before he entered. Instead, he had ensured that everyone saw the secretaries leave, gently pushing home the fact that this meeting would not be documented. History would not even know that a meeting had taken place.

Which was unfortunate, since today could turn out to be quite momentous indeed.

"Ladies and gentlemen. Thank you all for coming on such short notice. I know quite a few of you were Earthside."

There was a general murmuring of "Good evening, Mr. President," before the room became quiet once again.

"This board is in an envious position. Let me get directly to the point. Our research into interstellar travel, which we have been pouring money into for the last decade" — he nodded toward Yang — "has made a breakthrough."

Jeremy took a quick glance around the table. The president most definitely had all their attention now. The project had taken most of their reserves and had been a sore point amongst the cabinet for many years.

Yang leaned forward. "What kind of breakthrough are we talking about, Mr. President?"

"Several days ago, we sent one of our executive-class travelers to tour the Le Verrier mines on Neptune. When the specially modified ship reached the far side of Triton, the scientists on board initiated what they call a quantum jump. Twenty minutes later they initiated another jump, returning to Triton."

"Returning to Triton? Where did they go?"

Jonathon ignored the question and instead touched the screen embedded into the table in front of him. The image of Earth on the wall was replaced by a view of Neptune and Triton. The image zoomed into Triton, picking up a small ship on the far side.

"This, gentlemen, is a mock-up of the event."

The ship suddenly disappeared, leaving behind a quickly fading pinprick of light. The view changed, and the ship reappeared. Neptune and Triton were nowhere to be seen.

"The ship remained here for nineteen minutes and fifty-nine seconds, using all of its available scanning systems to collect data. It then returned."

The ship blinked out again, leaving the telltale pinpoint of light. The view switched back to Neptune and Triton.

"All systems checked out as normal, and the ship and its three passengers returned here. The passengers are still in quarantine, but so far they appear to be fine. Their names will go into the history books as the first to explore the Andromeda Galaxy, specifically thirty AU from the P1 nucleus."

The effect on the cabinet members was immediate, even on those who had no idea what an AU or the P1 nucleus was. Simply stating the ship had reached the Andromeda Galaxy was enough. Several of them stood so quickly their chairs bounced across the floor, impacting the richly wood-paneled wall behind them. The noise level increased until the president had to shout to be heard.

"People, please. Return to your chairs." He waited until everyone sat and silence had returned.

Yang was the first to speak. "Mr. President, have we been able to confirm the ship went where you say it did?"

"Yes. Mr. Adams has had a team examining the data for the last three days."

Jeremy stood and walked around the table, handing out folders to everyone present. "First, let me say that these folders will not leave this room. You may examine the data contained within as much as you wish, but they are to remain here when you leave." He sat back in his chair. "Ten years ago, Research and Development discovered the ability to send matter instantaneously across small distances. At that time, the project and its team were moved to my portfolio. In the intervening years, the distance and amount of matter we were able to move increased exponentially. Currently, the executive-class ship is close to our upper end. Most of the ship itself was converted to hold the engines required. We kept in the standard engines for interplanetary travel, which left us room for only three people and the high-resolution scanners."

Jeremy looked around the room at the mostly blank faces. Few registered how big the quantum engines needed to be to displace twelve executive-class suites.

"In the early stages, devices were required at both the sending and receiving ends to maintain integrity of the matter and accuracy at the destination. Once we managed to break through that barrier, the rest was a matter of increasing the object size. We believe Meridian is the only corporation or government to have this ability, which leaves us in a unique position of deciding what to do with it."

"Mr. President?" Yang had opened his folder and was running his finger down one of the columns. "We need to bring this project out of the military's purview and into sales. The cost of this development has been astronomical, and we desperately need to see some return on our investments."

The president leaned back in his chair and smiled. "I'm not sure that's the course we want to take."

"Mr. President?"

"Meridian has built its fortunes maintaining the Sat Cities," the president said, "as well as providing interplanetary vehicles to the other corporations. We are not the only ones to do so. Here we have the chance to forge ahead and grab hold of a market no other company has the ability to enter. If we sell this technology, we'll have half a dozen competitors before the year is out, and Meridian will be in the same place it always has been, a fair distance from the IBCs and SoCals of this world. I believe we, this cabinet, can bring Meridian to the front of the pack. This technology can do for us what the Cities have done for SoCal. Bring us into position number one."

Jeremy groaned inwardly. The president had taken this step too soon. The cabinet was old and comfortable, content with the way things were. Asking them to move the company into such a drastic venture without laying enough groundwork was sure to be disastrous.

"Sir," Yang said, "if we're not willing to sell this technology, the larger corporations could just take it from us. We don't have the military power to fend off an attack by IBC or SoCal."

The president waved his hand in Jeremy's direction. "Jeremy?"

Jeremy steepled his fingers and rested his chin on the

tips. This wasn't where he wanted to be, not so soon, but since the cards were on the table ... "I'm afraid, Mr. Yang, that I have not been entirely truthful about my portfolio's expenditures."

Yang's face started to turn red.

"Some of the funds allocated to the quantum jump project have been diverted into expanding our fleet. We have quadrupled our interplanetary fighters and trained pilots to fly them. We have also, under the guise of regular maintenance, reinforced this satellite's hull and armaments. In other words, we have been preparing for war to protect our investment. Since the return of our successful test, several executive-class ships have been taken out of service and are being retrofitted with jump engines and battle armament. By removing the scientific gear that was aboard the test ship, we believe we can fit a pilot and five gunners aboard. These ships are essentially weapons that can be anywhere at any time. We're also working on a prototype personnel carrier with a jump engine. Currently, the plan is unfeasible, but with the strides we have been making in this research, we expect to have something ready in the next nine months."

Yang stood up, his face so red that Jeremy thought it was going to explode. "You ... you falsified records to build an army? You stole from the corporation to build your own little empire! I will see you removed from your office for this."

The president coughed quietly. "Please sit down, Mr. Yang."

"But, Mr. President ..."

"I authorized the changes to his budget."

"You have no right!"

"But I do, Mr. Yang."

Yang sat and threw his pen down. It bounced off the folder in front of him and danced across the table.

"Please continue, Jeremy," the president said.

Jeremy glanced at Yang before continuing. "As I was saying, we should have a transport ship ready in about nine months. The transport ship can be used to carry anything, not just military personnel. For example, our scans of Andromeda showed quantities of water and metals. Quantities enough to supply Earth and its people for generations."

Fredericks leaned forward. "Mr. President, by withholding the technology from the other corporations and gaining access to resources no one else has, you are moving down the road to war. A war that, even with the extra resources just described by Mr. Adams, we have no hope of winning."

"That is correct, Ms. Fredericks. However, I do not plan on doing this alone. Tomorrow morning I have meetings with three other midrange corporations. I will be recommending a friendly takeover of their operations in exchange for access to our new resources. The transportation will, naturally, not be on the table for discussion, only access to the resources through us. If even just two of them join us, we will be able to withstand a SoCal and IBC standoff for some time. Long enough to get even more people on our side. If all three sign up, we will be in an even more powerful position."

"You sound quite sure of yourself, Mr. President," Yang said.

"I'm as sure as I can be, considering we are preparing for war." The president leaned forward in his chair and looked at everyone in the room. "Let's talk about what else we can do."

"Before we do, sir," Jeremy said, taking over the conversation again. "I believe that, once news of this leaks out, you will become a target for assassination. Before we go much further, we need to make sure you are protected."

"Why don't we discuss that when the need arises?"

"That will be too late, Mr. President. You have a meeting with the presidents of the United States and China next week. I'd like to increase our security measures to make sure you are safe."

The president raised an eyebrow in question. "Are you saying that I haven't been safe, Mr. Adams?"

"No, sir. But there are bound to be issues. If you still plan to make the announcement during those meetings, you will need extra security on the way home. All of the freaks will come out of the woodwork. I don't think we need to worry about the other corporations yet, but as soon as they find out you won't be sharing . . . In fact, I would like to convince you not to go to the meeting at all."

What the hell? Why the argument in front of the board? Jonathon was growing too big for his britches. Had he forgotten who got him where he was?

"And stand up the top two political leaders of the world?"

"You know as well as I that they are just puppets," Jeremy said. "China is under Kadokawa control, and IBC has the United States president. Their meeting with you is to further their own political agendas, which will end up helping the corporations behind them."

"True, Jeremy," the president said. "But in the next few months, none of that will matter. We will have access to enough water alone to end all the shortages on Earth. And we can bring the water here in less a day when the transport vessels are ready. Even now it takes months to bring ice from the outer reaches. I don't think the leaders will stay loyal to their corporations for long, once they see where the real power is shifting to."

"That is beside the point, Mr. President. The corporations will activate all of their moles and insiders. Some will try to get access to our technology, but others will be sent just to get you out of power."

"Do not misunderstand me, Jeremy," said the president. "I understand that attempts on my life will increase. I understand that we need to gird ourselves against an onslaught of attackers and protect the quantum jump drive. I just have a different opinion than you on which is more important. If I die, the corporation will still live on. It will still grow into the most powerful entity on Earth, and wherever else we decide to take it. Our resources will still be able to help the people of Earth."

That might be true, but Jonathon's replacement might not be someone Jeremy could control. If he still controlled Jonathon. "Mr. President, as of right now, you are the corporation. Without you at the helm, we would be lost. Looking for a new leader in the middle of battle results in the wrong type of leader being chosen. I'm not saying I wouldn't mind a more militant president"—he gave Jonathon a quick smirk—"but I don't think selecting one in a war situation will be good for the company."

"Jeremy, it's late and I'm tired. And if I stay much longer, my wife will wonder if I have a mistress." The president looked at the people sitting at the table, pausing to catch each person's eye. "Everyone in this room will have a specific job to do. There will be war, and we will be major participants in that war. I do not wish to lose. Think about that. We'll reconvene in the morning."

The president got up and left the room. The rest of the cabinet left the folders, some of them untouched, as they followed him out in complete silence.

Yang closed the door after everyone had left. He turned to Jeremy. "That went better than planned."

nine

I LED MIKEY OUT of the back lane and turned south on a narrow side street, away from the park. He stayed beside me the whole way. I thought I saw people following us, but I couldn't tell if it was just my tired brain playing tricks on me.

This whole thing was fucking bogus. Mikey and IBC seemed to think they owned me. Now they wanted me to finish the delivery . . . one that had almost gotten me killed last time, and led straight into this mess. The thought made me want to run as far away from here as I could. I didn't want to do this again. I had to dump Mikey.

But how? I needed to kick my brain into gear, but all

it wanted to do was shut down. Maybe if I just followed along for now. When we got to the car, I'd pass the package off to Mikey and run. Of course, I'd parked the damn car right in the open. At the time I'd thought it was a good idea. The more public, the less chance of anyone getting close to me or trying something. Now I wasn't so sure. Once I got the package in Mikey's hands, I had a lot of open space to cross. That would give him and his cronies plenty of time to catch me. Hell, this was beginning to sound damn near impossible.

Maybe I could get back to my own wheels. After I stole the van, I didn't want to go back home to get my bike. There was too much of a chance that Quincy or someone else was watching it. Chinatown was crowded enough during the day that they could have just grabbed me off the street before anyone knew what was happening. Now, if the IBC "protection" was solid, I might just be able to do it. I'd lost my lid, but the extra freedom of being on the motorcycle . . . Yeah, that would be good.

"If I'm going to help you, I want to get my bike first," I said.

"That wouldn't be a good idea."

"Why the fuck not?"

Mikey gave me a sideways look when I swore. "Because, young lady, you would be too exposed."

"Too exposed? I can move twice as fast on the bike as I can in this car. And I can go way more places."

"All very true. But you will also have no protection."

"What, your IBC guys can't keep up with a 'young lady' on two wheels?" I snorted as if the thought of it was funny.

"Don't you worry about us keeping up. That's our job. What I'm talking about is all the metal and glass the car puts around you. Frank made sure the car would stop almost anything. About the only thing that could hurt that car would be an antitank missile." Michael shrugged as if he was contemplating it. "They're tough to find on short notice, but SoCal might have a few. On your bike, someone could throw a rock at your head and bring you down. Oh, and your bike is tracked."

The car's capabilities dissolved in my mind, replaced by the new information. "What do you mean, the bike is tracked?"

"You really didn't know?" Mikey laughed. "I'm really beginning to believe you've been more lucky than skillful so far. Couriers have their vehicles tracked for record-keeping purposes. How else do you think your dispatcher knew where to send you next?"

"Duh, she knew the pickup and drop-off points of the current delivery. When we called in, she knew the general area we were in already. No tracking necessary." Was this guy just trying to freak me out or was he telling the truth? I had a tough time reading him.

"That would be accurate to a certain degree, but how many times did you call in after a quick run to the local donut shop? How did she get a delivery so close to where you ate, rather than where you delivered to? You're not a stupid girl, figure it out."

A cold knot settled in the pit of my stomach. Damn. He could be right. But then again, the quick stops were always close to the drop-off anyway. Just the thought of being tracked no matter where I went made me feel queasy.

I turned the corner, Mikey keeping step the entire way. "The car's right here."

"Unlock it and show me the package." He was all business again.

I went to the passenger door and keyed in the code. Pulling the door open, I grabbed the package out of the glove box. "Here you go."

I thrust the package at him before realizing I had nowhere to run. The bastard had blocked me between the open car door and my exit. He didn't take the package.

"Show me the labels," he said.

I angled the envelope so he could see the delivery label and the signature from the SoCal office.

"Good. Now get in the car and deliver it." He moved out of the way, but not enough to let me run.

My muscles twitched, aching to be released and run as far from here as possible. If I left the package, they'd have no choice but to take it. Instead, I threw the package onto the passenger seat and slammed the door shut before walking around to the driver's side. As I walked past Mikey, I got another whiff of coconut. I used to like that smell. The car started without any problems, and I gave Mikey the finger before driving away.

This was not fucking good.

LEVEL 2—WEDNESDAY, AUGUST 10, 2140 4:22 P.M.

I drove to the Level 4 down-ramp, stuck in rush hour traffic. It gave me time to try and piece together what had just happened. How the hell had I gone from trying to dump the package to going back to deliver it? *I* was supposed to be the one in control. *Me*. The protection IBC was supposed to give me didn't seem to be real either. I hadn't seen anyone following me when I left my parking space, and no one merged with me into this godawful traffic. Maybe Mikey was lying, and I was on my own again. Why the hell should I trust the fuckers?

I finally reached the ramp down to Level 3 and fought the traffic to Level 2. By the time I got there, my knuckles were white on the steering wheel. Whether from the traffic or where I was heading, I wasn't quite sure. I still hadn't seen anyone following me. Maybe it was time to test them and get off the route. Maybe if I pulled over and sat for a while, something would happen. Either I would get into more trouble, which was tough to believe at this point, or nothing would happen. If nothing happened, I was on my own again. I wasn't quite sure which thought bothered me more.

Up ahead was the damn Super Store again. Well, what the hell. It had been useful before. I turned the car into the lot and pulled into an empty spot near the road, beside a baby blue Kadokawa motorcycle. It reminded me of Howie's.

It only took a minute before Frank's comm unit beeped. I answered it.

"Anything wrong, Kris?"

It was Mikey. I looked at the comm's screen and saw the encryption indicator on. Even for this, they tried to keep things as secretive as possible. It must just be part of the way they lived and breathed.

"No, nothing wrong," I said.

"Why have you stopped?"

"I, uh . . ." I tried to think fast but my brain blundered from one incomplete answer to the next. What would they do if they knew I was testing them? "I . . . I dropped the comm unit and couldn't pick it up off the floor."

"You obviously have it now. Pull away from the curb and deliver the package."

"Yeah, o . . . okay. Bye." I closed the connection and placed the comm unit gently on the seat beside me. Fuck, they were watching me. I backed out of my spot and pulled out on the street before I realized something wasn't quite right. Mikey had told me to pull away from the curb. I was parked in the parking lot. Could he have just slipped up, or did he not know exactly where I was?

No way someone would make that mistake. That meant I wasn't being watched. I had some freedom.

They must have put a tracking device on the car. Or maybe they had managed to put one on me. I shivered at the thought, trying to remember when Mikey had gotten close enough to touch me. The answer took a while to pop into my head. When he pulled me from the park. I had been so busy looking over my shoulder, looking for Quincy, that Mikey could have done almost anything. I was used to owning my own space, and knowing when someone was in it. The lapse scared me almost as much as the events of the last day. I did a quick one-handed search of anyplace he could have touched me, and came up empty.

In the rearview mirror, I watched a tan sedan pull out of its parking space and merge with traffic. It stayed in my lane, two cars behind. Hadn't I seen that car when I left the park? Was it IBC's or SoCal's? I banged the steering wheel with the palm of my hand, my muscles aching from being held too taut. I was seeing problems at every turn now. Fine. *Fine* . . . Fuck. I would drop off the damn package. I just wished I had time to think.

San Angeles was huge. I would just have to find a place to hide afterward. Until it was safe to come back out. Get rid of the damn package. Hide. Maybe sleep for a week.

I turned down the street to Innotek and drove past the gray, square, five-story building, watching the entrance and the street in front. Everything looked . . . normal. There were no white vans parked anywhere. No tan sedans. It all looked quiet and calm, the sidewalk bathed in the yellow glow of the Innotek sign. But then again, nothing had looked out of the ordinary last time either, except for the security guard's new outfit.

I decided to park a block away and walk. If they were expecting me, maybe they'd be looking for the car. As I closed the door, the comm unit beeped again. I looked at it and slammed the car door shut, ignoring the damn thing. That felt good.

As I walked, the envelope tucked safely under my arm, a tan sedan drove past. The driver was watching the road ahead, and I couldn't see anyone else in the car. For a moment my feet felt too heavy to lift, and I plodded onward, stumbling over a crack in the sidewalk, almost falling to my knees.

Christ, now my mind was starting to play tricks on me. Every tan car that drove past would be the one I saw earlier. I needed to stop second-guessing what was going on and get the job done.

I approached the front door and the security guard unlocked it from the other side. This time, the uniform was crumpled and dirty. Obviously something that had been worn often, and a bit too long between washings. Deep smile lines surrounded the guard's eyes and mouth, though he wasn't smiling now.

"Evening, miss. We're expecting a delivery. That going up to the top floor?" he asked. His eyes flicked over my filthy and bloody clothes.

"Yes."

"You're a bit young to be making deliveries, aren't you, lassie? I think my granddaughter is about your age."

He kept flashing his eyes over my shoulder and nodding his head as if pointing at me with his chin. I could see the long gray hairs in his nose. I leaned against the open door, my legs too tired to support my weight anymore, waiting for the guard to move over so I could get in.

"In fact, if my granddaughter was delivering today, I kinda wish she would get a different job. Delivering here ain't safe—for a young girl." His lips continued to move after he stopped talking, shaping soundless words I couldn't make out.

"Can I get past? I need to get this thing delivered." I couldn't remember the last time I had met a guard so interested in chatting. Something was strange here. Either that or I was too freaked out by what had happened last time.

"Sure, though I wouldn't want to be a delivery person. No, sir."

I heard the roar of a motorcycle engine behind me and turned to see a flash of yellow and black on two wheels hurtle over the sidewalk toward me and the security guard. The bike seemed barely in control as it slid to a halt.

"Get on." The rider's voice was muffled through the helmet and closed visor.

My first thought was, *who drives gas anymore?*

LEVEL 2—WEDNESDAY, AUGUST 10, 2140 6:05 P.M.

Fear grabbed control and I jumped closer to the security guard, trying to push past him to get to the safety of the building. I could still hear the motorcycle behind me. The guard wasn't moving. I pushed harder, trying to duck under his arm. Just as he moved, a door behind the security desk swung open and Quincy ran out, pulling a gun from his shoulder holster. I stumbled backward onto the sidewalk.

A gloved hand grabbed my shoulder, yanking me closer to the bike. A man's voice bellowed in my ear. "Get on, now."

My stomach launched into my throat, stifling the

scream that threatened to erupt. How had he gotten here? How had he known? A gunshot boomed out of the lobby and the security guard crumpled.

Instinct took over, and I chose the lesser of two evils. I jumped on the back of the bike and grabbed the rider, the envelope jammed between us. I clamped down with my thighs as the bike surged forward, feeling Quincy's gun pointing at me, burning a hole in the middle of my back.

Whoever was riding the bike knew what he was doing. The bike flew off the curb and I felt it settle back onto its suspension, gaining traction again and accelerating. The driver made a beeline for the back alley across the street. Just before entering it, he locked the rear tire, sliding the bike's back end out and bringing us in line with the sidewalk. The engine roared and the back tire's sticky rubber grabbed the dry concrete, launching the bike forward, keeping the parked cars between us and Quincy. At the next block, he turned right on to the street.

After that, the driver did the same thing most of the couriers did and kept the tires on the cleanest part of the road. He weaved between the slower moving traffic and potholes, leaning the machine so far over that the foot pegs scraped on the ground, throwing a shower of sparks behind us.

Ahead lay one of the transfer elevators, an express to Level 4. As if on cue, the doors opened when we got close and we rode straight in and stopped. The driver locked the front wheel and twisted the accelerator as he leaned the bike to the left. The tail end swung out until we were facing the elevator doors instead of the back wall. The stench of burning rubber filled the enclosed space. The acrid air made me gag. Tears flooded my eyes, blurring my vision. The driver reached forward and pressed the close door button.

A tan sedan surged onto the street ahead of us just as the doors slid shut. The elevator rocked as it started up to Level 4. I realized I was still holding on to the guy in front of me and jerked my arms back. I grabbed the package as it slid down to the seat.

The driver raised his visor, keeping his face pointed away from the camera embedded just above the doors, and leaned to look back at me over his shoulder, revealing a young face with brown eyes.

"I didn't think we'd make it. You took long enough to get on the bike," he said.

I pushed myself off and pressed my back into the walls of the far corner, sliding the envelope into my pocket. My shoulders were shaking, and I hoped he couldn't see it.

"Relax. My name's Miller. We figured something was up when IBC let you go with the package." He patted the seat behind him and smiled. His smile went straight to his eyes. "You'd better get back on. When the door opens, I figure we got two minutes before they show up. Maybe less." He slammed his visor shut and faced forward again.

A wave of exhaustion blanketed me, pulsing outward until it reached even the tips of my fingers. Too much had happened in the last two days. Every piece, every particle of me cried out for sleep. I'd been wearing the same tattered and filthy clothes for days, and now they stank like I'd rolled through a burned-down house. I may as well have.

I was tired of running. Tired of people chasing me, commanding me, trying to kill me. Tired of the whole fucking mess.

The elevator doors started to slide open, and my body seemed to move of its own accord, as if knowing I had no control over it. I sat on the back of the bike and grabbed on again. The lesser of two evils.

This ride was less frantic. We made a couple of quick turns before riding into an interlevel parking garage. I watched the unpainted concrete walls zip past, blurring into a uniform gray. It felt like they were pushing in on me, squeezing the air from my lungs. I had to concentrate to pull air into my body. I think we went down a couple of floors before he—Miller—shut off the bike. The silence seeped into my numb skin.

Miller took off his helmet, pointing a thumb at the ramp we'd just taken. "The security cameras here have been disabled. No need to worry about them seeing our faces. They'll be switched back on in fifteen minutes or so. We need to change vehicles. Come on."

I slid off the seat and dropped to the ground by the rear tire. I couldn't breathe. I tried to suck the stale air in, but it never seemed to be enough.

"Now is not the time to give up. It'll take them a while to find the bike, and I want to be long gone before they do."

My eyes couldn't seem to focus. The walls still squeezed and pushed down on me.

"Come on," he said as he reached down and grabbed me under my arms. "Things are just about to get interesting. You don't wanna lose it now."

Miller half dragged and half carried me to a car. I barely noticed it, struggling to put one foot in front of the other. Somewhere in the back of my mind it registered that the sedan was a dark blue four-door. He opened the back door and laid me on the seat, my legs still hanging out the door.

"You just lie there and rest a while. I'll have you somewhere safe in no time. I just gotta make sure you're not being tracked."

He moved to the back of the car and I heard the trunk pop open. When he came back, he held a small scanner in his hand and began to move it over me. He whistled.

"Man, they weren't kidding when they said you were green. You've still got an active ID tag. With this damn thing turned on, they'll know where we are the second we leave the parking garage. Hell, they probably tracked us down here."

He ran to the trunk of the sedan and came back.

"Now, I'm gonna roll you over and stick this over your tag. I gotta block the tag from being read. You okay with that?"

Before my brain could even form a response he moved into the car and rolled me over, pushing my face into the back of the seat. My brain pushed through a thick fog, slow and sluggish. I wanted to stop him, but the signals didn't seem to be getting to my arms and legs.

"You could help a little bit, you know," he said.

Cool air hit my back as he lifted my jacket and shirt, sliding his hand in, to just under my shoulder blades, and pressed something cold and supple between them.

The fog lifted as the cold penetrated my skin, sweeping away the darkness. I squirmed and rolled over, kicking out with all the strength I had left. My foot missed Miller's head by a couple of centimeters.

Miller grinned, lighting up his whole face again. "Now that's more like it. Come on, we gotta get out of here. The car is out of the question. With your active ID tag, they'll already have the exits blocked. We need to move fast."

"What did you do?" I reached back and my fingers slid over a thin film stuck just below my shoulder blades.

"I told ya. I put a temporary block on your ID tag. The whole city's filled with scanners. The corporations, the government, anybody with access knows where you've been since the day you were born. Come on, we gotta move!"

I pulled the envelope out of my pocket. "I have this package. IBC told me to deliver it—"

"I know."

He grabbed it out of my hands and pulled me from the car. Without letting go, he started walking to the far corner of the garage.

"There's a service entrance on the next level down. We can jump between the levels here and get into the service area," he said.

I followed him, although I wasn't sure how much choice I had. When I slowed down, his grip tightened and he pulled me along. I focused my attention on the manila envelope in his hand, the reason I was in this mess. It didn't seem like much really. Just some paper glued together. What could be in it that could ruin my life so completely?

We reached a low wall. The drop on the other side was about two meters to the next parking level.

"I'll go first. You follow me, and I'll catch you if you slip, okay?"

I couldn't take my eyes off the envelope.

Miller grabbed the front of my jacket and pulled my face close to his. "Look, I don't feel like dying here today, and I can't leave you behind. You saw the guy at Innotek? He's a killer; it's his job. And he's after you, so pay attention and follow me. I'm going first. When I'm down, you follow."

The sound of tires screeching on the level above echoed around us, pulling me back from the edge.

"That could be them. We gotta move. You need to trust me."

"I don't know you," I said.

"No, you don't. But it's either me or them, and you know them." He pointed over my shoulder with his chin.

I made my decision. I had seen Quincy's handiwork.
"I'll follow."

"Good." Miller climbed over the wall and lowered
himself to the other side. His feet touched the ground
before his hands had let go.

Leaning over the wall, I saw him standing below, waiting. Tires squealed again. I moved over the wall, my arms
and shoulders holding on to the top. Suddenly, I was
back in the elevator shaft again, slipping slowly down.
My grip froze. The sound of a motor joined the squealing
tires.

"Just drop, I'll get you. Now!"

I closed my eyes and listened to his voice. I could hear
the urgency in it. I remembered his smile, how it touched
his eyes, and another wave of exhaustion cascaded
through me. I didn't know who he was, and I really didn't
care anymore. I let go and felt myself fall back, putting
my trust in a stranger.

Miller caught me before my feet hit the ground.

"Okay, just over here."

He stopped in front of an old service door, rust crawling through its gray paint. It looked as though it hadn't
been opened in years. Miller pulled a key from his pocket
and slid it into the rusted lock. It turned without making
a noise and the door swung open.

"Always be prepared," he said, looking at me.

He pushed me ahead of him into the yawning black
opening and closed the door behind us, locking it again.

"I don't know if they'll look in here. If they decide to,
that door won't hold them back long," he whispered. He
turned on a flashlight and handed it to me. "At least
there's no cameras in here. Just follow the corridor to the
tee section and turn right. I'll be right behind you."

I was lost. Miller had led me through so many doorways and up and down so many flights of stairs that I wasn't sure we were even on the same level anymore. The areas we had passed through had changed several times, from the dingy and dark one we had entered to a clean one painted industrial gray, to one almost hospital white. Now, twenty minutes after we had entered the maze, we were standing in front of another door. It was all a hazy mess.

"These service corridors pretty much go on forever. It's easy to get lost in here if you don't know the way."

Was that a threat or a warning? Either way, it didn't matter. I stumbled in the darkened tunnel and fell against the wall, sliding into a sitting position. I closed my eyes as the flashlight slipped from my loose grasp.

"Easy there. We should be okay for now. When was the last time you ate . . . or slept?"

"I don't know. This morning? Yesterday?" Everything over the last two days had become a blur in my mind. Had I eaten today? Somewhere in a remote part of my brain, it scared me that I couldn't remember.

Miller slid to the floor beside me. "Another ten minutes or so, and we'll be out of here."

"Who are you?"

"I told you, the name's Miller."

"Who do you work for?" I opened my eyes and looked at him.

Miller examined my face, his brown eyes felt like they were boring a hole into my soul. He seemed to come to a decision.

"All right. I work for ACE. You heard of us?"

I nodded. "Yeah, you're a bunch of taggers and vandals, destroying corporate property." I knew as I said it that the description didn't fit Miller.

"Yeah," Miller chuckled. "That too. ACE is a lot bigger than that. We fund and lead the anticorporate movement, both on the corporate side and as environmental hackers. We're actually bigger than some of the wannabe corporations. Not bigger than the Big Three, of course, but we're pretty good. I'd say we got about half a million people on the payroll, which would put us somewhere at the low end of the middle range."

"And your job is to rescue couriers in trouble?"

"Good." He smiled and leaned his head against the wall beside mine. "You're getting your wits about you again. C'mon, we'd better keep moving. You've got a meeting, and we're late."

I sighed and struggled to my feet, fighting the urge to just lie down and sleep. I figured as long as I kept moving, I had a chance. A chance at what, I didn't know.

About ten minutes later we were in another gray hallway. The pipes on the ceiling were covered with insulation and labeled with cryptic sequences of letters and numbers. We stood in front of a door while Miller looked me over a couple of times. He shrugged and grinned, his eyes lighting up again, and opened the door. It swung open to bright white fluorescent lights.

"Where are we?"

"Level 4, the Hotel Chevrier. Right where we need to be," he said.

After all the walking and stairs, we were still on the same level. I followed Miller out and closed the door behind me. We were obviously in a laundry room. Washing machines stood silent along one wall, stretching from the floor to the ceiling. The other wall held huge tumble dryers, their doors hanging open.

"Our timing's good. No one's here," Miller said.

He led me out through a blue tiled hallway and into an elevator. No music, thank god. The doors opened onto a spacious lobby. Warm Ambients flooded in through the large windows.

TEN

"**W**HERE DO WE go from here?" Yang moved away from the closed door and back to the large conference table.

"Let's not move too fast," said Jeremy. "The president surprised me today, and I don't like it. He wasn't supposed to tell anyone our plans to overtake the Big Three. It forced my hand and made me reveal the higher level of our own forces. Some of the cabinet will not be impressed."

"Do you believe they will block the president?"

"It's too late for that, much too late. Any extra scrutiny they bring could hamper the plans though."

Yang moved over to the president's chair and sat down, spinning it to look at the view of Earth. "And what is the status of our plan?"

Jeremy stopped the retort that was already forming. *Our plan, yeah right.* If Yang hadn't caught his extra skimming, there would be no *our*. Jeremy would be the one reaping the rewards that war brought, the flow of unmonitored money that would move through his office. It would be easy, so easy to build his own little empire. First, he needed that war.

"Plans for the Quantum Jump Project have been in our mole's hands for a week. He's fed a copy into the SoCal systems and shipped another copy to Kadokawa."

"Shipped? How?"

Jeremy felt a twinge. This wasn't like Yang. He wasn't this forceful unless he felt he had the upper hand. Was it possible he knew what was going on? *My god, if he knows—How the hell did he find out?* There were only three people involved in the Kadokawa delivery, and he was the only one with all the details. He made a mental note to look for leaks immediately.

"A courier package containing a memory card with the plans, documentation, and the successful Andromeda mission."

Even with the plans, SoCal and Kadokawa would be at least a year behind, making the war one-sided until then. Quincy's interruption of the first delivery using the SoCal hardware would guarantee the two would start fighting between themselves immediately. By the time they had their own quantum jump drives, the president wouldn't be able to trace how they'd gotten them. Hell, he'd probably ask someone in the defense portfolio to look into it, and that person reported straight back to Jeremy.

"I have heard there are problems with the courier?"

Jeremy wasn't sure if it was a statement or a question.

Yang spun around in the president's chair and looked at Jeremy. "From the information I gathered, SoCal met the courier in one of Kadokawa's ancillary buildings. They tried to intercept the package and kill the courier."

Jeremy breathed a quiet sigh of relief. Yang had the planted information: setting up a strong rivalry between SoCal and Kadokawa. "Yes, well. It seems our mole leaked the information to SoCal too soon. They must have been monitoring him more closely than we thought."

"They knew what the package contained then? And what of the mole?"

Jeremy stood straighter, showing that he was still a military man, a man of action and results. "The mole has been eliminated, and the courier is about to be."

"How?"

"I've taken care of it." Yang was starting to feel too important. Jeremy watched him spinning lazily in the president's chair, as if he belonged in it. Soon, it wouldn't matter. Once the war had started, officially or not, Yang would cease to be a problem. Just one of the many casualties leading up to the final conflict. "I have my best person on the job. The courier will be eliminated and the rogue package will be back in our hands."

Yang stopped spinning and looked Jeremy in the eye. "If you are discovered, I will wash my hands of this matter. The signatures on all the documents belong to you and," Yang waved his hand over the chair he was sitting in, "the president."

Jeremy raised his voice a notch. "This is not the time for threats, Yang. Especially not empty ones. We both have enough on each other to ensure that if one of us is caught, the other will hang beside him."

"And now who is making the threats?" Yang changed tactics. "And what of Kadokawa?"

"They already have the information they require."

"Good. Are you sure you want to leave IBC out of this?"

"Yes. If one of the top three doesn't have the jump drive, it divides them. If they fight amongst themselves, we will fare better, much better, in the end."

"Good. Very good." Yang stood and walked to the door. "Keep me informed if anything changes, will you? I hate getting my information secondhand."

Jeremy watched Yang leave. *What a pompous ass. He actually seems to believe he has control over me. That won't last long.* Jeremy turned back to the vid screen. The sun was setting behind the curve of the Earth and large swathes of light from the cities below glittered in the dark.

LEVEL 4—WEDNESDAY, AUGUST 10, 2140 7:00 P.M.

Miller led me past the windows lining the lobby. I had a hard time grasping where I was. Yesterday, I'd managed a few hours of sleep in my old Level 1 hole, covered in mouse shit and garbage. The day before that I had been sleeping in my own bed above Lee's Fish Market. Now I was walking on lush carpet, passing real green plants, in a fancy hotel I wouldn't have been able to get near if I was alone. I tried to brush some of the dirt off my jacket and only succeeded in spreading it to my hands. I had never felt more out of place, more like one of the bums on Chinatown's streets, like unwanted filth. The urge to turn and run, to get back to where I belonged, burned in me, and I fought it as best I could. I brushed my sweaty hands on my jeans, trying to get rid of the dirt, and ended up just jamming them into my pants pocket. My fingers curled reflexively around the key chain that wasn't there.

The Ambients that flooded in through the windows dimmed a notch and changed their tone to a more subtle orangey yellow. The joys of Level 4. On Levels 1 and 2, and most parts of 3, the Ambients just dimmed or turned off abruptly at night. I wasn't used to it, and it added to my feeling of not belonging.

The far wall, away from the windows, held a small gift shop. Souvenirs of the city lined the shelves with colorful t-shirts and handbags, rows of candy, and the prerequisite shelf of miniature toothpaste tubes and headache remedies.

At the end of the lobby was a small coffee shop, open to the outside with cute little tables and chairs on the patio. Beside it, inside the hotel proper, was a more up-scale place with a hostess waiting to seat you. By the look of it, they shared a common kitchen between them.

I angled toward the coffee shop before Miller pulled me across the hall toward the hostess.

"I'll be right back, okay? I just gotta fill the AD in on what's been happening. Wait here."

I nodded and moved closer to a potted palm near the front door. The hostess smiled at Miller when he walked past her, and then turned to me with a look of disgust on her face. I pretended to look out the windows. If the bitch had been through the same crap I had, she'd probably be dead already. The second the thought entered my head, I felt ashamed of it.

A few minutes later, Miller came back, brushing past the hostess as if she wasn't there. He didn't have the package anymore. It felt strange, not having it near me, as if it had become a part of who I was.

"Come on, Kris, we'll get you something to eat," he said.

I followed Miller into the restaurant, pretty sure that if he hadn't led the way, the hostess would have stopped me. Rich wood panels covered the wall, and the tables were draped in crisp white tablecloths. In front of each elegantly carved wooden chair was an almost see-through plate topped with a beige napkin, rolled and tied with a red ribbon. On either side of the plate were more knives and forks than I knew what to do with. Two wineglasses stood near each plate, reflecting the light from the flickering candle set in the center of each table.

I didn't belong here. Hell, nobody I knew belonged here. What was I getting myself into? This place was way above my comfort zone. Way above my social status. With every step, I felt more uncomfortable with where I was and what I was doing.

Thankfully the tables were mostly empty. In the center, close to the door where they could see anyone that walked in or out, was a group of old ladies. They held teacups in their hands and on the table was a tray of dainties. To me, they looked like wannabe society ladies, imitating what they had seen on the old vids. Their open looks of disdain as I walked past, coupled with the way they covered their noses, mirrored those of the hostess. I looked at Miller's feet. I hated feeling uncomfortable in my own skin.

Miller stopped and pointed to the far corner where a large man sat alone. "That's the assistant director."

I hesitated.

"It's okay, Kris. Just walk up and grab a seat. He really wants to talk to you. I'll get the waitress to bring over some food for ya." He gave me a gentle push in the direction of the table and turned back to the hostess.

I looked back just as the hostess disappeared into the kitchen separating the restaurants. Typical. The fanciest-looking places in the world got their food from the same place as the run-of-the-mill coffee shop. I found it comforting.

Pulling out a chair, I sat across from the assistant director and took off my jacket, laying it on the empty chair beside me. I must have really smelled as bad as I looked; when I removed my jacket, he pulled back a bit and covered his nose with his hand, just like the old ladies. He moved it so it only covered his mouth, trying to make it look like that was what he had meant to do in the first place. I sunk lower in my seat and gave him points for trying.

"Kris Ballard. You've been a very busy girl. It seems as though everybody wants a piece of you."

"Yeah, I guess." I was pretty sure he did as well.

He laid his hand on the envelope beside him. "And this is the reason why?"

"Yeah."

He stared at me for a second. "You don't trust me, do you?"

I looked him in the eye and pulled myself up from my slouch. "I don't know you."

"Ah, of course! Where are my manners?" He raised his bulk and reached a hand across the table. "My name is Nigel Wood." He leaned in and lowered his voice, as though sharing a big secret. "I'm an assistant director of ACE. I knew your parents."

I just looked at his hand, but didn't reach for it. My brain had gone numb.

"Perhaps after we've talked a while then." Nigel sat back down and replaced the napkin in his lap. He was acting as though he hadn't said anything *wrong*.

A waitress dressed in black pants and shirt left the kitchen, the door swinging behind her, hinged to go both ways. She held a tray as if it was contaminated, and moved toward our table. Without asking, she placed the food in front of me and left.

"Please forgive her," Nigel said, waving at the food.

"Serving cheeseburgers, french fries, and strawberry milkshakes is not part of the norm here. I'll have to check with Miller to see how he managed to get them to do it."

Somewhere in the back of my head, a thought pushed through the numbness—*He must have just smiled at her*.

"Please, eat. We can talk while you do."

I just sat and stared at him. I couldn't get past what he had said. He knew my parents?

As if just realizing what had happened, Nigel looked down at the table like he was embarrassed. "Sorry. Maybe I shouldn't have dropped that on you so . . . fast. I didn't mean to upset you." With the last words, he looked into my eyes. He seemed sincere. "Please, eat. I'll explain everything when you're done."

I didn't realize how hungry I was until I picked up the burger. When I took my first bite, the tomato slid off the melted cheese and fell with a plop on to the plate. Suddenly it was as if I hadn't eaten in weeks. The first bite wasn't enough. I barely swallowed before I jammed the burger into my mouth again for another bite.

Nigel leaned forward. "Whoa, slow down. We'll stay until you've finished eating." He laid his hand on the envelope again. "Now, did you open the package?"

The food must have been working its magic; I bristled at the question. "Is the envelope open?"

"Obviously not," Nigel smiled, "but it has happened that carefully opened envelopes were resealed."

I took a gulp of my milkshake, not taking the time to use the straw. "No, I didn't open it. I've never opened a package I delivered." I wasn't about to tell him how close I got.

"Okay. Good. Do you know why you were picked to deliver the package?"

"You first," I said, the words coming out in a harsh rasp. "What about my parents?"

Nigel sighed and looked down at the table again. "Okay, that's fair. I really don't know how to say this, except for the way it is. And I do dislike beating around the bush. Your parents worked for me—for ACE—before I was an assistant director."

I must have showed some sign of disbelief, because Nigel stopped looking at the table and looked back at me.

"Oh, nothing like Miller, no. You see, one of ACE's goals is to bring equilibrium back to the planet. The corporations have stripped or covered up so much land and water that sustainability has become almost impossible. Without the mines on Mars, without the water they are extracting, we would be on the verge of extinction. Your parents believed, truly *believed* we could achieve sustainability. But in order to do it, something had to change. They tried to be the catalyst for that change, and were killed for their efforts."

"It . . . it was just a random attack," I stuttered. "A gang looking for money."

"That's what we thought too, at first. But we take care of our own. When the police stopped looking, we kept on, we dug deeper. We don't know which corporation ordered the hit, either SoCal or Meridian, but we're sure it was a hit. The gang that did the work didn't exist before that day, or after. Nothing else made sense."

I just sat there. My brain had gone from numb to speeding at Mach 10. What if Nigel was telling the truth? I remember going to friends' houses for a couple of days at a time. Was that when they took off and did their work for ACE?

"I know it's a lot to take in, Kris. Our memories of our parents when we were kids are seldom correct. This change is just a bit bigger than most. We'll have plenty of time to talk about that later. I'll make sure we do. This package"—he tapped his hand on the envelope again—"is somewhat time critical, so I'll ask again. Do you know why you were picked to deliver it?"

"No. I figure Dispatch had a problem with me somewhere along the line." I felt the beginning of a brain freeze headache from the shake and pressed my tongue to the roof of my mouth. It was supposed to work, and it stopped me from asking more about Mom and Dad.

"Maybe. We've looked into your dispatcher's background, as well as yours. Besides the fact that she collected a Meridian paycheck, we didn't find anything offbeat. We couldn't find a connection to you at all, aside from the obvious work-related one. Certainly nothing that ties back to your parents. The best we could figure was that you have no obvious family ties. No one who would worry about why you didn't come home at night."

"You're telling me I got fucked over because I'm a loner?"

Nigel took the swearing in stride, not even pausing in the conversation. I was beginning to like this guy. Better than Mikey from IBC anyway.

"It would appear that way," he said.

I shoved the last piece of the cheeseburger into my mouth and slowed down. Leaning back in my chair, feeling fuller than I had in days, I started in on the fries. The thin film attached to my back pinched my skin and I leaned forward again, resting my elbows on the table. "When can I lose this damn blocker, or whatever Miller called it?" I had so many other questions to ask, but was afraid to.

"Ah, yes, I'd almost forgotten. It's actually your ID tag that's caused a lot of your problems. Pretty much everyone born in the last fifty years is implanted with a tag at birth. It's part of the cancer and heart disease vaccination given to young children. In specific terms, small carbon flakes are injected into the pleural cavity with the

vaccination. They collect around the upper superior me-
diastinal lymph nodes and send out coded, low-pulse
signals with every heartbeat."

Nigel was beginning to lose me and I stifled a yawn.

"It's the city administration's, essentially SoCal's, way
to track people. What it really does is it allows them to
probe into people's private lives, and if it's helpful to
them, use that information to their benefit. It removes
our freedom without most of us even knowing about it.
A monitored population is a controllable population.
Very *1984*."

I had no idea what he was talking about. Nigel must
have seen my eyes lose their focus. I didn't remember
being this bored in school.

"But I'm preaching again. Sorry, I was in med school
when ACE recruited me." He shifted in his seat, obviously uncomfortable. "At any rate, the blocker will remain attached until we can get you to a facility that can
modify the tag. It's not a surgical procedure, but does
require special equipment. It allows you to program
pretty much any information into the tag as well, giving
anyone access to anywhere."

"Like Level 6 and up?" Had my parents ever been to
Level 6?

"Exactly."

"I've seen Level 6 security examine people's backs.
Are they looking for these blockers?"

"Yes, we used to use blockers exclusively, and the first
editions were pretty bulky. When they started checking,
we turned to surgery, but that left obvious scarring, of
course. We lost a lot of operatives when they started
checking. Since then we've gotten smarter. We override
the carbon fibers with our own transmitters. It took us
years to develop the tech, but so far, it's been highly

effective. They haven't caught on yet." Nigel paused. "Now, back to our questions."

LEVEL 4—WEDNESDAY, AUGUST 10, 2140 7:15 P.M.

Looking through the scope of her rifle, Abby could see the entire lobby of the Hotel Chevrier. It was pretty much deserted this early in the evening. The coffee shop was open, as was the bar at the other end of the lobby. Those didn't interest her though. The formal dining room beside the coffee shop, with the pretty hostess trying to lure customers in, did.

From Abby's vantage point across the street, she could look through the big plate glass windows covering the front of the hotel and into the restaurant. There was a bit of glare from the Ambients, but not enough to stop her from looking in. A group of old ladies quietly sipping their tea blocked her view all the way inside. She wouldn't have been able to see to the back of the room anyway. Her angle didn't allow it.

She had been here for about two hours already, peering through the scope normally attached to her rifle. In fact, she had been almost ready to pack it in when her target showed up. Four others showed up with him; two walked into the hotel lobby about a minute ahead to check things out. The other two followed him into the restaurant like shadows. A few minutes later one came out, and three stood in the lobby.

Her target was, of course, Nigel Wood. Meridian Black Ops knew he was high in the ACE echelon, high enough to need a shadow team. Unfortunately for him, he was a creature of habit, and this was his favorite restaurant. It made her job easier; she didn't even need to verify against the profile picture in the dossier. Her target had arrived. Now she would wait until he came out, unless she was called off to chase a child on Level 1 again.

Abby looked back through the scope. It would take two shots: one to break the glass and one to make the kill.

Just under an hour later, she caught movement in the relative quiet of the hotel lobby. A young girl emerged from the elevator and was led to the restaurant by a face Abby knew all too well. Miller. Her job had just become more difficult, but then, she knew that was going to happen when she ran her star charts this morning.

The goons supporting the suit would have been easy, but Miller had a strange way of knowing when something was going on. Last time she'd dealt with him, she'd barely made it out alive. Too bad he wasn't her target today. Maybe she'd get lucky and get a chance at him as well.

When they paused at the entrance to the restaurant, Abby took a closer look through her scope at the girl. It was the courier from her failed Level 1 hit, looking worse for her troubles. Miller went inside, hiding the courier behind a potted plant just inside the entryway. Bastard probably did it without even realizing it.

Abby could have shot through the plant and taken out the courier, but that was too risky, and would give her primary target a chance to get out. If she wanted a chance to fix her previous error and still get her primary, she would need to move in closer.

She packed the scope back into her padded briefcase with the rest of the disassembled weapon, and a few minutes later walked into the lobby of the hotel like she owned the place. Every movement, down to the selection of her posture, proved she knew what she was doing, that she belonged. Abby moved back toward the elevators the courier had come from and pressed the down button. The Chevrier had its service areas in the basement, where she knew she would be able to find hotel uniforms.

Fifteen minutes later, Abby walked out of the women's changing rooms. Her shoulders had taken on a stooped look, and her feet dragged a bit when she walked in the low-heeled shoes. The damn things hurt like a demon, but it was the best match she could find in the staff room.

Her outfit, stained and smelling of stale coffee, matched what the coffee shop waitress was wearing, which was exactly what she wanted. It was loose enough to cover the rifle parts hidden under it. She relaxed the muscles on her face, letting them droop, making her look ten years older.

She knew staff wouldn't be allowed in the front lobby, so there must be a back entrance to the restaurant kitchens. Abby turned away from the elevators and followed the hallway to a set of stairs leading up. She opened the door and, placing a hand on the rail to help her up, walked to the top like she hated being at work.

One of Nigel's goons stood at the top of the stairs. He didn't even give her a second glance. If anyone found out he'd held the door open for Meridian's best assassin ... Abby let a ghost of a smile touch her lips once she stepped past.

The kitchen itself was almost divided in two. The portion facing the front of the building—the coffee shop— contained a few flat tops and deep fryers. The other section contained a much more modern and complex kitchen, including gas stoves and charcoal barbecues. Abby moved to the restaurant side of the kitchen and began to assemble her weapon.

LEVEL 4—WEDNESDAY, AUGUST 10, 2140 7:42 P.M.

I took the last gulp of my milkshake and put the glass on my empty plate, smearing the ketchup around, and leaned back. Now that the hunger had passed—I'd eaten way too much—the exhaustion set in again. I had a hard time keeping my eyes open.

"Listen, Kris. I know you're tired, but I have a few more things I need to talk about before we can go. The next few days are going be pretty busy for me, and I need an answer from you quickly so we can move forward."

Using my elbows, I pushed myself off the back of the seat, sitting up straighter. Here it was. The bullshit price I had to pay for the help they had given me. Fuck that. All I wanted was a place to sleep and hide out for a while until things blew over, and for Nigel to tell me more about my mom and dad.

"You showed some quick thinking in the last couple of days, Kris . . . thinking that we could use in our organization. I believe we could use each other, and both come out the better for it."

Nigel was starting to sound like a used car salesman, and I didn't want anything to do with it. "I just want out. I'll find a place to hide for a while, and when this blows over . . . we'll see." I picked one of the extra forks off the table and started spinning it in my hand, trying to look bored with the whole thing. Spinning a fork was harder than spinning a pen.

"I'm not sure that's going to work for you this time."

He leaned over the table and dropped his voice. "Meridian is plenty mad. The information we're picking up off their lines says they got a couple of teams looking for you. I don't think they care if you still have the package or not. It sounds like you've caused them a whole lot of grief, and they want to get rid of you."

"So? I can go back to IBC. They were willing to help me." And Nigel didn't think IBC was behind the attack on my parents.

"And did they? Who was there to look after you at Innotek? If Miller hadn't shown up, you'd be dead right now."

I knew he was right, and the spinning fork faltered for a second. I had seen Quincy move out from behind the security desk when Miller drove me out of there. If I had walked in, the second the door to the building locked behind me, my life would have been over. I don't think Quincy would have made it quick.

"We need an intelligent courier. One who can think on her feet and get the damn job done." He waved his hand indicating something bigger than the room around them. "And not just here. The world is bigger than this city. Did you know that there are still areas of Earth open to the sky? It's not all shrouded in layers of concrete and humanity.

"Have you ever seen a sunrise, Kris? A real sunrise. This . . . this ball of flame just seems to pop up from the horizon, throwing its light and heat everywhere it can."

Christ, this guy was laying it on thick. True, the only sunrise I had seen was on the vids, but I hadn't missed it. You can't miss something you've never had.

"How about the Sat Cities? You can look out your view port and the whole world will be out there. It's like you can just reach out through the glass and hold it in your hand. And if you're not facing the Earth . . . my god.

The stars. So many of them shining from distances your mind can't even grasp.

"We can give you those things, Kris."

He made it sound like I was winning the lottery. As if I was ever going to be on a Sat City. They wouldn't even let me onto Level 6. How the fuck did he think they were going to let me off-planet?

"What do you say, Kris?"

"What would I deliver?" What the hell, I figured I would play him along for a while, see how serious he was.

Nigel leaned back in his seat again, looking comfortable with the direction the conversation was taking. "It would pretty much be the same stuff you do here. Electronic communications between the Sat Cities and Earth, and between each other, is as bad as it is down here." He gave a small grin. "Communications to the mining colonies are even worse. Anything secure goes through couriers, with enough fake messages that no one knows which courier is carrying real information."

"I'm not sure if it's what I want to do, Nigel." Two could play at this game. I'd been in situations before, usually with guys that wanted to get into my pants, where they would say my name more often than necessary. It supposedly made the conversation more personal and immediate. Though it never worked on me, it seemed to have an effect on Nigel. The bastard slouched a bit more in his seat and he looked on the verge of a smile.

"We would train you, Kris. Not the kind of training you get for city runs. It's a bit tougher out there, and you need different skills."

"Like you trained my dad?" The twirling fork slipped from my fingers and its spin carried it to the floor. I bent down to retrieve it and started spinning it again. By the look on Nigel's face, it bugged the hell out of me. It was either that, or the question I'd asked.

"Your parents were environmentalists and pacifists. They didn't need or want training. We'd give you weapons experience. Teach you how to properly shoot that gun you have in your pocket. Pistols aren't just aim and pull the trigger. Well, they are—" He gave a small chuckle, finding humor in his own mind. "—it's just that the aiming part is really tough to get right. I've heard stories of security guards emptying an entire clip at a guy that wasn't moving, and missing every single shot.

"We'd also get you hand-to-hand lessons. By the time we were done, people like Quincy wouldn't be able to get close enough to you to use that knife of his."

"I could just leave the city."

"I don't think you understand how big these corporations are. SoCal pretty much owns this city, and this is only one of dozens. Meridian has access to all the trackers. If you make it to another city, and that's a pretty big if, you'd be in the same mess as you are now. Meridian has a Quincy in every city, probably more than one."

"What, and they don't in the Sat Cities?"

"Of course they do. But if you're up there, that means you're working for us, and you would be trained and prepared to deal with it."

Despite my doubts, I was beginning to fall for the spiel. If it was good enough for Mom and Dad . . . It must be the lack of sleep. My thought process felt bogged down, unable to latch onto a single item for any length of time. Maybe they had put something into the food? I didn't think so though. I felt pretty much the same now as I did when I walked in. The food just compounded the exhaustion. Besides, the drugs I knew about tended to do a bit more of a number on you. Once, a guy I was seeing bought some Sweat off a street punk. Sweat made you do exactly that: if you were on it your whole body would be drenched in sweat. But the ride was supposed to be awesome. He had tried to get me take a hit, but there was no way I was getting into any of that shit. I stopped seeing him after that.

"When would this happen?" I asked.

"We could start the second we walk out of here. We'll move you to a safe house and get your ID tag neutralized. Then we'd move you up to one of our training facilities outside San Angeles. You'd be up and running in about a year."

Damn. It was starting to sound good. Especially the part about getting out of the city right away. I watched the fork spin in my hand, trying to buy some time to think.

LEVEL 4—WEDNESDAY, AUGUST 10, 2140—7:44 P.M.

The rifle barrel slid into the stock and locked in place with a soft click. Abby held it close to her side, hiding it from anyone who might approach. She was surprised at how empty this side of the kitchen actually was. She figured at least there should have been a cook waiting in case an order came in. Maybe on the slow nights they crossed between the kitchens, working wherever they were needed.

The weapon itself reached from her waist almost down to the floor. The barrel came in two pieces and screwed together, then clipped into the stock. Its long, rifled barrel made it highly accurate over distances, and accuracy was what she was looking for. Meridian wanted Nigel Wood, and Jeremy wanted the courier out of the way, with no mistakes.

Abby approached the front counter of the kitchen, moving around the barbecue grill. Beside the swinging door leading to the restaurant was a long pass-through window the chefs used to slide the orders to the servers. She moved to the corner and peered over the counter-top. Nigel and the girl were both sitting at the far corner table. She could use the counter to help balance the weapon's barrel. Nigel's face was just to the left of the courier.

Nigel leaned forward in his chair, hiding his face behind the courier's head. At this range she might be able to kill two birds with one stone, one shot through both heads. She'd actually seen a bird once. Jeremy had something called a "bald eagle" stuffed and mounted in his office. He said they used to fly free. Big deal. Abby lined up her shot and slowed her breathing, praying for a straight trajectory.

<hr />

LEVEL 4—WEDNESDAY, AUGUST 10, 2140 7:44 P.M.

"This is a one-time offer Kris. If you say no now, we won't be seeing each other again." Nigel put his hands flat on the table, trying to press home his point. He reached out and touched my hand. "You really need to understand how good this would be for both of us."

I snatched my hand back, the fork in the other hand lost some of its spin before my fingers automatically corrected and stabilized it, keeping it going. My forced calm exterior was beginning to erode.

Nigel's smile was gone from his face. "Some of our couriers pilot their own vessels to the mining colonies. They figure it's safer than taking the transports. If you want to go that way, we could look into it for you."

Pilot my own ship? This guy was really fucking reaching now. Either that, or he thought I was an idiot. From what I had seen on the vids, the training took at least two years and cost a fortune. And where the hell was I going to get a ship? Were they just going to give me one? I barely contained a snort. This was getting too far-fetched. Still, if I could get a safe place to sleep, I'd play along.

"I need some time to think about it. I'm so fucking tired right now, I don't think I can make any choices," I said.

Nigel sighed, obviously mulling it through. "No problem. We'll put you in a safe house tonight. We'll need an answer by morning."

"Okay. When can I get the ID tag removed?"

"We don't remove it, we alter it. And that depends on your answer."

"So, if I don't work for you, I don't get the tag removed?" The fucking bastard. If I didn't get the tag removed, or altered, or whatever, I would be dead meat in days, if not hours.

"We don't actually remove the tag, it's too much a part of the lymph node. We just modify it. But essentially, you are right."

"I've still got this blocker, that'll work."

"For a few days, at most. After that, the power source runs out. There's no way to recharge them. You get one use, and that's it."

"You bastard."

"Sometimes I have to be."

"Is that how you treated my mom and dad?" The fork spun out of my hand, and I automatically bent to pick it up. A loud crack split the air and I bolted upright. It was a sound I recognized. Nigel had fallen over backward and blood was spattered on the wall behind him. Without thinking, I slid under the table. The corner of the chair pulled at the back of my t-shirt and gouged into my skin. I grabbed Nigel's legs, pulling him under with me.

His head bumped the chair leg on the way down, leaving a red smear.

This wasn't happening again. This *couldn't* be happening again. He was supposed to be a fucking bigwig. Didn't he bring some sort of protection? Fuck!

"Miller." I screamed as loud as I could. I was a fucking sitting duck out here. I had no idea where the shot had come from. There was no place to hide anyway. Even under the table, I felt exposed. Where the hell was he?

Wait, there was one place I could hide.

I rolled on top of Nigel, shuddering when I felt his still-warm body, but I didn't stop to dwell on it. The center table leg smacked into my back as I tried to roll off him. I ended up wedged higher off the ground between his body and the table. I wiggled my shoulders and pushed with my legs until I could feel myself starting to slip. I got a shoulder down and pushed against the table leg, my brain screaming at me to hurry. Nigel's body shifted and I slipped down to the floor, stuck between Nigel and the table leg.

I heard another loud crack and Nigel's body twitched, the force of the bullet moving him as though he was still alive, could still feel pain. The old ladies at their table started to scream, finally realizing what the hell was going on. I reached for the gun in my pocket and lay as close to the ground as I could get, trying to control the fear rising in my throat like bile. My face felt warm and I reached a hand up. It came away covered in blood.

I had no idea if it was mine or Nigel's.

ELEVEN

MILLER WANDERED BY the elevators for what felt like the hundredth time. This kind of shit wasn't his gig. He wasn't a delivery boy or a bodyguard. The waiting was beginning to wear a bit thin. He glanced over at one of Nigel's bodyguards. The guy had been standing there for almost an hour, and he hadn't even moved yet. Except for his eyes. They just kept on flicking back and forth, covering as much of the lobby as he could see. A sniper could have taken him out in a heartbeat.

A loud crack punctuated Miller's thoughts. Out of reflex, he dropped to the floor and rolled behind a large potted plant while pulling out his gun. The bodyguard just stood there, a look of shock and confusion on his face. When Miller realized that no one in the lobby was the target, he stood and ran for the restaurant at the far end. The bodyguard ran after him.

By the time he reached the restaurant, he had to fight his way through the old ladies, each one trying to get out of the restaurant first, and to hell with their friends. Their screams, at such close range, almost drowned out the sound of another rifle shot.

He shoved the ladies out of the way, pushing one to the floor and jumping over her. At first glance, the corner table was empty. One spot on the dark paneling was shining, as though someone had thrown a cup of coffee at it.

A third shot rang out from Miller's left, and he dived under the nearest table. As his eyes adjusted to the darker room, he saw the assistant director and Kris under the table. It looked like Nigel had protected her with his body, except that he was lying facing outward. Most people, when protecting someone else at close range, faced the person they were shielding, covering them with their arms.

The bodyguard came running in. "Kitchen!" Miller yelled and waved his gun in the general direction before putting all his attention back on the corner table. He moved closer to it, crawling from table to table, trying to keep as many obstacles between him and the kitchen. He realized the AD was dead before he even got close.

"Clear!" The shout came from the kitchen and a bodyguard ran out and sprinted to the AD's table. Miller stood from the table he was behind and followed.

LEVEL 4—WEDNESDAY, AUGUST 10, 2140 7:44 P.M.

The barrel lay flat on the smooth counter, and Abby held her breath. She had one shot left in the small cartridge. One shot to get this right. She could see the courier's shoulder just above Nigel's body, and aimed for where the head should be. Her second shot had been in the same place, but with the inherent weakness of the put-together rifle, the bullet didn't have the power to go through Nigel's bulk.

This one just might be able to do it. She let her breath out in one slow smooth motion and squeezed the trigger again. From where she stood, it looked like the third bullet had entered the hole created by the second one. With some luck . . .

Now it was time to move quickly. She stashed the weapon under the counter, behind rows of clean and shiny plates, and pulled a small tube from her pocket. She popped the lid and placed the tip of it in her nose and squeezed. Blood, her blood put in the tube earlier, flowed from her nose to her chin, soaking the front of her borrowed uniform. She resealed the tube and put it back in her pocket. From her other pocket, she took a plastic bag with a sponge in it and patted it over her fingers. She placed her hand onto her cheek, leaving red finger marks across it. She quickly wiped her hand on a small cloth and put both items in the bag.

Abby moved to the far corner and kneeled, whimpering and holding her hands behind her head, and waited.

The sound of the kitchen door banging into the wall, and then back into whoever slammed it open, almost made her laugh. She turned her shaking shoulders into part of her act. The frightened woman. Brutalized by a man with a gun.

"Get up!" A man's voice. Probably one of the four who walked in with Nigel.

"No, please!" She cowered in the corner, trying to make herself appear smaller, drawing short sobbing breaths.

"I said get up!"

A rough hand grabbed her shoulder and spun her around. She watched his eyes widen and flick from her cheek to her bloodied shirt.

"Christ. Did you see who did this?" he asked.

She shook her head, still cowering and sobbing.

"Okay, okay, you're safe. Stay here and I'll get a medical team over to see you." He ran around the corner, heading to the front kitchen.

Abby stood and stumbled to the door leading back downstairs. If anyone was watching, she had to maintain the act. Reaching the door was easy, and the guard placed behind it had already left. Most likely running around like an idiot looking for a man with a gun. She took the stairs two at a time and ran to the changing room.

Two minutes later, a lady walking tall and assured left the unguarded front door and walked down the street. She wasn't carrying a briefcase this time.

LEVEL 4—WEDNESDAY, AUGUST 10, 2140 7:48 P.M.

Blood ran into my eyes, partially blinding me. My world had, once again, turned into blur. I remembered waving my gun over Nigel's body, but I didn't know if I had pulled the trigger.

The gun had been grabbed from my hand at the same time Nigel rolled away from me. I shook my head slowly, trying to clear it. He couldn't do that, could he? He was dead.

Miller's face swam into view and I latched on to him like he was the last person on Earth, a familiar face with soft brown eyes in the hell my life had become. Somewhere in the back of my mind I realized I had only known him for a few hours, but somehow, here and now, it was enough.

I felt myself being dragged out from under the table and carried a short distance away. The sounds of plates and glasses smashing to the floor filled my ears, drowning out the sounds of voices, before I was laid on a table. Miller had a napkin and was wiping the blood from my face, a look of concern on his.

"It's okay Kris, you're okay. You're safe now. None of this blood is yours, you're not hurt."

Somehow, the thought didn't seem to make me feel better. I still felt the warm, sticky stuff on me. Some of it had run down under the front of my shirt. My stomach twisted and I rolled onto my side. Miller placed his hand on my hip, stopping me from rolling off the table, and got a wave of cheeseburger and strawberry shake as a reward. I didn't hear him complain.

A man in a dark suit swam into view. "The extraction team is here. Back delivery door."

"Good. Did you find the shooter?"

"No. We had a witness, a waitress, but . . ."

Miller turned quickly and looked at him. "But . . . you can't find her now."

"That's right." The bodyguard stood a little taller, as if waiting for Miller to pick a fight. Instead Miller took one last wipe of my mouth with the napkin and lifted me up.

"C'mon. Let's get out of here."

I must have passed out somewhere along the way. I remember a van, and someone lifting my shirt up over my back. I struggled a bit at that, but Miller came back into view.

"Just checking the ID blocker. It's okay."

My world faded to black.

LEVEL UNKNOWN—WEDNESDAY, AUGUST 10, 2140
7:43 P.M.

The only light in the office came from the two glowing displays and the small lamp sitting on the desk. Hunched over the desk, Devon was trying to find a new way to optimize his algorithms, to make the computer perform its function with a higher degree of accuracy and speed.

Yet he knew it was all a ruse. If he was away from his computer he wouldn't have access to all the data. Without the data he was useless to his employers. Every two minutes, he looked at the screens and scanned them, hoping to see something new.

Sitting alone in this room gave him a degree of separation from the jobs performed by other members of ACE. But this time, he was feeling it even more than normal. The computer had still not been able to find a common thread between all the individual pieces of information related to the courier. Some of it tied together, but nothing formed a complete whole. But Devon knew the computer didn't have all the information yet.

What the systems had managed to figure out was disturbing. It appeared as though the package source, the individual that sent it, was a Meridian mole. Someone who had ingrained himself in the SoCal systems so well that he was part of the machine. What he had sent to Kadokawa was still a mystery, but the computer gave it a sixty-two percent chance of relating to the executive-class cruiser that had stopped sending its positional beacon for about twenty minutes several days ago.

Besides sifting through the old information, the computer was still watching all of the new raw data coming in.

The courier had arrived at the hotel meeting about an hour ago, and Devon listened in on the conversation. It sounded like the AD was getting what he wanted, as usual.

Suddenly, the screens flashed. Remote audio monitors detected gunfire in the hotel, somewhere just off the lobby. Devon sat and listened to the scene unfold a couple of levels away. He knew the information he had supplied was now being used to change the real world. The data that lived briefly on his screen was alive, was real. With his help, it was changing, shaping reality. Devon smiled, flipping his ponytail over his shoulder.

LEVEL 5—THURSDAY, AUGUST 11, 2140 7:00 A.M.

I rolled over in a bed, pulling the sheets higher around my neck. Something square pushed into my back and brought me to full wakefulness.

Opening my eyes, I found myself in a small room with a real bed and clean sheets. Warm light streamed in through the frilly yellow curtains and splashed against the far wall. A plain black dresser sat in the corner by the closed door. From what I could see, there were no other furnishings or decorations in the room. It didn't feel like a place people stayed in for long.

I ran my fingers through my hair. It was matted and dirty, but my hand came away blood free. The thought of blood brought back a rush of memories; the cheeseburger, Nigel, the way his body twitched when the bullet hit him. Then there was the blood, warm and sticky, running down my face, into my eyes and down my shirt. He was dead, and with him, any information he had about my parents.

I sat up, pulling the sheets away. My head felt like it was stuffed with cotton, and I leaned back against the headboard, feeling the square object press into my back again. The cool air in the room touched my skin. I was naked, or almost anyway. Whoever undressed me had left me in just my bra and panties. Dried blood still clung to the straps and the top of the cup. Two strands of thick tape, white and textured, wrapped just under my breasts. I reached back, following the tape. It held on a small box, strapped securely to my back.

There was a quiet knock at the door, and the knob turned slowly. I dropped back down on the bed, pulled the sheets up, and closed my eyes, leaving them open just enough to look out from beneath my eyelashes.

Miller stepped in, carrying a bundle of clothes in his hand. He took a quick glance over at me and placed the clothes on the dresser before leaving and closing the door behind him. From what I could see, his own clothes looked freshly washed, with no trace of yesterday's supper on them.

I waited a minute before slipping out of bed, every muscle groaning in protest. I limped to the dresser, grabbed my clothes, brought them back to the bed with me. On top of the pile was my—Frank's—gun. The spare clips, still full, sat beside it. Between the gun and my clothes was the package, its flap torn and open. Under the package was my envelope of cash. I moved them off my clothes and quickly got dressed, pausing only long enough to examine the purple bruise forming on my calf. It still hurt, but it could have been so much worse. I left the box taped in place, tugging at my shirt when it snagged on a corner. I wanted to know what it was before I tried to do anything with it.

When I was done, I did a quick search of the room. Starting with the dresser, I pulled each drawer open, making sure I made no noise. The drawers were all empty. They didn't even have a piece of lint or thread in them to indicate they had ever been used.

Behind the curtains lay a quiet suburban street. If I was still on Level 4, it was a pretty high-end neighborhood. Tall trees lined the empty street, casting shadows across the pavement and into the neighbors' front yards. The Ambients overhead were on tracks, simulating the motion of the sun during the day. I never really understood that. To me, the lights came on slowly in the morning and dimmed again at night. What was the point of moving the light source? Somewhere in the distance a dog barked. Dogs. High-end for sure.

I was pretty sure if I opened the window I'd hear kids screaming from the backyards and lawnmowers running. The mythical suburbia in all its glory.

The smell of bacon wafted in from somewhere in the house, and for a second I was back home with Mom and Dad. My stomach growled in appreciation, bringing me back to reality. I moved to the door and twisted the knob, half expecting to find it locked. The knob turned easily and the door opened into a carpeted hallway. Two other doors were open in the opposite wall, and I could see bedrooms behind them. I followed my nose to the kitchen.

Miller stood by the stove in a kitchen right out of the vids, huge and apparently well stocked. He glanced up from the frying pan and must have seen me looking around.

"Yeah, the kitchens are always the best part in the

safe houses. If you're in one of these, you never know when or where your next meal will be, so they keep 'em stocked up." He went back to moving the bacon around the frying pan. "Did you sleep good? You were pretty out of it by the time we got here."

"I must have been." I couldn't remember anything after the restaurant. I took a second to study Miller. He looked different today, younger than he had last night. And not too bad looking either, now that I had time to really see.

A blush crept up the back of his neck. "Y ... Your clothes were pretty messed up. I ... I figured I'd better get 'em clean for ya."

"And the box on my back?"

Miller's blush deepened. "You tore the blocker at the restaurant. We had to replace it in the van on the way. That old box was all we had."

"And the tape?" I couldn't help giving him the little extra jab. The way he stuttered and wouldn't look at me was something I'd never seen a guy do before. It made him seem like more of a real person instead of some top secret agent.

"Yeah, uh. The black box was falling off, and I, uh, I needed to keep it on."

Feeling a bit uncomfortable myself, I let the subject drop. "You got any coffee to go with that bacon?"

He raised the spatula from the frying pan and indicated the counter beside the fridge, dripping bacon grease on the floor. "It ain't decaf."

"Thank god for that." I opened the cupboard above the coffeemaker and found the mugs. Pouring two cups, I passed one over. "If you put anything in it, you'll have to take care of it yourself."

"No, just black. Thanks," he said.

The Ambients shone through the window above the

sink. I could see why I thought he was older last night.
The left side of his face had a fine network of scars, miniature white lines and cracks lacing a pattern across his
cheek and temple. In the daylight, he didn't look like
he'd even reached thirty yet. Maybe a lot closer to
twenty-five, or younger. For some reason, thinking he
was younger reassured me. Maybe because he was almost in my age group, and by the looks of things, knew
what rough times were. Someone like me.

The silence stretched out as Miller placed the bacon
between two sheets of paper towel. I watched him drain
some of the fat down the sink, followed by a copious
amount of hot water from the tap, and then crack four
eggs into the pan.

"Sunny side up?" he asked.

"Over hard."

"Okay. You wanna get plates? They're just above the
sink. Knives and forks are beside it, on the right."

I made myself busy setting the table. The activity reminded me of home, of my little space above the Fish
Market. Granted, I didn't have a kitchen, and I hadn't
been able to afford bacon since I ran away, but just the
motion of setting a table and drinking a cup of coffee did
it. It just seemed so normal, as if nothing strange had
happened. Who would have thought that I'd feel nostal-
gic about the smelly, cramped place?

"You okay?"

Miller had turned from the stove and must have seen
me lost in thought.

"Yeah, I'm fine. I just . . . this doesn't seem real."

He placed the bacon on the table and reached up to
touch my cheek. "I know."

Tears suddenly flooded my eyes and overflowed, falling down my face and on to the floor. It was as though I
could feel the barriers it had taken me years to build drop

as reality set in. I moved into Miller's arms, wanting . . . needing some form of human contact, and pushed my face into his chest.

The memories of the last few days, images of blood and death, of running afraid for my life, washed over me. My legs turned to rubber and my sobs came out in huge gasping breaths. Miller's arms tightened around me, supporting more of my weight as my sobs started to quiet down. His arms were strong and warm. I felt safer in them than I had in days. In years. I wanted nothing more than to sink into the warmth and never come back out.

But I wasn't some snot-nosed kid who needed help. I couldn't be. Not now, not ever. I pushed myself away, angry at myself for acting like a wimpy baby.

"I'm, I'm sorry. I don't know why . . ."

"It's okay, don't worry about it."

I smiled, feeling heat creep into my cheeks, and reached for his shirt, pulling at the wet material. "I think I've ruined your shirt."

"It'll dry. Sit and have some bacon, I'll bring your eggs."

I looked into his eyes, feeling the heat increase, and noticed they weren't really brown at all, but more of a deep hazel speckled with flakes of gold. They created a feeling in me I didn't know I had anymore.

I tore my gaze away and moved to the table, picking the chair that put my back to the wall. An old habit. I pulled over the plate of cooling bacon and filled my own. By the time Miller came back with the eggs, I was already halfway through them.

Miller sat down across from me and started moving bacon on to his own plate. "Damn, I forgot the toast." He jumped up from his seat and threw bread into the toaster. "It'll just be a minute."

I wanted to ask him if he knew my parents, but even thinking of the subject almost brought me back to tears.

The rest of the meal passed in silence. When the toast popped, my whole body shuddered and my heart lurched into my throat, beating a million times a minute. If Miller noticed, he didn't show it, and I forced myself to relax.

When we were finished, I leaned back in my chair. The black box dug uncomfortably into my back, and I leaned forward instead, resting my forearms on the edge of the table.

"So, is Miller your whole name?"

"My friends used to call me Ian, back when I had time for friends."

"And what do I call you?"

"Miller will do."

I looked down at my dirty plate, the second good meal I'd eaten recently, and felt a too-familiar hole open in my chest. "I can't call you Ian?" Even to me, my voice sounded small and plaintive.

"No one does. I'm not sure if I'd even respond to the name anymore." He pushed himself away from the table and collected the dishes, putting them into a dishwasher under the counter.

I moved into the living room. It was pretty much the same as the rest of the house, sparsely furnished and a little cold-feeling. There were no pictures on the walls, no little knickknacks on any flat surfaces. Barren of all personality. A giant vid screen took up one wall. It was the biggest one I had ever seen outside of a corporate office.

Was this my life now? Is this all I would know if I signed up with ACE?

When Miller walked in behind me, I moved and sat on a black couch by the window, careful not to lean back too quickly, and looked at him. "Tell me about ACE."

"What do you want to know?"

"Everything. Where I come from, ACE is just a bunch of kids spray-painting buildings. Nothing serious. That's not what I see here," I said.

"That is ACE, just not all of it. ACE is a counter-corporation entity. That's the words they want us to use. What it comes down to is, we don't think our lives and the lives of everyone else, on- or off-planet, should be controlled and monitored by the corporations. They've grown into things, beasts, bigger than any government. The top three pretty much make the rules and control what happens in our lives down to the smallest detail.

"If—" He looked around the room, trying to find an example. "If plastic couches became all the rage next year, you can bet that one of the big three planted the seed that started the trend, and they'd be making money hand over fist. The human race has turned into bunch of mice running around a maze, being controlled by our corporate masters."

"And ACE wants to stop that?" I asked.

Miller started pacing across the living room, from the vid screen to the kitchen door. "Stopping it would be impossible. Sure, there are a few radicals higher up the food chain that think destroying the corporations would solve all our problems, but most of us just want some control back. We need checks and balances against the corporations. We need to make sure they aren't controlling us for their own benefit, for their own profit margin. We need to stop them from destroying the planet for their own purposes."

That was, supposedly, where my parents came in. "And how do you do that?"

"You know, there used to be laws in place that limited what a company could tell you. If they advertised a new drug to cure the common cold, they had to list its side effects, no matter how nasty. The government . . . the people ... decided there was too much sugar in kids' cereal, so they placed limits on how the corporations could advertise those cereals. They put down guidelines on how they could advertise to children. The government used to limit a corporation's size, forcing them to split if they got too big ... too powerful. We need to get back to that, we need to be able have our checks and balances. We need to speak up and have our voices heard."

"You sound like a political activist, and stop pacing, you're driving me nuts."

"Sorry." He moved to the loveseat and sat down. "I guess in a way, we are. Except politics doesn't work anymore. The corporations feed so much money into the lobbying groups that the government has just become another pawn in their game. It's been decades since our voices, our words, have made a difference."

"So what do you do, then? If your vote is worthless and you don't have enough money to play the game, what can you do?" It all seemed kind of pointless to me.

"We go underground. We find out the corporations' secrets and expose them. Some of them reach down to such a fundamental level, you start seeing them spray-painted on the sides of buildings. Others just need to be spread around. If you can spread the knowledge, the power, to the little guys, then it helps everybody. Not just the mammoths."

"Where do you fit in to all of this?" I asked. "You can't just go around rescuing female couriers all the time."

Miller laughed, a good deep laugh that started way down in his stomach. A laugh that, when I looked into his eyes, made me feel warm inside. A laugh that took a few more years off his face. I couldn't help but laugh with him.

"No, not every day." He stood up. "Can I get you more coffee?" He walked into the kitchen.

My mood changed almost immediately. What the hell was that all about? He didn't want to talk about his job, or what?

When he walked back into the living room with two coffees, the smile was gone from his face.

"If you don't want to talk about it . . ." I said.

"No. I think you need to know before you agree to sign up." He looked at his watch. "Before they get here and pressure you into a decision."

LEVEL 3—THURSDAY, AUGUST 11, 2140 8:00 A.M.

Quincy pulled his vibrating comm unit from his pocket and looked at the caller ID before answering. Maybe now he'd get some information he could use. "Quincy."

The voice on the other end sounded shaky. "I don't want to do this anymore."

"You don't have a choice."

"I—"

"You're on the Meridian payroll now, mister. And there is only one way out, with no benefits, for you or your mom."

The phone went quiet for a while. Quincy waited, letting his threat sink into the dweeb on the other end of the connection.

"I know where they are." The voice sounded defeated. "If I tell you, ACE will go into shutdown. They will know someone has been leaking information."

Quincy stopped to think. If they lost this source, Jeremy would be mighty pissed off. Then again, the girl had gotten away from him more than once, and that didn't make him a happy man.

He reached for his pen and paper. "Tell me."

LEVEL 5—THURSDAY, AUGUST 11, 2140 8:00 A.M.

Miller began pacing again. "I started out pretty much like you. A young kid with street smarts. My parents dead." His hand moved involuntarily to his scarred cheek. "They died and I was left alone on the streets. I was fifteen then. So full of myself, of what I thought I knew. ACE likes people like us. No family ties to worry about if things go wrong. So they recruited me as a courier, like you. I did mainly Earthside jobs for a couple of years, before they shipped me off-planet. That's when things changed.

"I was making a standard run to the Mars mining colony. One of our guys had some new information for us. I don't know if it was low-level garbage or some high-end stuff. They don't tell us, and it didn't matter to me. On the trip back, I was attacked. Someone didn't want the information in ACE's hands. The training took over, maybe too good. By the end of the trip, I had three bodies stuffed under my bunk. The AD you met last night, Nigel, figured my talents were wasted. I was moved to the Black Ops team, and I've been here ever since. That was three years ago."

I just sat there. I knew, somewhere deep inside, that Miller had killed before. But hearing him just come out and say it made it feel colder and more calculated. His story also made him about twenty-one years old. Way younger than he looked.

"Do you still think I'm a cool guy?" He gave me a half smile.

"I . . . We all need to do things we're not proud of to stay alive. You just . . . well, you did what you had to." I couldn't help but think about Frank on Level 1, and what I had done. The coffee in my cup had gone cold. I leaned forward to place it on the table and settled back into the couch. The top of the black box dug into my shoulder blades again. "If I decide not to become a courier for ACE, what happens?"

"We let you go. We'll drop you off wherever you want. I can even move you to another city if you want. When we get there, I take the black box and you never hear from us again."

"And once the box is off, they can track me again?"

"Yeah."

"That doesn't leave me much choice, does it?"

Miller moved to the couch and sat beside me. "Sometimes running free is better than the alternative. It's possible that when they realize you don't have the package anymore, they'll leave you alone."

"How possible?"

"I don't know. All I can say is that they'll know you don't have it anymore. I can't promise more than that."

Impulsively, I reached out and grabbed his hand. "Thanks." I knew this was more honesty than I had gotten from anybody since this mess started.

"For what."

"Everything." I reached up and touched his scars with my fingertips. "How . . . ?"

He stood and moved to the vid screen wall.

"I'm sorry."

"No . . . No, it's okay. It's just something I don't think about too much." Miller started pacing again. "When I was fifteen, our house got broken into. They busted in through a window, and before my dad could do anything, he and Mom were in the middle of the living room, tied to chairs. Well, by the time they were done, I had these scars, and my parents were dead. But I was alive. I ended up in foster homes for a few months before I decided I'd had enough. I ran away. ACE picked me up a few months later, and the rest is history. What about you, what's your story? You're what, seventeen or eighteen?"

"Sixteen . . . but I'll be seventeen real soon." For a split second I thought I saw disappointment flicker across his face. Maybe it was just wishful thinking. "I just got tired of being a victim, you know? I left home when I was fourteen, and I've been alone ever since. Until now, that is. It's as though . . . as though I'm the victim again. The one being controlled instead of being in control." I wasn't sure why I was talking to him like this. I guess Miller just made me feel safe.

"We're a lot alike, you and I. You'll do good in ACE."

"If I decide that's what I want."

"Yeah, if you decide." Miller filled the awkward silence that followed by moving back to the kitchen. "Look, I'm gonna finish up in the kitchen. Why don't you relax a bit? The guys from ACE should be here in about forty-five minutes."

"Okay. I'm going to take a shower, if that's all right."

Miller looked at me, and I wondered if he was seeing me half naked again or just realizing how grubby I looked.

"Last door down the hall. Take your time. You might want to double up on the tape holding the box on." He turned and walked back into the kitchen, his ears turning a deep red.

It made me like him more.

The shower was soothing and deliciously warm, though the hot water stung when it hit my recent injuries. I must have stood under the running water for over half an hour, until my skin started to look wrinkled.

I didn't close the bathroom door behind me when I went in, leaving it open about a centimeter. But it may as well have been locked. Miller didn't even stick his head in to make sure I had a towel.

I wasn't sure if I should be disappointed or relieved. And I wasn't really sure why I did it in the first place. This wasn't the time to get involved with anyone. Maybe I just wanted some human contact, something to show me I was still part of the real world.

As I toweled off, the sound of voices drifted down the hallway. I gently closed the door and flicked the lock.

It sounded like it was decision time. I wasn't ready, but delaying it wouldn't change anything. I got dressed, straightened my short hair with my fingers, and walked back to the living room.

"Ms. Ballard? I'm Assistant Director William Clark, and this is Ted, from ACE Human Resources." They both sat on the couch, indicating the loveseat for me. Miller stood by the entry to the kitchen.

"Before we start anything else, where is the package?"

"On the dresser in the bedroom," I said.

"Miller, get the package and give it to the driver outside. We need to find out what this is all about."

William turned to face me and spoke again. "I understand AD Wood talked to you about joining our organization. Although we don't know why he wanted to recruit you, we trust his judgment. So, we need an answer. Ted?"

"Hi, Kris. It's good to see you. Let's talk about salary and career paths, shall we?"

I made Ted go through his whole spiel. It was some of the most boring shit I had ever listened to, but he seemed to be really enjoying it. At one point, I looked up at Miller and he had to leave the living room so no one could see him laughing. I don't think Ted ever caught on, even when William stopped him.

"You've had a chance to talk to Nigel, and to Miller here. I'm sorry for forcing the issue, but we need to move forward. Your little package is at the center of a very big crisis."

"Before I answer, Nigel said he knew my parents, said they worked for ACE."

William and Ted looked at each other before William answered. "We don't know anything about that, but we'll look into it if your answer is yes."

"You don't leave me much choice," I said.

"What do you mean?"

"If I choose not to join you, I don't get to find out about my mom and dad, and I die. You remove the black box, my ID tag goes live again, and SoCal or IBC or whoever finds me and kills me."

"We don't know that's going to happen."

"We don't know it won't."

William looked over at Miller, standing behind me near the kitchen. I didn't turn around to see what he did, but whatever it was, William came to a decision. "The possibility is pretty high."

"Well then, seeing as I'm not fucking suicidal, I guess I'm in."

William and Ted rose from the couch. "Good. Miller knows what to do. Welcome aboard, Kris." They turned and left the house.

I had made up my mind in the shower. Saying it out loud to people who could do something about it seemed to flip a switch in my brain. I was actually looking forward to the training regimen Nigel had described. It wouldn't be like my old life, which had to be good, and there was bound to be a nice place to live, and in my own way, I was following Mom and Dad's footsteps. I felt lighter, as though a world of worries and stress had been lifted off my shoulders. No one would try to kill me, not yet anyway, and I could move on with my life.

LEVEL 5—THURSDAY, AUGUST 11, 2140 10:45 A.M.

"Welcome aboard," Miller said. "It's not an easy life, but it has its benefits. I'll get the car out of the garage. Grab whatever you need from your room and meet me on the front street."

Miller turned and left through the side door. The house seemed suddenly empty without him.

I went back to the bedroom and grabbed my jacket. It was still filthy. Someone must have taken it off the chair in the restaurant. Probably Miller. I took the gun and extra clips, shoving them into the jacket's pockets. It really seemed like too nice a thing to leave behind. Maybe when Miller dropped me off, I'd give it to him as a gift. I figured I had to do something, he'd been so helpful. He was one of the few guys I'd met that didn't seem to want something from me.

I remembered the feeling of strength in his arms when he put them around me. How, for that brief moment, I had felt safe. It was how I'd felt when my dad held me when I was little, like nothing in the world could hurt me, especially not the monsters under my bed. This time the monsters were real.

I folded the envelope of cash and stuffed it into my back pocket.

I looked through the frilly curtains and saw the car nose out to the end of the driveway. Miller got out and started to walk back to the front door. A silver van drove slowly down the street, passing the house and pulling into another driveway a few doors down. The driver kept his eyes straight ahead, not looking at Miller or the house, but something wasn't right. There was something about . . .

Oh god. No! It was Quincy. It was fucking Quincy. I yelled through the closed window while Miller kept walking to the front door. He didn't hear me, couldn't hear me through the fucking glass. I had to get out there, get to him. He was a sitting duck. The side door, the one Miller went out to get the car. It was the closest. I ran for it, slipping on the hallway carpet and banging into the wall. My shoulder left a dent in the drywall, and pain flared in the pulled muscle. The door pushed open into a garage. Three stairs led down to concrete. Barely slowing down, I took the stairs in one leap. My left heel clipped the last stair and I launched forward, landing on my hands and knees. I screamed as loud as I could. "QUINCY!"

Through the open garage door, I could see the van back out of the driveway and launch toward the house. Its tires squealed on the dry pavement. From the other direction I saw Miller turn and run toward me. He was too far. He wasn't going to make it. I pushed myself to my feet. My pants were cut and my knees bled through the torn material. The skin on my hands was scraped, but there was no blood. I barely registered the pain.

The van accelerated and jumped the curb onto the grass, swerving between Miller and me. I briefly saw Miller turn and run back the way he had come, back toward the front door of the house. The van slid to a stop, gouging deep furrows into the green turf with its tires. A gunshot sounded in the quiet neighborhood.

I stood in the garage, swaying on my feet. What was I supposed to do? The gun. I still had the fucking gun. I pulled it from my pocket and it almost slipped from my grasp. The sweat on my hands made the gun wet and slick and difficult to hold. Now what? Was I supposed to run out there like a fucking commando? I'd never fired a gun in my life.

Another shot sounded from the far side of the van.

The car. If Quincy stayed on the far side of the van, there was a chance I could still get to the car idling in the driveway. Two more shots sounded, followed by the sharp twang of metal being hit. I ran and opened the door, sliding behind the wheel. I threw the car into drive and stomped on the pedal, hurling the car onto the street, the motor whining as it went to full power.

I kept going until I had a full house-width between me and the van. Slamming the car into reverse, I stood on the pedal again. The car jumped backward, quicker than I had expected, and flew toward the driveway. I kept the van centered in the rear window. The car's right tires jumped the curb, almost twisting the steering wheel from my grasp. I kept my foot to the floor and slammed into the side of the van. My head snapped back from the impact. I kept the car moving. The car's rear end crumpled, pushing the van across the front lawn and past the concrete stairs leading to the front door.

Miller jumped from behind the shield created by the stairs and raced to the passenger door I threw open for him. Before he was fully in the car, I had thrown it back into drive and slammed down on the accelerator again.

I sped down the street, leaving the safe house and Quincy behind. I hoped he had been flattened by the van.

"Left! Turn left here! Good, now the next right, or we'll get to a dead end. When you get to the next intersection, turn right again." Miller lay back on the seat, sweat running down his face.

"Are you hurt? Did you get hit?" I asked.

"What?" Miller looked at me.

"Did you get hit?"

"No . . . no, I'm all right, I'm okay."

"How the fuck did he know where we were?"

"I . . . I dunno. Let me think for a minute." He turned toward the window.

I turned right and merged with traffic moving down the busy road.

Miller kept looking out the window.

"If one of our safe houses has been compromised, ACE is in trouble. They'll be going quiet until the leak can be found," he said.

TWELVE

A HALF HOUR LATER we were driving through the outskirts of a business section. Nearby, the buildings stretched from the ground to the ceiling. Miller didn't talk during the drive, lost in his own thoughts about what had just happened. He was the first to break the silence.

"Did you call anybody from the house?"

"No. I don't even remember seeing a comm unit."

"That's twice, maybe three times, they knew where you were. Once, I can count off as a fluke, but twice? I don't think so. There's either someone in ACE feeding them information, or you still have a tracking device on you." He was silent for a minute longer. "I don't think you're being tracked. My scanner would have picked it up in the parking garage. Nothing gets through that thing without being detected."

I weaved through the slower, thicker traffic, never exceeding the posted speed limit. This wasn't making sense to me either. "If there's someone inside ACE, then why are they still coming after me? I don't have the package anymore."

"Good question. They could have been after me. I've made more than my fair share of enemies."

"That was Quincy. It couldn't be a coincidence," I said.

"True. It took them a while to find us. If the mole is in a low-level position, it would take them some time for them to get the information. ACE is pretty compartmentalized."

I caught Miller looking at me and tried to smile. His gaze moved down from my hands to my knees.

"We've got to find a place to clean up. We need to wash out your cuts. You're not going to be much use looking like that."

I gave him a dirty look.

It was his turn to smile now. "I mean with your pants all shredded and bloody. Turn right at the lights. There's a mall just up the street. We'll have to get rid of the car as well, if we can. The crumpled back end will be pretty noticeable."

I turned right and saw the mall just ahead. I turned right again and into the parking lot.

Miller sat up straighter. "The trick with parking lots this big is you don't want to end up somewhere you can get boxed in. You also don't want to park too far from the building. If you have to make a quick exit, the last thing you want is to be running across a whole parking lot. See over there? There's a two-level parking garage. You'll want to park on the first level, the second is too exposed to potential snipers and limits your escape routes. There's a spot right by the entrance. Back into it. If we need to, we can pull out really quick, and if someone tries to block us from leaving they'll need two vehicles, one in the front and one in the back. Most people don't immediately think of blocking off a curbed area, so we might be able to back out over the curb and onto the street, just in case."

I parked where he told me to and followed him into the mall. I could see him watching me in the mirrors around the elevators.

"Walk like you belong here, Kris. Stand up and look around, not at the floor."

"I don't belong here," I mumbled. "I can't afford anything in this place."

"Maybe not, but if you want to become one of the crowd, you have to act like one of them, even more than look like them. The human mind works off of first impressions of body language."

I looked around. Sure enough, several of the people in the mall gave us more than one look. And the look only seemed to drop down to my bloody knees on the second or third glance. Most of them wouldn't be able to see the blood at that distance, but the tears in my pants were plainly visible.

"Where did you learn all this?" I asked. And there was something else . . . "You sound different, too." Gone were the slang words, the imprecise pronunciations. It was as if Miller had suddenly become more educated, more upper class.

"ACE, and on the job. You use your courier status to get you in and out of places you normally wouldn't have been allowed to go. It gives you a sense of belonging, even temporarily, that influences your body language without you knowing about it. Being a courier for ACE doesn't give you a uniform or a sense of fitting in. It has to come from inside you. The voice is part of it. If I sound more educated, people will automatically believe that I am. If I project the right body language."

I followed Miller's lead and began to look around. We were bombarded with advertisements for clothes and electronics. Everywhere you looked you were hit with a new deal, a better price. Spaced evenly between the ads were cameras, watching people's reactions to what they were seeing and adjusting if specific ads weren't working. When I first saw the cameras, I quickly looked down at the floor again. Miller nudged my shoulder and grabbed my hand, squeezing it. I could feel his strength pass into me, and began to walk with more confidence.

He strode into a small specialty shop, full of jeans and t-shirts and jackets. The place was way out of my league.

Fifteen minutes later we left with a bag filled with new clothes. I stepped into the public washrooms and changed in a stall, placing my old clothes into the emptied bag. When I walked out, I forced myself to walk a bit taller and to look around. Trying to believe I fit in. The clothes helped. The stiff material in the new jeans rubbed my knees, and I could feel the soft scabs peel away. I didn't dare look down to check if blood was seeping through.

My new attitude must have worked. When I walked toward Miller he gave me one of his heart-melting smiles, and we moved back to the parking lot. No one gave us a second glance.

Once we were back at the car, Miller got behind the wheel. "Now we need to dump this thing," he said.

I sat carefully, pulling my pant legs up to lessen the pressure on my knees. I didn't see any blood yet.

"I have my bike on Level 2," I said.

"Nah, they'll still be watching it. I have a car in the

garage we went into last night. We should be okay going back there. It's about an hour away from here. Why don't you grab a nap? You look exhausted."

I was. It was as though the morning had never existed. The shower, the breakfast, the bed, all vanished in the blink of an eye. But I sure as heck didn't want to sleep now, didn't want the loss of control that went with it. "I'll wait."

"Suit yourself. Once we have the car we'll zip down to Level 3 and check into a motel."

"Won't ACE wonder what's happening?"

"Maybe."

By the tone of his voice I figured it would be best if I dropped it.

My eyes closed and I drifted into sleep without knowing.

I was sitting in my bedroom, afraid to come out, and almost as afraid to stay in. My Auntie had left for work an hour ago. I tried to leave before she did, but she wouldn't let me, saying I had too much housework to do.

Now I was alone in the house with him *again. I slipped on my runners and grabbed a coat from the closet. If he had fallen asleep, or was watching a vid, I might be able to sneak out the front. I opened my bedroom door a crack and looked into the living room. The vid screen was on, throwing its flickering light onto the walls. I could see his hand hanging off the side of the easy chair, a bottle dangling loosely from his grip.*

I crept across the floor, holding my breath and avoiding all the creaky parts. I made it all the way to the front door.

"Where the hell 'r you going?" His words came out slurred.

I turned to look at him, my breath coming back in a

whoosh. He was still in his chair, leaning over the arm and looking at me. Sweat covered his upper lip, or spilled booze.

"I said where the hell 'r you going? C'm here."

I grabbed for the doorknob and twisted, yanking the door open. It slammed to a sudden stop, leaving only a few centimeters of space. My heart thudded in my chest. The chain. He'd clipped the chain. I slammed the door shut and fumbled with the chain. It jammed and I twisted and pulled until it came loose and I slid the chain out. I twisted the knob again and jerked the door open. It ripped out of my grasp and crashed shut.

His hand was just above my head, holding the door closed. His breath reeked of booze.

"I don' think so."

He squinted at me, trying to look through the alcohol-induced haze. I tried to push my back through the door into the hallway.

"You haven't tol' your aunt, 'ave you? I tol' you I'd kill you if you did."

I shook my head and whimpered. Tears filled my eyes and my world became dark.

"Good. Now come 'ere."

He grabbed my arm and twisted, dragging me back to his easy chair. I was too scared to resist.

"I got you a present," he said.

Sitting beside the chair was a small, pink striped bag. He reached his meaty hand into it and pulled out what looked like a small shirt. It was made of see-through red lace. He thrust it in my face.

"Put it on."

When I didn't reach for it, he grabbed my hand and jammed the negligee into it.

"I said put it on."

He let go, and my hand dropped to my side, the negli-

gee dangling from my loose fingertips. I turned toward my bedroom.

"No! Here. Put it on 'ere, in fron' of me."

I hesitated. His hand swung out, hitting me across the face. I fell to the floor, giant sobs escaped from my throat. I lay there, quivering.

"Stop yer whining, an' put it on."

I pushed myself into a sitting position and groped at my shoelaces. I finally got them undone and rose to my feet.

By the time I managed to slip on the sheer red material, he had his pants down to his ankles, lying in his chair and taking another gulp from his bottle.

"Now git to work."

Minutes later, I lay huddled on the floor, too scared to even cry. The skin on my face felt tight and swollen. I thought his first swing had broken my nose. The rest landed on my back and chest. I could feel the bruises already forming. He flopped back into his chair.

"Bitch don't even know how to help a man get it up." *He took another drink from the bottle, emptying it.* *"Get me 'nother one, bitch. Take that thing off and get dressed, you look like a slut."*

I struggled to my feet and got him the bottle before even trying to get dressed. As he opened it, I grabbed my clothes and ran back to my room.

The sound of the road changing woke me up. We were underground, in another parking garage. I pushed the memories back where they belonged, back into the careful box I had built for them over the years. They made me realize that even though what was happening was different, the feelings were almost the same. I had become the victim again.

This time, I didn't think running away was going to

help. The memories didn't want to stay in their locked box anymore, forced out by feelings of hopelessness and loss of control I hadn't felt in a long time.

"You didn't look like you slept well," Miller said.

I stared out the side window at the cars parked in their spots. "I didn't."

"When we get the car, we'll need a place to hole up for a while. There's a cheap motel near the Kadokawa offices. I don't think they'll look for us there."

Without turning my head, I said, "Okay."

MERIDIAN SAT CITY—THURSDAY, AUGUST 11, 2140
12:00 P.M.

The view from Jeremy's office wasn't as good as the one from the boardroom, but that was mainly by choice. The wall of vid screens could have displayed anything he liked, from the Earth from orbit to windswept plains full of bison. That, however, was too extravagant at the best of times. Today, it was so completely out of the question that he would have happily shot anyone who dared to bring it up. Only data and maps, filtered and precise, flowed across his screens.

There was a soft knock on his door before it opened.

Abby had just arrived in his office.

He looked at her as though she was a streak of rust on an otherwise pristine fighter craft. The fact that she had shown up here, completely unannounced, did not bode well for the state of her mission.

"What are you doing here?" The sound that came out was almost more of a snarl.

"I came to report on the status of my mission."

"You left Earth just to tell me something I already

know? What kind of fool are you?" The words were snapped and precise.

Most people would have started to make excuses. At the very least, they would have tried to get out of the office as fast as they could. Abby moved deeper into the viper's den, to a low couch against the wall opposite the vid screens, and sat down, crossing her legs as if nothing that happened was unexpected.

"Yes," she said.

Jeremy moved behind his desk and sat down, turning off the data flow to the screens. When dealing with Abby, it was best to lose all outside distractions.

"Our reports indicate you failed. What more can you tell me?"

"Probably not too much more. The girl met with Nigel Wood, an assistant director of ACE."

"I know who Nigel Wood is. I assigned you his case."

Abby continued unfazed. "Wood opened the package and read the documents inside. As far as I could see, he did not scan the data chip. All items were returned to the envelope before the girl joined him."

"At least he's dead."

"Yes. He was my primary target at the time. I tried to get the girl, but . . ."

"This girl has got to be one of the luckiest I've ever seen," he said.

"Luck has nothing to do with it."

Jeremy knew when he'd made a mistake, and this was one of them.

"The girl was fated to live through my attempts to kill her. She may be fated to live through them all, I don't know. If you could supply me with her birth date and time, as well as the location of the happy event, I will be able to plot her charts and discover her weak points. Armed with that information, my next attempt will most likely be successful."

As far as Jeremy was concerned, it was all bullshit. People made themselves. Some of it based on being in the right place at the right time — luck — or by the people they associated with. Either way, the alignment of the planets and the stars had nothing to do with it. He wasn't about to say that out loud, though something must have shown in his face.

"You still do not believe," Abby said softly. "I've worked for you for over ten years, and you still attribute my success to luck?"

"No, to skill."

"My skills arise from knowing how the person I'm assigned to thinks. How they will react in any given situation. Nothing can delve as deep into a person as the stars. Nothing else can give me the level of information I need to understand my assignment."

Jeremy sighed. He knew this could go on forever. He looked Abby in the eye; it was time to get back to the business at hand. "What I believe is your success rate. Which has been tarnished by this last . . . twist of fate?"

"Am I to believe I'm still on the case then?"

"Yes, you are. You will not, however, be working alone."

At those words, Abby stood up and strode over to his desk. "I always work alone." Her voice was still cool.

"This situation has gotten out of control. I need to know it will not extend past the end of the day. Quincy . . ."

Abby winced at the sound of his name.

"*Quincy* has also failed. Together, perhaps you can succeed. Your job will be the elimination of the girl. With the package open, who knows what information she now has? Quincy's job will be to retrieve the package and return it to me personally. Do you think you can handle that?"

"I'd prefer not to."

"Your preference doesn't matter."

Abby let out a soft sigh and smiled. "I can do it."

"Good. The trace on the girl has been blocked, so we don't know where they are. After her escape from Quincy at the ACE safe house, they were sighted briefly at a mall on 4th Street West, Level 4, Los Angeles. We should know their location as soon as her . . . protector . . . calls in."

"And the information I require?"

Jeremy flipped through a stack of paper on his desk and pulled a data chip out of a file folder. He tossed it to her. "It's all in here."

He watched Abby turn and walk out of his office, closing the door softly behind her. She was becoming a touch too arrogant. He would have to look into taking her down a notch or two.

≡≡≡

LEVEL 4—THURSDAY, AUGUST 11, 2140 12:30 P.M.

Switching to the new car took only a couple of minutes. I watched as Miller took most of that time cleaning the old car of anything that could be traced back to us or the safe house. It made me feel useless to just be standing around.

When he finished that, he scanned the dark blue four-door for any trackers, making several passes and punching codes on to the scanner touch screen between each one. The car was clean. We got in and drove to the exit.

"So, what's the plan?"

"I think we'll skip holing up in a hotel. Right now all I want to do is keep moving. A moving target is harder to find and harder to hit," Miller said.

"What about ACE? Why don't you contact them and get some help?"

Miller slowed the car as he exited the garage and merged with traffic. "With the information we have, I have to assume ACE is compromised. Talking to them may be as bad as talking directly to SoCal or Meridian. I think we're on our own."

We. Miller had said *we*. It felt like a weight was lifted off my shoulders. I leaned back into the car seat and relaxed a bit. I guess I didn't realize how much having him around meant to me. His obvious skills might be my only chance of getting out of this. If I was being honest with myself, he was nice to be around.

The black box dug into my back, but instead of being a pain, it had become almost a source of comfort.

"What about this tracker thing in me? Nigel said the power source on the blocker would only last a few days at most. Is this box any better?"

"Worse, and yeah, that's gonna be a problem."

The fear I had just managed to push into the background forced its way back to the front. "A problem? I think it's more than just a problem." I cringed hearing my voice go up an octave.

"I figure we've got one and half, maybe two days before the power source fails. A lot can happen between now and then. Still, it is our priority."

I sat up again, relieving the pressure the black box put on my back, and looked through the front windows. I didn't dare look at Miller. "You could just drop me off. I could try to get out of the city."

I sounded and felt weak.

Miller rested his hand on my knee and I grabbed it, squeezing his fingers tight.

"Look, I'm not going anywhere. Nigel assigned me to protect you, before he was killed. I plan on doing that."

My heart sank deep into my chest. Is that what it was? Was he just following orders then? Was that the only reason he stayed with me?

I gave myself a mental kick in the pants. It was time to stop acting like a forlorn kid. I felt like getting out of the car and walking away. Instead, I sat still and let go of his hand. Whatever his reason, I was still safer here, at least until the tracker was removed.

Miller gave my knee a hesitant pat, sending shards of pain up my leg, and put his hand back on the steering wheel. "We need to get up to Level 6."

I could tell by the tone of his voice that he had made a decision.

"ACE has a small medical facility there where we can get the tag modified," he said.

"I thought you didn't trust ACE."

"I don't, but in this business, you have to trust your favors. One of the docs there owes me a big one. He can block the tag without ACE knowing we're even there."

"Will he do it?"

Miller sighed. "I don't know."

"Even if he will, I'm not allowed on Level 6."

"I'll get you in." Miller turned into an empty parking lot. The building stood vacant. Broken windows reflected the Ambients, and yawning black doors faced the street.

"What are we doing here?" I didn't like the look of this place at all.

"We need some privacy, and this is probably the place we'll find it."

Miller maneuvered through the piled up garbage and stopped in the dark alleyway behind the building. When he opened the door and got out, the smell reminded me of Level 1: garbage and pee mixed with other, less pleasant things.

"This place used to be a skateboarder hangout, until

the police forced them to move down to Level 3. It's been empty ever since, as far as I know." He opened the back door of the car and reached a hand in between the bench and the back of the seat, searching with his fingers. His hand stopped moving, and he pushed whatever he had found sideways toward the passenger side of the car. With his other hand he grabbed the front of the seat and pulled. The whole bottom seat section slid out, revealing a box the width of the car. He looked at me and asked, "How are you with small dark places?"

LEVEL 4—THURSDAY, AUGUST 11, 2140 12:40 P.M.

"You want me in there?" I stared at the dirty, tiny cubbyhole. The box was barely wider than my shoulders, and not nearly long enough. What the hell was Miller thinking, that I was a contortionist, or worse yet, a child? The thought rushed into my head, filling it with dread. He thought I was just a kid.

"It's the only place we have. I'd put you in the trunk, but there's no promise they won't look in there. I can't bring you in with me. They'll scan you and wonder why you're not transmitting; then they'll find the box. If we remove the box, they *might* let you up with me, but then the corporations will have a lock on you."

"Can't we . . ." I racked my brain for a solution other than getting into that coffin. "Can't we sneak through the service corridors between levels, get in that way?"

Miller shook his head. "There are no service corridors up to 6. Level 5 used to be the top. When SoCal decided to expand, they kept the new system completely separate from the old. They didn't want anybody to get above Level 5 unless they allowed it."

"What about—"

"There is no other way Kris. I know you're not too happy about it, but we're kinda short on time."

I stared at the box. It couldn't be worse than the tunnel on Level 1, could it? "Are you sure I can fit?"

"Climb in and see."

I opened the side door and took another look at it. The damn thing wasn't even a coffin, it was just a small wooden box, barely big enough to hold a glass of water. I stepped over the seat bottom and sat on it, one leg in the box and the other one still outside the car. It refused to move.

"I can't."

"You have to, Kris. We're running out of options. You'll be fine." He reached across and rested a hand on my shoulder for the last words.

I hauled my other foot into the car and placed it in the box. Sweat dripped down my forehead and my breath was ragged. I slid off the seat and into the box, wiggling down until my feet touched the side wall. By the time I got the rest of myself in, I already felt like I'd pulled a couple of muscles, and my clothes were wet with sweat.

"You'll have to get a bit lower than that, or the seat won't latch."

I looked at him like he was insane. Instead of voicing my thoughts, I angled my hips a little and pushed my shoulders to the bottom. The black box dug in, and my chest hurt from when Frank had hit me.

"Do you have a pillow or a blanket? Something to soften the box?"

"Sorry, no. You'll have to suffer for a while. I promise I'll have you out of there in a half hour. Okay?"

Miller's eyes were filled with concern, and I nodded, barely moving my head. I trusted him. I'd barely known him twenty-four hours, and I trusted him.

"Good. I need to move some stuff from the trunk in with you. If they pop it and see what's in there, we'll never get through."

"In here, with me? Where the hell do you plan to put the stuff, up my ass?"

Miller gave me a quick grin I couldn't help but return.

"I don't think we'll have to go that far," he said.

By the time he had moved most of the stuff from the trunk to my box, I was so wedged in it felt like a crane would be needed to get me out. I kept my eyes focused on the Ambients through the back windows and slowly counted my breaths.

"How ya doing?" Miller asked.

"Fucking great."

"Good, I'm gonna put some of this other stuff out here, under the garbage pile. Hopefully no one will find it until I get back."

He left my limited field of view. I heard some more rummaging around the trunk, followed by the scraping of wood and stone outside, before Miller came back.

"Okay, I'm gonna close you in. No matter what happens, you've gotta stay quiet, okay?"

"Yeah, okay," I promised. I could hear the fear in my own voice, hoping Miller couldn't. I almost wished he would just get the fucking thing over with.

When the seat was lowered, I wasn't sure I would be able to keep my promise. My entire world became a black tomb. The box taped to my back seemed to have grown sharper corners that cut into my skin. The other equipment held me in a tight grip, each piece pressing in on me, crushing me.

I let out a little whimper when the car started to move. Some of the equipment settled more tightly against me, and the black box grew steel talons that dug into my back. I couldn't breathe. I tried to bang the side of the box, but my hands were jammed too tight. Each bump brought new waves of pain, from the pressure on my torn knees to something scraping against the bandage on my neck to the black box. Tears tracked across my temples, dripping into my ears.

When the car finally stopped, I almost laughed with joy. Only Miller's whispered warning to remain quiet stopped me. Still, the thought of getting out, of seeing the light and feeling the air move against my skin, swept through me. I fought a losing battle until voices came through the seat, muffled and distorted by the thick material.

The car door opened and slammed shut again. I felt more than heard a key slide into the trunk lock and it popped open. A thin line of light pierced the box just to the left of my face. I wanted to shout, to scream. *For god's sake, let me out. Let me out!* Air rushed into my lungs, ready to explode outward with sound. Instead, I held it, feeling the searching hands of the guard get closer to my little sliver of light.

The sounds of searching stopped, and the trunk slammed shut, throwing me back into my dark piece of hell. A moment later the engine started and I shifted to the back of the box as the car nosed up the ramp to Level 6.

Time became measured in the bumps and turns that tightened the box's grip on me. For a while, I counted them, before losing track. My world had become six walls that pressed in on me. If I could raise my head, it would scrape against the seat bottom. I forgot how to breathe, forgot how to exist, thinking it would be better if Quincy had gotten me. I pushed the thought from my head, willing myself to breathe in and out. The air grew stale and I was sure each breath would be my last.

I don't know when the car finally stopped. I couldn't hear, I couldn't see, I couldn't feel. I was helpless. The sky opened up above me and a rush of air and light invaded my senses.

My body reacted immediately, pushing off the bottom of the box, through everything that shifted above me during the drive. I hurled myself from the prison I'd been in, throwing my arms around Miller, pushing my face into his chest, no longer caring if he, if anyone, thought of me as weak or scared. The steady sound of his heart beating calmed me down, and I slowly got myself under control. I realized his arms were wrapped around me, holding me as tight as I held him.

"We made it. You're okay, we made it," Miller whispered softly. "Come on, let's get you out of here."

He let go of me and pried my arms away, keeping hold of my hands. He backed out of the car door, gently pulling me along with him.

"I'm sorry it took so long, I couldn't find a place to open the seat."

I refused to let go of him. "How . . ." I breathed in deep. "How long?"

"About forty minutes, give or take a bit. But we made it. Come on, I'll close the seat. You get in the front and I'll be right there."

I finally let go of Miller and moved around the car. I didn't want to get in the front seat, didn't want to be enclosed again away from the vastness of the parking garage, but I pulled the door open and slid in, closing it behind me.

LEVEL 6—THURSDAY, AUGUST 11, 2140 1:15 P.M.

The feeling of being in a huge open space increased when we left the garage. I leaned forward and gaped out the front window. The ceiling was so far above us, I almost didn't believe it was there. It was painted a light blue that faded in the distance. The Ambients lay in giant tracks, slowly moving across the huge expanse. As Miller drove through a business section, I counted at least twenty stories in the building that touched the sky.

We stopped at a gated community. Miller typed in an access code and the gates slid open in front of us. The second we were through they slammed shut.

"The doc's in here," Miller said. "He works at a small outpatient clinic, does minor surgeries and stuff like that. A couple of years ago I was on a run from the Mars colony back to Earth. One of the guys sitting at my dining room table started choking. The stewards came over and tried to get whatever it was unstuck, but no go. By the time I decided to do something, the guy was already turning blue. I slit open his larynx and stuck a straw in the hole. You shoulda seen it; the cut closed around the straw like it was supposed to be there. The guy started breathing again.

"When we made Earthfall, the doctors came and took him. Turned out a sliver of chicken bone had lodged in his throat. Every time the stewards tried to get it out, they just ended up pushing it in deeper.

"The guy's father worked for ACE. One of our doctors to boot. When we finally met, he made it pretty clear that he thought he owed me, big time, for saving his son's life."

"And you're using that favor on me?" I asked.

"I gotta keep you safe. With ACE out of reach, and that tracker in ya, I gotta use what I can."

I tore my eyes away from houses and lawns around us and looked at him, making eye contact and holding it. "Thanks." I couldn't remember the last time anyone had done so much for me without expecting something in return.

"No problem." He paused. "That's the place." Miller indicated a small three-story building on the right. The parking lot was half full. "ACE runs it, and SoCal foots the bill. Neat little setup. It looks normal enough. I'll drive past one more time to make sure."

Miller drove down a side street and pulled into a driveway, backing out to go the way we had just come. His comm unit started to beep.

"Shit."

"What?"

"It's not part of the procedure, calling me like this. If there's any chance of ACE or one of its operatives being compromised, all communication will cease until proper confirmation of the situation can be made." It sounded like he was quoting directly from a book.

"They've got to realize that ACE is compromised. Losing an AD and having a safe house hit is no simple coincidence," he said.

"Maybe they caught the guy."

"Yeah, maybe," said Miller.

I could hear the doubt in his voice. The comm unit beeped again.

"Are you going to answer it?"

Miller pulled the unit from his pocket, pressed the speakerphone, and laid it down on the dash between us. He raised his finger to his lips, telling me to keep quiet.

"Yeah."

"Miller? Miller, it's Devon, from ACE."

"What can I do for ya?"

"I have an activation code: golf, echo, romeo, alpha, lima, delta, wun, seven, fower." Devon used the phonetic pronunciation of four.

Miller nodded at me. I guess the code was right. He hesitated before answering.

"Code is a go," he said.

"All hell's broken loose here. They figure there is a mole in place. They're shutting it all down."

Miller stepped on the brakes and pulled the car over to the side of the road. "Could you repeat that, please?"

"They're shutting it all down. They've got no idea where the leak is, so they're doing a purge and rebuild. You still got the courier with you?"

"How complete is the shutdown?"

"Umm, hang on." The comm unit was quiet for a while before Devon came back. "Looks like everything. Several safe houses have already been sold off, the rest are on the market. All couriers and operatives are being told to go into hiding until they're notified. All on-going missions are being contacted directly with instructions."

"Shit."

"Do you still have the courier with you?" Devon asked again.

"Yeah."

"Where are you?"

"Level 6, just outside Doc Searls' offices."

The line went quiet again for a minute before Devon came back. "His office was told to close a half hour ago. It's probably empty by now. Are you or the courier hurt? Can you go somewhere else?"

"Nah, we're fine. I was hoping to get her tracker fixed," Miller said.

"Unless Searls is still there, that isn't going to happen," Devon said.

Miller pulled away from the curb and sped toward the doctor's office. "I'm gonna check. If the doc's gone, where else can we go?"

"Nowhere, man. We're shutting down. You're to stop your mission and wait for further instructions."

"Her tag will activate soon."

"Not our problem. Your mission is aborted. Dump the courier and await further instructions."

Miller closed the link on his comm unit, put it back in his pocket, and kept his eyes on the road.

LEVEL 6—THURSDAY, AUGUST 11, 2140 1:22 P.M.

Devon closed the link with a gentle touch to his screen. The call had been made, as he had been instructed to do. He walked to his Level 7 exit, pulled another unit from his pocket, and dialed.

"It's done." He listened quietly for a while before continuing. "Doc Searls' office. Green Heights Community, Level 6."

After listening a bit longer he hung up and put the comm unit into an inside pocket. It was time to head back to his office.

With Nigel gone, it was a lot easier to get out and make his phone calls. There was no one that contacted him over the hard line. Not yet anyway. And with ACE going into full shutdown mode, there wouldn't be for quite a while.

He would stay here as long as he was needed. He smiled to himself. Or as long as it was safe. Whichever came first.

The door to his office rolled open when he approached and closed again behind him. Devon settled into his chair and watched the screens.

LEVEL 6—THURSDAY, AUGUST 11, 2140 1:22 P.M.

"What's going on?" I realized my voice sounded too high again.

"You heard. ACE is shutting down until they find the leak."

"What about me? What happens to me?"

"They want me to dump you. Leave you out here for the corporations to find."

I just stared at him.

"It's not going to happen." He turned in his seat to face me. "Look, Kris. I'm not going to do it. I don't care what they say. It's just not right."

Without thinking, I reached out and brushed the scars on his face with my fingertips. "Thank you."

Turning to face forward again, Miller pulled past a slow moving car. "First things first, we see if Doc Searls is still in."

Two minutes later, he spun the wheel and the car rocketed into the parking lot. "When we stop, get out and follow me. I'll do all the talking."

"What if he's not here?"

Miller paused. "Let's just hope he is."

Miller turned the wheel again and the car slipped into a parking spot. I threw my door open and ran toward the building, just behind Miller. The doors were still open, and I felt some hope rise in my chest.

"It's on the second floor. Stairs." Miller ran past the elevator and pulled open the door to the stairs. He took two at a time. I followed as close behind as my short legs allowed.

We came out into a reception area. The waiting room was empty and no one sat behind the desk. Two hallways went to the back of the building, one on either side of reception.

"Fuck. Come on, we'll look in the back." He grabbed my hand and pulled me along with him, taking the closer of the two hallways.

The corridor was as deserted as the front. All of the

examination rooms stood empty. The hallway took a ninety-degree turn, and at the other end it turned again, toward reception. In the back were two operating theaters. One looked recently used, with surgical instruments and blood-soaked gauze scattered on the floor. We stood by the table, both of us trying to catch our breath.

"Now . . . Now what?" I asked.

"I dunno. We might be able to find a black market doc, but that's a pretty risky—" Miller held up his hand, telling me to stay quiet. "I think I heard something," he whispered.

He motioned for me to stay low, and when he pulled out his gun, I followed suit. My ears strained in the silence, trying to hear whatever it was Miller had heard. From down the hall, I thought I heard a soft footstep, but I wasn't sure if it was real or just my imagination.

We left the operating room and moved toward the hallway we had just come from. No other sounds came from the front room. I mimicked Miller and placed my back to the wall, stopping just before the corner. Miller dropped into a crouch and looked around it, pulling his head back quickly. He pointed at the other hall back to reception and stepped past me to lead the way. Dropping to a crouch again, he looked down the other hallway. He stood and stepped around the corner. I followed him. I was sure he could hear the pounding of my heart.

When we reached the reception area, Miller repeated the process, this time crawling around the desk. We moved past the elevators, staying under the cover of the receptionist's desk, and moved to the stairwell door. Miller pushed the door open and waited until I was through before closing it quietly behind us.

We went slowly down the stairs until we reached the turn, and then sped up, taking two or more stairs at a time. Each step pulled the new jean material across my knees, sending a sharp pain through them. When we reached the first floor door, he stopped and turned to face me.

"Quincy was up there."

"What? Oh god." I felt the blood drain from my face and an icy hand grab at my pounding heart.

"Yeah. How the hell did they find us? And so fast? They must have our entire comm system tapped, and already been in the area."

"Let's just get in the car and go." I started to push past him.

"Wait! If I was them, I wouldn't have let Quincy work alone again. You've escaped from him a couple of times already. Somewhere out there may be a partner . . . or more than one."

I froze in my tracks. Why didn't I think of that? "What do we do?"

"We can't stay here, we're sitting ducks." He leaned against the wall and closed his eyes. "Okay, on the count of three, we run for it. I'll go for the car. You go out the back door and run for the first cover you can see. I'll meet you at the driveway we turned around in. Stay out of sight." He tucked his gun back into his pocket. I hesitated and did the same.

"Separate? Are you sure?" The moment the words were out of my mouth I felt a wave of embarrassment. Of course he was sure. It was me that wasn't.

"I think we have a better chance to get out of here separately. And *if* Quincy has a partner, they're probably watching the car. The back exit may be safer."

"What if someone's watching the back as well?"

"That's a chance we have to take. Just run as fast as you can to some cover, and keep going."

"Yeah, okay."

Miller turned toward the door.

"Wait!" I reached up and pulled on his shoulder, turning him to face me again. The thought that this might be it, that this might be the last time I saw him, filled me with the urge to hold him, to feel his lips on mine.

"What?"

What if he didn't like me like that? He would think I was a stupid young girl. I gave him a quick hug instead. "Good luck."

He awkwardly returned the hug with one arm. "I'll see you at the driveway," he said.

Miller pushed the door open and ran for the front entrance. I turned, bolting for the back. Before I reached it, a loud crack split the air and my step faltered. I resisted the urge to turn around. I didn't dare stop to see if Miller had been hit.

I ran to the doors, pushing them open without slowing down. As soon as my feet hit the pavement outside, I veered toward the right, away from the street Miller had specified as a meeting place. There was no point in leading anyone who was out here directly to the spot. I reached the back of the parking lot and scrambled over the fence, scraping my neck on the top. The bandage covering where the bullet had grazed me peeled off.

Dropping over the other side, I found myself in a backyard, but not like one I had ever seen before. The grass was green and lush; flowers bloomed in beds that lined the edges. Clumps of dirt stuck to my shoes as I ran through the flowers. A pool, blue and glowing in the Ambients, was near the house.

I ran to a shaded corner, made darker by the gnarled tree growing there. I touched my neck and looked at my hand. There wasn't any blood; the wound must have closed. A car door slammed in the parking lot behind me, the sound echoing off the house. Just as I climbed over the fence into the next yard, another car door slammed shut in front of the house.

By the third yard, I changed direction and started heading back to the meeting spot. The driveway was only a few streets over. I still moved in what I hoped was an erratic pattern, trying to confuse anyone who might be following me. I raced through a yard and down someone's driveway, crossing the street without even looking down it. I kept running into the next yard, the next place of relative safety. By the time I'd run several blocks, the fear-driven adrenaline rush started to fade, and I stumbled to a halt and collapsed.

I'm not sure how long I lay there. My legs felt like rubber and my lungs hurt with every breath. I pushed myself upright and scanned my surroundings.

This backyard was pretty much like the first one I had run through, without the swimming pool. As my breath came back, I looked around and realized I'd gotten myself trapped. This yard had a two-meter-high fence all the way around it, and nothing to help me climb over it. I moved back to the open gate and looked through. Nothing. The street was empty of cars and people. Either I hadn't been followed, or I'd managed to slip away from them.

I limped through the gate and closed it behind me, keeping my hand on the gun in my pocket.

THIRTEEN

LEVEL 6—THURSDAY, AUGUST 11, 2140 1:24 P.M.

ABBY WAS SURE her first shot had hit, though it was tough to tell with all the people. She had caught glimpses of Miller in the crowd heading through the doors. His timing couldn't have been better; the people made perfect cover. The moment he had moved away from the crowd, she had squeezed off a shot. The crowd froze for a split-second. After that it was pure mayhem, and she had lost him.

She thought she saw Miller running and took another quick shot, but it wasn't him. Just another casualty. Six cars left the parking lot in quick succession. Any one of them could have been Miller. She memorized the makes and colors.

A minute later, Quincy walked out of the building without the girl. Abby broke her new rifle down into three pieces and started packing it up. In the distance, she could hear the police drones moving toward them.

They'd gotten lucky, being close enough when the location call arrived. Lucky to have found Miller and the girl still in the building. She hoped their luck held out a bit longer, that Miller was hit, and the girl would be easy to find.

By the time Abby had ducked into the roof stairwell, the drones had arrived, buzzing around the area, trying to figure out what was going on. A couple of them skimmed to the ceiling to get a bigger picture, looking for something out of the ordinary. Quincy would know to blend in, wouldn't he? Damn, she hated working with someone else.

Five minutes after leaving the roof, Abby was walking out of the building, looking like a businesswoman on her way to a meeting. When she passed Quincy, he joined her.

"Did you get the girl?" she asked.

"No. I didn't even see them. I heard your shots though, so I'm assuming you saw them?"

"Just Miller. He won't go far. I'm pretty sure I got him. It's just a matter of time until he shows up. With ACE shutting down everything they can, he'll have to go somewhere public to get the wound looked at."

"Damn. We'll take the car and cruise the neighborhood. If the girl is here, she'll be on foot now, and she doesn't know her way around this level."

"I have a couple of cars to check on as well. One of them might be his," she said.

Abby walked to the car in silence. There was no excuse for Quincy missing them inside. This should have all been a done deal.

MERIDIAN SAT CITY—THURSDAY, AUGUST 11, 2140
1:25 P.M.

Jeremy's desk was as cluttered as it always was: stacks of paper and folders, data chips and old coffee cups lay over every visible surface. Yet he always managed to find what he was looking for.

"I think you're starting to run your department the same way you keep your office. An unorganized mess." The president had walked down to Jeremy's office, which was either a good sign or a really, really bad one. Any official meetings with the president always occurred in his office.

"It's just for looks, Jonathon. You know that. If I look disorganized, anyone who comes in here will think that's the way I am. It puts me at an immediate advantage."

"I'm not so sure, Jeremy. I've heard some rumors today. Some pretty bad ones. What's going on?"

"I'm not sure what you mean."

"Then let me lay it out for you." The president's voice hardened and he sat down on the leather sofa. "My sources in SoCal tell me they've had a leak. A leak that, as I understand, they've sealed. The leak leads back to us. It sounds like one of our people tried to send information out to Kadokawa."

This was a bad visit.

"We sometimes use our people to feed information to other corporations. You know that, Jonathon. If we can destabilize some of the existing relationships, then we have a chance to move up."

Jeremy felt a wave of distrust come from the president, one that quickly vanished.

"I've been led to believe that the information he tried

to pass involved documentation and specifications on new spacecraft," Jonathon paused to let the news sink in. "SoCal does not deal in space travel or spacecraft design, Jeremy. What do you think they have?"

This was a really, really bad visit.

Jeremy sat down behind his cluttered desk and looked at the president. What did he know? "I'm not sure. If they've closed the leak, then we've lost our man. I'll check with his team leader and see what he has," said Jeremy.

"Yes, you will. I've also heard that the information was never delivered, that it's either in the hands of a courier, or ACE."

Christ, when the president said he had sources, he wasn't kidding. Where did he get the information from?

"I want this courier brought in. Here. I want to question her on what happened. Make it happen, Jeremy."

"Yes, sir, Mr. President. I'll put a team on it right away. Do you think they have the data on the jump drive?"

Jonathon sighed and stood up again. "Let's hope not, Jeremy. Let's hope not. I want the courier here as soon as possible, and I want all the data you have on our SoCal guy and ACE's connection with this."

"Yes, sir."

"If we lose this advantage, heads will roll. Yours will go before mine. I'll see to that." He turned and walked out of Jeremy's office, closing the door softly behind him.

Jeremy slid open a drawer on his desk and pulled out a small comm unit. This one was not part of the Meridian network. It was untraceable. At the touch of a button, his call was routed through several networks.

"Where is the courier?"

The voice on the other end sounded panicked. "I don't know. I called them a while back, like Quincy asked. I told Quincy where they were. They're trying to get the girl's tracker tag adjusted, but ACE is shutting down. They know they have a leak. If they find me . . ."

"If they find you, you die. That's the risk."

"But I—"

Jeremy killed the connection and dialed a different number.

"Yes," Abby answered.

LEVEL 6—THURSDAY, AUGUST 11, 2140 1:29 P.M.

Two police drones passed overhead and slowed down as they approached the building. The Ambients caused their shadows to chase them over the ground, trying to catch up to the speeding devices. Abby saw Quincy glance up before quickly looking at the ground just in front of his feet.

"Just walk normally. Look up like you're curious, but don't try to skulk near the building or do anything to attract their attention. We're just a couple of people walking down the street, okay?"

"This isn't my first party," Quincy said.

"Yeah, yeah, just keep walking."

They reached the parked car, a small black sports model still shining in the Ambients like it was new.

"Get in, let's see if the Net can get us some information on the cars."

Abby slid in behind the steering wheel and fired up the onboard computer. She connected to the Net and created an encrypted tunnel to the Meridian systems. Three cars in, she got a hit. The car had no registry entries. It was as if the thing had never existed. Kind of weak for ACE to do that, almost as though they wanted the car found and traced. Abby displayed the car on the screen, a red Mitsubishi.

"Keep your eyes out for this car," she told Quincy. "If you see it, let me know." She pulled away from the curb.

"Where we going?"

"The closest hospital. We may get lucky."

"He's not going to a hospital. No one with training would."

"No, but he may not have a say in it," said Abby. "If he's hurt bad, the girl will be in charge, and she'll take him straight there."

"That's a big if. We need to search for her around here first."

Abby's comm unit rang. She picked it up and looked at the screen. Encrypted link. Jeremy. Shit.

"Yes."

"Where are you guys?"

"Heading to the hospital. I managed a shot on the guy covering the courier. With ACE shutting down, I figure they're gonna have to head there."

"And the girl?"

"Quincy says he never saw them. I only saw the guy come out the front door."

"You sure they're still together?"

"No, but the last time we saw them, when Quincy bungled the safe house job, they took off in the same vehicle."

"I agree," Jeremy said. "And so do my sources. As far as we know, she still has the package, unless she made a transfer at the safe house."

"If she has it, I'll get it."

"Good . . . good. Remember you're working with Quincy on this one. I expect both of you to get this done. I want to talk to the courier whether she has the package or not." Jeremy switched tracks. "Things are changing up here, people are beginning to sniff around, so we have a change of plans. We need to find out what she knows. If she does have the package, destroy it first. Get rid of the guy anyway."

"We can do that."

"You'd better, or it's your asses on the line."

Now she knew how Quincy got on board. They were both idiots. If Jeremy thought he controlled her, he was kidding himself. She had more outs than anyone could know about. You didn't get as high in this field as she was without being able to cover your own assets.

"I want the girl found tonight. Make it happen, Abby."

Abby ended the call and pulled a U-turn, heading back to the building.

"What now?"

"Jeremy wants the girl found. I think we should search the area first."

She saw a smirk on his face as he pulled out his gun, double-checking the cartridge.

"He wants her alive."

The grin disappeared.

LEVEL 6—THURSDAY, AUGUST 11, 2140 1:35 P.M.

I wandered the residential streets, each step bringing home the grim truth. I had no idea where I was. All the houses were a blur of manicured lawns and flowerbeds filled with gnomes and birdbaths.

How could I be lost? I tried to go over the path I'd taken since I left the doctor's office. How many streets had I crossed? Was I even heading in the right direction? I knew I'd gone in a loop. That meant I'd passed the street Miller was on. The only problem was, I had no idea which street it was.

Okay, I'm a courier, and we don't get lost, no matter

where we are. I remembered turning around in the driveway. From there we had turned left to get back on the main road. Then it was only a few blocks to the building. Okay then, if I walked back along the main road, I should be able to find the building and backtrack to the right street. Of course, if Quincy was still there waiting, that would be a bad idea. My chest tightened and my breathing became shallow.

When I looped around, I swung pretty wide, which meant I was heading the wrong way. The main road had to be behind me. Right?

Christ, I really was lost. I felt blood rush up to my head and pound in my ears. My stomach felt like it had dropped down to my feet in a sudden rush. How the fuck did this happen? I was a courier for chrissake.

Okay, okay, get a grip. All I have to do is find the main road again. Breathe! When I reach it, turn left and keep going. I'll either reach the office building or the end of the gated community. Either way, I would know where I was, and things would be okay. As long as Quincy didn't see me.

Three blocks later, I passed the house with the high fence again and kept walking. I counted the blocks, trying to sync the new information with what I remembered of my panicked run. Nothing seemed to fit. I ducked behind a hedge when a shiny black convertible drove past. I was close to turning back again when I saw a large street ahead. I ran the last half block and stopped at the corner of the last house.

My stomach lurched. Nothing looked familiar.

That's okay. No problem. If I'd run as far as I thought I had, then all of this would be new anyway. I reminded myself to breathe again before turning and walking down the brightly lit sidewalk. This wasn't safe, but I didn't know what else to do.

It was another twenty minutes before the sign for the

office complex showed up, still a few blocks ahead and partially covered by the sign from a fast food joint. I breathed a sigh of relief and ducked back onto a side street, anxious to get off the main road before venturing out to find the right one. At every intersection I turned backward, recreating the same view I had in the car.

There! That huge rock on the front lawn. I had seen that before. Hadn't I? I turned down the side street, hoping it was the right one. If not, I would have to double back and go down another street, until I found Miller and the car.

Suddenly, it was there. Not in the driveway where I had been looking, but parked with one front tire on the curb. As I got next to the car, I saw Miller slouched low in the driver's seat, his eyes closed.

LEVEL 6—THURSDAY, AUGUST 11, 2140 2:00 P.M.

A wave of anger flashed through me, replacing the relief I felt at finding Miller. Just fucking great, here I was lost and worried I'd never find him, and he was sleeping. What the fuck? I whipped open the passenger door, sliding into the seat next to him, pushing his comm unit out of the way.

"Wake the fuck up—"

The blood was the first thing I noticed. My anger disappeared faster than it came.

"Jesus Christ, what happened?" I asked.

Miller lifted his head and gave me a half smile. "Someone was waiting out the front door. A sniper, I think. He got me as soon as I moved out of the crowd." Miller struggled to sit up, his face turning white.

I leaned over his seat and looked at the bloody shirt.

I thought I saw a hole in the material, but it was tough to tell. "We have to get you to a hospital."

"We can't. The police will want to know what happened."

"Fuck the police. You're really bleeding."

"There's a . . . a kit in the trunk. Get it out and bandage me up. I'll be as good as new."

I pulled the keys from the ignition and stumbled from the car. Miller didn't look too good, and I had no idea what to do.

The first aid box was the only thing in the trunk. Everything else was still in the box under the rear seat. Slamming the trunk shut, I ran back to my door and got inside.

"What do I do?"

"Take off my shirt . . . uh, careful." He sucked in a few breaths between clenched teeth. "Take off the shirt and clean around the hole. Pour some of that hydrogen peroxide, the brown bottle, on it. Then . . . then put a big wad of gauze on it and tape it down. When you're done with that, do the same to the exit hole."

I shook my head. "Exit hole?"

"Where the bullet came out."

"Yeah, yeah, okay."

My hands shook as I unbuttoned his shirt and peeled it away from his shoulder. Fresh blood seeped from the bullet hole. This wasn't what I was thinking of when I'd thought of undressing him.

As I worked, Miller's face blanched again, and his jaw muscles stood out on his cheeks from clenching and grinding his teeth. The hole was in his right shoulder and remarkably small, no bigger than my pinky finger really.

"Are there . . ." Miller spoke through his teeth. "Are there any bubbles coming from the hole?"

"No. No, I don't see any. Is that good?"

"Yeah, it means I may not die today. Cover it up and look for the exit hole."

I poured more hydrogen peroxide on the wound and covered it with the gauze pad before taping it all on. I moved Miller carefully, until he was leaning against the steering wheel.

There wasn't any hole. "I don't see anything."

"You cleaned off the blood?"

"There's no blood back here. There's no exit wound at all."

"Shit."

"What?"

"That's not good. It means, uhh," Miller grunted as he lay back against the seat. "It means whatever hit me is still in there."

"Does it have to come out?" I pulled back, afraid he'd ask me to do it.

"Yeah."

"I . . . I can't do that."

"Yeah."

"I'm taking you to a hospital."

Miller only grunted in reply. By the time I managed to move him to the passenger seat, he had passed out, and blood had soaked through my makeshift bandage. His breathing sounded ragged and shallow.

I slid behind the wheel and started to drive. Where the hell was the hospital? Miller's comm unit lay on the dashboard and I grabbed it to turn it on. The GPS took a while to lock. There were three hospitals relatively close. Fighting my better judgment, I chose the one farthest away.

I glanced at Miller. He was ghostly pale. I hoped I hadn't made the wrong decision.

FOURTEEN

LEVEL 6—THURSDAY, AUGUST 11, 2140 2:15 P.M.

I LEANED ON THE horn for about the fifth time, using all the swear words I knew. Every car ever made must have been on the road, and they were all driving in fucking reverse.

"Get the hell out of my way!"

The yelling didn't help the cars move, but it made me feel a bit better.

A blue compact cut in front of me and slowed down. I jerked the wheel, trying to fit my car into the spot left by the blue one. The sound of squealing tires and honking horns came through the open window. They weren't mine, this time. I accelerated and swerved back in front of the blue compact. Idiot.

I could see the light beige walls of the hospital ahead, a red cross tacked to the side of one of its various buildings. I cruised past most of it without seeing an entrance to the emergency room.

Where the fuck was it? The hospital itself must have covered at least five square blocks. It was really just a bunch of buildings connected to each other through walkways, or built right up against each other. I swerved down a street that cut between the buildings. The next sign I saw was for Columbia University. Fucking great. I spun around the drop-off circle by the front doors and headed back out the way I came. Miller groaned in the seat beside me.

Why the hell did they have to hide these things anyway? There should be huge signs pointing the way to the emergency room. What, they didn't want people to show up?

An ambulance sped past me on the crossroads ahead, its lights flashing and siren wailing. It turned down the next drive and cut its sirens.

That had to be it.

I pulled out onto the street, oblivious to any cars that may have been coming, and followed the ambulance to the large doors. With a look at Miller, I got out of the car and slammed the door shut.

"Hey, this is the ambulance drop-off lady, you can't be here." It was some skinny shithead in an oversized security uniform.

"I've got a guy hurt in here."

"You'll have to take him around the building, to the normal entrance." The skinny fucker started to put out a hand, trying to stop me from opening the passenger door. I slapped his arm away and pulled the door open. Miller fell to the ground. The bandage I had put on earlier had soaked through and his pants were covered in blood. Oh Christ, how much more could he lose? There was so much of it.

The security guard blanched and stood stunned.

"Don't just stand there, moron, help me get him in." I had my hands under Miller's arms and was trying to drag him to the doors. Every pull seemed to pump more blood from the wound, and my hand slipped in it. I should have picked a closer hospital.

"I'll . . . I'll go get a doctor."

"No, help me carry him." But it was too late. The security guard had turned as fast as he could and run back to the doors. He had disappeared into them before I could take two steps.

He came out a second later. Two doctors rushed past the gurney being rolled into the hospital from the ambulance, ran past the guard and reached us. When they saw the blood, they paused long enough to pull on latex gloves.

"Lay him down, let us look at him. What happened?"

I collapsed to the road and laid Miller's head in my lap. "He was shot."

One of the doctors gently wiped Miller's shoulder and pried away my makeshift bandage. Without looking up, he said, "He's lost a lot of blood, we need to get him in right away. Prep surgery room two." He looked up at the security guard hovering over them. "Go get a gurney and tell them to prep Surgery Two. Now!"

By the time the gurney came, Miller's hands had gone cold. I helped the doctors lift him up while the security guard just stood and watched. As I followed back to the entrance, he grabbed at my shoulder.

"You're gonna have to move the car, lady."

Without missing a step, I twisted free from his grip and yelled back. "The keys are in it, move it yourself!" I followed Miller into the hospital.

The doctors wheeled him into a small operating room, smaller than the one I'd seen at the office. The walls were tiled in a light green, and the white floor looked clean enough to eat off of. Three displays hung from the ceiling around the table and came to life when Miller was moved onto it.

One of the doctors looked over my shoulder. "Get her out of here."

I felt a hand touch my elbow and I jerked it away. "I'm not going anywhere."

The nurse stepped in front of me. She was small, maybe a bit shorter than me even, with blonde hair and blue eyes. Eyes that practically leaked with compassion.

"We have to go and let the doctors get to work," she said.

The nurse took a step closer and I stepped back, increasing the space between us.

"That's right, we can wait out here." The nurse took another step closer.

This time I didn't back up. The nurse put her arm around my waist and turned me around. I let her lead me back into the hallway.

"Come on. Can I get you some water?"

I looked over her shoulder and watched the doors to the operating room close. Just before they shut, I saw Miller on the operating table, a needle pushed into his arm. Tubes carried various liquids from hanging bags down to the needle. A mask had been placed over his face.

"The waiting room is right through here."

I walked numbly beside the nurse. It was just a shoulder wound, it couldn't be that bad.

"Will he be all right?"

"Let the doctors look at him first. We'll let you know what happens."

The nurse maneuvered me into a chair and forced a paper cup of water into my hands.

"Drink it, you'll feel better."

My body went cold and the cup shook in my hand. I took a sip of the ice water, like a puppet obeying her master, and waited.

I didn't know what was up and what was down, wrong from right, day from night. The last three days had become a giant smear. I had gone from being a courier barely scraping out a living to being the most wanted person in the city. Or so it seemed. And all over a package I didn't even have anymore. The only constant I could find, the only thing that had kept me alive and sane, the only thing that mattered, was Miller. He had to make it. It was all my fault.

Chances were, by this time tomorrow, the power source on my black box would be dead, and I would be vulnerable again. Easily tracked through the multitude of sensors laid throughout San Angeles. What would happen if I was still on Level 6 when the tracker kicked in again? Would there be alarms and a mad rush of police to put me back into my rightful place, amid the scum of the city?

Whatever happened, I wasn't prepared to do it alone any more. Three days ago I would have told the world I was ready to handle anything, handle it on my own with no outside help. Now, reality had smacked me right in the face, and I knew how unprepared I really was. Sure, I could function in my own small corner, pretending everything was in my control. But now the world had flipped over and forced me to face the facts. I was just a stupid sixteen-year-old girl. Scared and lost and alone. I wanted Miller back. He had to make it.

My only connection to reality, my only chance at life, lay on a table in a cold operating room, and I had no idea if he would die or not.

There was so much blood, so much . . .

LEVEL 6—THURSDAY, AUGUST 11, 2140 5:30 P.M.

I felt a hand on my shoulder, a gentle shake pulling me
from my sleep. I had no idea when I had drifted off. I had
just been sitting here, waiting. How much time had
passed? Looking out the double doors, I thought the
Ambients might have dimmed a bit. It must have been a
couple of hours at least.

"Kris? Are you Kris?"

The same nurse that had led me out of the operating
room earlier stood beside me, a gentle smile on her face.

"Yeah, yes, that's me."

"Your friend is out of the operating room and waking
up. He's in the hallway, asking for you. I shouldn't let you
see him until the police come, but"—she glanced over
her shoulder at the entrance doors—"a short visit should
be okay."

"Thanks." My brain felt fuzzy. It was tough to put all
my thoughts together. Miller's image rose to the surface.

The nurse turned and walked away before I was fully
awake. I stood and hurried after her, through more
swinging doors into a long hallway. It was tough keeping
up. My legs were still numb from slouching on the hard
plastic chairs, and I couldn't feel my butt at all. The nurse
walked past a bed, one of many lined against the walls of
the corridor, and tapped the person in it on the leg before moving on, as though oblivious to my being there.
Miller raised his head and smiled.

"Hey, how you doing?" I reached out a tentative hand
and pushed a lock of hair off his forehead.

"I'm all right." His words came out mumbled. "The
docs took a chunk of metal out and patched me up. They
musta shot me up with something, I was feeling pretty

good for a while." He reached up and grabbed my hand, moving it to his mouth and kissing my palm. "Thanks for bringing me here. It was a stupid thing to do, but thanks."

I felt my entire body flush with heat. "You'd lost so much blood, I didn't know what else to do."

"It's okay, it worked out. The cops will come and ask me how I got a bullet in my shoulder. They'll tie me to the shooting at the doc's office. I'll just have to sit in a cell until ACE gets their shit together and gets me out."

I sat down on the edge of the bed, my fingers playing with a crease in my jeans. My emotions were a jumble of incoherent feelings, spinning out of control between relief for Miller and fear of being without him. I couldn't stop the tears.

"I don't know what to do," I whispered.

Miller squeezed my hand tighter. "You got some money off the IBC guy right? If you look in the box under the back seat of the car, you'll find more. It should be more than enough to get you out of the city. Your best bet is to get up to Level 7 and catch a shuttle out of here. From there, get a car and just drive until you don't know where you are. Get out of San Angeles."

"I don't think I . . . can do it without you." I almost said *want*.

"I know you can. Look how far you got before I got here. It's tough to stay alive when the corporations are hunting you down. You did good. Just keep it up and you'll be out of the city in no time."

"I don't *want* to do it alone, without you." I didn't, I couldn't hold back this time.

"You have to." Miller put my hand on my lap and let it go. "And you have to do it now, before the cops come. If they see you talking to me, you'll never make it out."

From down the hallway, I could hear the sound of the double swinging doors banging open.

I turned to look. Quincy strode down the hall, looking into rooms as he passed. Behind him walked a woman. She locked her eyes onto mine and grabbed Quincy's arm.

"Oh, god. They found us." I froze where I was, watching Quincy.

A hand reached into my jacket pocket. Miller reaching for my gun. He slipped it out and I heard a soft click as he cocked it.

The woman stopped dead in her tracks. Her hand reached behind her back, grabbing at something stuck in her pants. I didn't see the gun in her hand until it was too late. Miller didn't make the same mistake.

I felt rather than heard the bullet flying out of the barrel of my gun, the blast of air pressing my shirt against my waist. It was surprisingly quiet. The woman dropped where she stood, a perfect round hole in the middle of her chest.

Miller pushed me off the bed, and I landed on the floor, my butt no longer numb. The gun pointed over the side, aiming at Quincy.

I heard the gun pop again, and a doorframe shattered behind Quincy as he ran into one of the rooms. Doctors, nurses, and patients, originally frozen where they stood, began to run at the sound of the exploding doorframe. I stood up and Miller jammed the gun back into my pocket.

"Run."

"No!" I wasn't leaving him behind.

The double doors flew open again and two uniformed policemen ran through them, ducking and hugging the walls. Their weapons were in their hands.

"Run, I'll be okay," Miller hissed again.

A nurse ran past us, bumping into my shoulder. Miller gave me a push and I stumbled after the nurse down the hall. We ran through the doors to the ambulance stop.

I hesitated in the cool evening air, spinning back to face the closing doors. One cop stood by Miller, the other I couldn't see. I headed to the drive where I'd left the car.

It was gone. For a second I felt dizzy and my shoulders started vibrating. The security guard must have parked it for me. He seemed pretty lazy, so it had to be close. I ran across the driveway and into the parking lot, scanning the rows. I found it almost right away.

I pulled open the door, praying the keys were still inside it. They hung from the ignition. I started the car and drove out of the lot, forcing myself not to speed or drive erratically, as more police drove in.

Two blocks away, I pulled down a side street and parked. My knuckles stood out white on hands clenched around the steering wheel. Miller. I had left Miller with Quincy right there, and Miller had stuck the gun back in my pocket.

I turned the car around and drove back toward the hospital. There were already three more police cars by the ambulance entrance, and I heard the sound of sirens in the distance. Drones flew through the air overhead. More were on the way.

I drove right past, keeping up with the other traffic that had slowed down to gawk at the spectacle.

FIFTEEN

ONCE KRIS RAN past him, Miller concentrated on
the door Quincy had ducked through. One of the
police had reached the opening and stood just outside. If
Quincy had decided to shoot, she would be dead; indoor
walls just didn't stop bullets that well. She rushed in,
swinging her gun wildly, while her partner ran toward
Miller's bed.

Had Kris made it out? If there were any more cops
outside, there was a chance she would have made it past
them, lost in the general rush of doctors and nurses and
patients. He clung to the thought, allowing himself the
feeling of relief it offered.

Something had happened. The job had changed from

simply protecting and delivering Kris to . . . to something more. He wasn't sure when it had happened; it wasn't as though someone had flicked a switch. Could he be falling in love with her? There was a four-year difference between them, and with her being only sixteen years old (another part of him chimed in, almost seventeen) the age gap was way too big. So what was it then? He'd never had a sister. Was this how you felt about a sister, protecting her? Somehow he didn't think so.

His wound had opened up again, and blood oozed slowly through the white bandages wrapped around his shoulder. He lay back down and closed his eyes, too weak, too tired to keep looking at the door anymore. Exhaustion plus the drugs they gave him were working their magic. If Quincy didn't get him, the cops would anyway. At least with the cops he had a chance. Quincy would probably just gut him.

He heard voices beside his bed, and the slight click of the wheels unlocking.

"We need to talk to him." It was one of the policemen. The other was on her comm unit by the room Quincy had run into.

"You'll have to wait a minute. I need to check his bandages. Can't you see he is bleeding again?" A woman's voice, used to giving instructions by the sound of it. The policeman wasn't cowed though.

"Can I talk while you work?"

"He's lost a lot of blood, and he needs to sleep," she said.

Miller felt his good arm being lifted and moved to the side of the bed. Hard plastic wrapped around his wrist, pinning it to the steel frame.

"Fine. He ain't going nowhere now."

The bed started to roll.

"And I think I'll stay with him as well."

Tenacious bastard. Not like he was going anywhere soon. Miller's whole body felt light, as if it could float to the ceiling. The motion of the bed rocking slowly down the hall brought on a new feeling. His stomach churned. He turned his head and vomited.

"Fuck!"

The cop . . . good.

Sleep came again, wrapping him in a soft blanket of warmth. His last thought was of Kris's face. An angel asleep on the pillow back in the safe house.

MERIDIAN SAT CITY—THURSDAY, AUGUST 11, 2140
5:40 P.M.

The vid screens showed Earth, overlaid with dots of color and text. Jeremy stood watching it, watching the world's military and paramilitary organizations move through their daily routines.

From here, everything seemed normal. His distance from the action induced an almost euphoric feeling, as though he was in control of each and every piece in play. But the information displayed here was nothing without the knowledge contained in his head. Knowledge gained through years of being down there. Moving through the ranks. Obtaining the power and control he needed to end up where he was: in charge of the next superpower's security forces, a complete military in its own right. And now, with the added support of the jump drive and a president willing to fight to move up the ladder, he was set.

Supplying SoCal and Kadokawa with the jump drive plans had been motivated by pure greed. He knew that. But it was a greed that he controlled, not one that controlled him. Having it look like SoCal had killed the

Kadokawa representative proved that. A protracted corporate war, and one that Kadokawa wouldn't join, meant that his domain, his control, would only expand.

And now he felt it all slipping away because of a courier, a fucking sixteen-year-old girl.

He hadn't interrogated a prisoner in over a decade. It would be fun to get his hands dirty again. By the time he was done, she'd do and tell him anything. He would crush her spirit, crush her will, until she was his. Then he would kill her. Jonathon wouldn't have a chance to see her.

His anger bubbled through to the surface, and he smiled. Enough bullshit, enough hiding behind facades. He was Jeremy Adams, dammit, Jeremy fucking Adams! And he had worked too hard and too long to lose everything now.

He moved away from the vid screen and looked at his desk, papers and file folders still strewn across it. All of it useless. Interoffice memos and company hierarchical charts. Simple diagrams displaying fake information. Hell, over half of the paper was blank, put there to make the piles bigger and messier. The same thing with the data chips. All of them were empty, labeled with important-sounding names.

Jeremy put his arm across his desk and slid it from one side to the other. Everything, the papers, the data chips, everything, moved and fell off the end into a box he'd had delivered earlier in the day. Beneath the mess lay a desk as pristine as the day it was installed. He moved around to the chair and touched the display that still sat on the corner.

"Yes, sir?"

"Get maintenance to remove this garbage."

"Yes, sir."

He pulled open a drawer and removed a pen set and name tag given to him when he'd first walked into this office. The name tag moved to the far end of his desk, in line with the door. The pen set slid just behind it.

"Welcome to the real Jeremy Adams," he whispered.

A comm unit beeped and Jeremy removed it from the open drawer. He glanced at the screen: full encryption and routing protocols were on.

"Yes?"

"We got some trouble." Quincy's voice cut through Jeremy's new sense of freedom.

"What kind of trouble?"

"Abby's dead. I think the cops got the courier and Miller."

Jeremy took in a long slow breath and released it. His voice hardened. "You think, or you know?"

"The cops came in right after Abby was shot, so I ran. I barely got out myself. I had to climb out the ceiling tiles."

"You *think*, or you *know*?"

After a short silence at the other end, Quincy answered. "I think. I didn't hang around to find out, you know?"

"Wait."

Jeremy muted the call and started using his display. A knock came from the door and a tall man in a green jumpsuit walked in.

"Get out."

"I'm here to get the garbage."

"I said get . . . the fuck . . . out."

The maintenance man turned and ran out the open door like a scared chipmunk.

"Close the door!"

The door snicked quietly shut.

The police bands didn't show too much. They picked up the guy, what was his name, Miller? The police had him in custody, still at the hospital. There was no sign or mention of the girl. He started a watch on her tracker. If the cops had her, the first thing they would do is get rid of the blocker. He'd pick up her signal right away.

The display stayed blank.

He reached for his comm unit and unmuted it. "They don't have the girl."

"Are you sure?"

"You're not questioning me, are you, Quincy?" Jeremy's voice had turned into a soft purr. "That wouldn't be good for your health."

"No. No, sir. I . . . no."

"Good. Now find the damn girl and bring her here."

"Yes, sir. What about the guy?"

"He's just an ACE gun for hire. Leave him to the police."

"Yes, sir."

Jeremy closed the link and put the comm unit back into his desk drawer. He stood, moving back to the vid screens, and zoomed in to the city. His city.

Abby was the best he'd had. She'd gotten the job done countless times, and now that asset was gone, a gap in his infrastructure that would be difficult to fill.

What the hell, it would make him feel good to pay back the man who killed her. He walked back to his desk and spun the display on it around to face him, touching the top corner.

"Yes, sir."

"Get me the Level 6 Police Chief. What's his name?"

A slight pause, then, "Philip Beard, sir. He's coming through now."

Yes, getting rid of Miller would make him feel good.

"And get my shuttle ready. I'm going to the city."

With some luck, Quincy would have the girl soon as

well. He could take care of her while he was down there. He grabbed the comm unit and dialed Quincy as he walked to the door.

LEVEL UNKNOWN—THURSDAY, AUGUST 11, 2140
5:40 P.M.

Devon's screens blanked and displayed a map of the area surrounding his office. It took him a minute to figure out what was going on; he hadn't seen these maps since everything was installed.

The proximity sensors had triggered.

Three green dots moved along three different corridors, all of them toward his office. Two more appeared along two different corridors.

It was time.

One by one, the green dots turned red. The sensors had picked up weapons.

Devon moved as though he had done this every day of his life. When he first moved into the office, that's exactly what he had done. Practicing until he could escape in less than a minute.

Now he typed in the reset command on his computer, his finger hovering over the enter key. Back then, he had simply told his systems to erase themselves, but he couldn't do it with the cube. He pulled the box away from the wall, yanking the cables out as he did it. He took his lunch kit and emptied it on the floor, replacing the contents with his computer. The hard line rang.

Devon ignored it. He had to get out. He pushed at the ceiling in a place that looked no different from the rest. A section of it clicked and dropped down on hinges and pneumatic sliders, a rope ladder falling with it. Devon slung his lunch bag over his shoulder and started up, taking one last look at the room that had become his life. He pulled the rope ladder up behind him and pressed a button. The ceiling section moved back into place.

Climbing over the small railing, Devon moved to a catwalk suspended above his office. The sensors were embedded up here as well, but with the computer gone, no one would be able to track him. He moved quietly in his running shoes, following the catwalk to safety.

They'd finally found him. The knowledge filled him with joy and shame. He'd known it couldn't last forever. He only wished he knew who had managed to outsmart him, who had tracked him down. Though in the end it didn't really matter.

He stopped where the catwalk turned into a ladder, steel rebar rungs set in the concrete when they built the place. He reached down underneath the catwalk and searched. There it was. He got a firm grip and pulled, ripping the small bag off the fasteners holding it in place.

This was his lifeline. He'd created it when he first started working for ACE, and updated it with newer information every year. More often than that, recently. The packet contained a new life, a new identity. One ACE, SoCal, Kadokawa, or anyone else didn't know anything about. With this, he'd be long gone before anyone figured out what had happened. And they'd never find him again.

He thought about his mother, his only link to the world of ordinary people. She'd never see him again either. Still, he had set her up pretty good, too. It would take a while for his "death" to be discovered, but when it was, all of his known assets would go to her. His mother's life would be a good one. Devon didn't feel any remorse.

He climbed the ladder and pushed open the top

hatch, emerging into a corridor much like the ones around his office. He'd only used this route once, when he set everything up. He closed the hatch behind him and walked down the corridor, a smile on his face.

＝＝＝

LEVEL 6—THURSDAY, AUGUST 11, 2140 5:30 P.M.

Quincy had replaced the ceiling tile and moved as quickly as he could away from the police. Hanging from the roof supports, he knew that one mistake and he would fall through the weak T-bars and flimsy tiles. When he thought he was far enough away, he moved a tile and dropped down to a desk below. He had come down somewhere in an administrative section, which was a good thing since everybody seemed to have gone home for the day. It took him another ten minutes to figure out how to get out of the maze of offices and cubicles before he placed his call to Jeremy. He knew Jeremy wasn't going to be happy, but it had to be done.

The phone call itself had been short and sweet, and by the sounds of it, Jeremy didn't think he was responsible for the woman being shot. Hell, if she had waited before pulling her gun, he would have been in range. Boom, done. No more problems. He knew it was going to happen, though. You get one of these snipers, so used to being removed from the carnage, you get them in close, and they panic.

He was lucky she didn't scream. That would've given him a headache. He hated screamers. He always made sure he taped up his target's mouth before getting the job done. It just made life easier.

Now he had to find the girl. How the hell was he supposed to do that? She'd fallen off the detection net like water off the Level 2 ceiling. And to top it off, he didn't have access to a car. Abby wouldn't get into his, and then refused to give him a set of keys to hers, just in case. He should have cut them out of her.

When they got to the hospital, the third one they had tried, they had checked the front parking lots, looking for the car. They didn't find it. They were walking to the back lot when he looked in through the emergency doors, and saw the girl inside. Close timing, too; she had just gotten up and walked further inside.

Well, if the girl's car wasn't in the front, it had to be in the back. And if it wasn't there, then she was already in it. An untrackable girl in an untrackable car. Life was just getting better.

Jeremy said to find the girl. He didn't say how, or to keep it quiet. So be it. He was going pull in some people. His best bet was to watch the ramps in a ten-kilometer radius. Both up and down. She was more comfortable on the lower levels, so she'd probably head that way. Get out of sight and try to hide.

It's what he would do.

The back parking lot was huge. It was going take forever to walk the aisles and look for the damn thing. Better set up the ramp watches first. He pulled out his comm unit and started dialing. When he was done, he entered the lot and started walking through the rows of cars.

It would take a while for the people he called to cover all the ramps, but with some luck, they'd see her car.

After twenty minutes of walking and searching, his eyes were starting to cross. Every red car in the lot looked the same. What happened to the damn car companies trying to make their stuff look different? He sat down on a curb and rubbed his eyes.

"Hey, bud, did you lose your car?"

Quincy looked up. A security guard was walking up to him. Quincy moved his hand to his pocket and stood up.

"No, but I'm looking for one in particular." He glanced over to the ambulance entrance. Several police cars were still there. "They sent me to look."

"I thought the uniforms were assigned jobs like this."

"Yeah, well, the shit rolls down, you know. I pissed someone off and I get the crap jobs. I guess I'm lucky I'm not on foot patrol." Quincy started walking again. He turned and stopped. "Hey, you haven't seen this car, have you?" He gave a description.

"Nope, but I already told the guys in the ER. The guy that was shot drove up in a blue one. Well, the girl was driving. I had to move it out of the lane for her, you know. If an ambulance came and the drive was blocked, I'd lose my job."

Blue? Damn Abby. "I hear ya. Where'd you park it?"

"A couple rows over. It had blood all over the front seat."

Quincy started walking toward where the security guard indicated.

"I wouldn't bother. The car's already gone. I'm surprised the other cops didn't tell you. I went looking for it as soon as things settled down."

"Figures. They're getting a good laugh out of me this time."

"Yeah, well. It isn't there."

"Thanks for the help, you saved me a lot of walking."

"No problemo."

Quincy pulled out his comm unit again and confirmed the ramps were being covered, updating them on the car. Most of the down-ramps had people watching. The up-ramps weren't quite there yet.

He had everything covered. Or did he? Quincy knew what he would do, but every time he thought he had this girl figured out, she went and changed something on him. What if she wasn't heading back down? What if she was heading up, running away as fast as she could?

Two cars drove into the parking lot and stopped by Quincy. The driver got out of one and Quincy got in. He'd check out the shuttle port, just in case.

SIXTEEN

I LEFT THE HOSPITAL area and drove until I found an up-ramp. I felt lost and out of control. It was strange, not knowing where I was and how to get around. I'd spent the last year memorizing every shortcut, every detour on my levels and in my area. But Level 6 was new territory.

Was I doing the right thing? Miller had made it very clear he wanted me to get out of the city. With the black box running out of power, I had to agree it was probably the best idea. As soon as that thing went down, I was a goner. But I wasn't sure it was the *right* thing to do.

He had kissed my hand. You didn't do that if you're just doing your job. Do you? Maybe it was my imagination taking off, just being a stupid little girl. Miller made me feel different. New. Like I wasn't damaged goods. Maybe I was just pushing what I felt onto him. Was running away from that worth it?

Every thought was driven from my mind when I reached the Level 7 up-ramp. My world turned upside down and I felt weak and nauseous.

There wasn't anything above me.

The vertigo increased when I pulled off the ramp into a parking lot and got out of the car. Other people had pulled over as well, all of them staring into the darkening blue sky.

Sky.

I felt like I could see forever. I fell against the side of the car, another wave of dizziness rushing through me. I had seen open sky before, of course, but the vids just didn't do it justice. There was *nothing* above me. It was as if someone had cut open the top of my head and let the whole universe rush in.

A cloud moved overhead, pushed by some unseen and unfelt wind. The light felt . . . warm. And the colors. The grass was greener, my skin looked whiter, almost sickly.

The concrete under my feet radiated heat collected throughout the day. My mind tried to grasp the vastness of everything. Tried and failed. It went way beyond my wildest imagination. A shuttle roared across the deepening sky, leaving a soft white trail in its wake.

I climbed back into the car and sat staring through the windshield, thankful for the roof of the car over my head. The sun had turned a musky yellow, fat and pregnant near the horizon, and the sky was layered in vivid oranges and reds turning to a dark blue as it went higher.

The shuttle's contrail deepened, the bottom still

reflecting light from the setting sun while the top faded into a dark gray.

The experience left me breathless. Miller had probably seen it before, but still, all I could think about was sharing this moment with him.

I sat in the car until the sun moved below the horizon, watching the shifting colors play across the darkening sky, reminding myself to breathe when I realized I was holding my breath. Tears rolled down my cheeks and I wiped them away roughly with the back of my hand. I started the car again and moved onto the street, following the shuttle's trail back to the shuttle port.

Finding a road that went in the right direction was relatively easy, but finding the entrance to the shuttle port wasn't. I drove down dead-end streets in the middle of low-slung warehouses, and once, through what must have been lower-cost housing. I could almost hear the glass rattle in the windows when another shuttle came down.

Even here though, the houses were better than anything I had seen below, except on Level 6. Each house was self-contained. Individual bungalows with play sets and palm trees in the backyard.

It felt so far from where I had come from. These families had more than I ever did, more than I ever would. They probably didn't even care.

When I finally found the entrance to the shuttle port, I drove along the winding approach and parked as close to the terminal as I could. The parking garage was actually above the ground. Each level open to the sky at the sides.

I was tempted to walk to the edge and look out over the city; I could see the lights and signs twinkling in the dusk. But time was running out. I had no idea how long it would take to get on a shuttle, or even where they all went. I took all the money from under the back seat, shuddering when I saw the tiny box again, and put it in the envelope with Frank's money. I found the stairs back to ground level and took them. My body ached after sitting in the car. It hadn't been that long, but the previous days were taking more than their toll.

The terminal itself was exactly as I had seen it in all the vids. The front doors opened on to a massive concourse, all chrome and glass. The floor was tiled, mostly white with angled grid lines of light and dark gray spaced about two meters apart. Ticket counters with smiling people in brightly colored uniforms lined the far wall. Overhead, extending about a quarter of the way over the concourse, was a second level filled with restaurants, bars, and stores. The lower level reminded me of the hospital where I had left Miller behind, and regret again settled into my gut.

I moved toward the counter, reading the displays posted overhead. The departures listed places whose names I only knew from being forced to read about them in school: New York, Budapest, Paris, SoCal Sat One, Moscow. The list went on and on. None of them were places I could go.

Off continent would be too obvious, and I'd be asked questions about luggage and passports, neither of which I had. Would I need them for local flights? I had no clue. I moved to the next board and started reading local destinations: San Francisco, San Diego, Las Vegas. Everything along the west coast was part of SoCal's city, San Francisco would just be a flight into a different neighborhood.

Las Vegas was IBC territory. Not my first choice, but the flight was leaving in an hour, and from there I could catch another short hop somewhere else. Maybe Denver or Minneapolis. They were still owned by the government outright. So were the corporate cities, in theory, but in reality the government had no control over what happened in them.

I must have starting walking to the counter a dozen times, each time veering away before I got close, before they could see me coming. Once, when the line was long, I stood in it for a while before chickening out and walking back to a bench.

How was I going to do this? I didn't have any ID, except for my driver's license and my courier's ID card. Was that enough? Or would they alert the police? By my tenth time up, I was in such a panic, I was sure they could see me shaking from across the entire airport.

I had to get myself under control. I found a washroom and went inside. My jacket was stained brown—Miller's blood—and there was a streak of it on my face as well.

I pulled Frank's gun from my pocket and tucked it beneath my shirt. A few minutes under warm running water and a few more with the dryer, and the jacket looked pretty good. A wall dispenser sold toothpaste and combs and other assorted items. I dropped in some coins.

With my hair combed, teeth brushed, and face washed, I felt like a whole new person. The shuttle I wanted to get on left in fifteen minutes, and I hadn't gotten a ticket yet. There was no way I was going to get on that flight now. I had to go back to the board to see what was available.

I left the bathroom, but not until I dropped the gun into the garbage can, burying it under the used paper towels. The thing may have made it through the security check, but it wasn't a risk I was willing to take.

I picked the next flight to Las Vegas, leaving in a

couple of hours, and started the same pattern of trying to buy the ticket. It only took me three tries to realize it just wasn't going to happen. For the first time, I noticed cameras mounted high on the ceiling. Was one of them watching me?

Miller had told me to leave the city. He had told me to get on a shuttle. But just the thought of leaving filled me with guilt. Why? I was only doing what he told me to do.

He had kissed my hand.

I knew he wouldn't, didn't, leave me. But he was trained for this shit, I wasn't. Thinking it made the words sound hollow. Before I fully realized what I was doing, I had walked away from the ticket counters, back down the concourse. I needed my gun if I was going to do anything.

The way I figured it, I still had at least until noon tomorrow before the black box stopped working. I still wasn't sure what I was going to do, but I knew that running away again was not going to solve this problem.

Taking a quick glance at the cameras, I walked into the bathroom and retrieved the gun from the garbage. As I left, a large hand grabbed my arm, jerking me off to the side.

"Move or scream, and you die right here."

I looked up at the face of my attacker. Quincy.

LEVEL 7—THURSDAY, AUGUST 11, 2140 7:00 P.M.

Quincy put his arm around my shoulders and smiled. I tried to wrench away and he tightened his grip.

"It's okay," he said, speaking louder. "Mom will come back soon." People had stopped to look at us, the scared girl and the thin man. He stepped forward, forcing me to keep up with him, and lowered his voice. "You've been quite the little bitch, haven't you?"

I tried harder to twist away. "Let me go!"

"I can't do that now, can I? It took far too long to actually get hold of you."

"I'll scream."

"I've already warned you about that."

I felt something hard press into my side.

"This will make a bit of a mess. I like 'em powerful, no chance for a mistake."

He jabbed me with the gun again. It felt as though he pushed it right through my ribs, and I gasped in pain.

Quincy dragged me through the concourse and out the large doors to the parking garage. When we were in the stairwell, he moved his grip to my upper arm, squeezing with a viselike grip.

"Where are you taking me?" I couldn't keep the quiver from my voice. I was sure his plan was to get me someplace quiet and put a bullet in my back. Or worse, use his knife on me.

"On a little trip. The boss wants to see you. Figures you know a lot of stuff."

"I don't know anything. Please, let me go." Panic and begging had crept into my voice. I hated the sound of it. "I . . . I can make it worth your while." I still had a fair amount of cash left.

He leered at me and grabbed my chest. "What are you going to offer me that I can't just take?"

I knew then it could be worse than being sliced open.

When we reached his car, he slammed me against it, pressing a hand into the back of my neck while the other one searched. He found the gun and the cash and put them both into his pocket. When his hand hit the blocker he grunted.

The rest of his search got more personal before he opened the door, pushing me in ahead of him. I crawled into a shell I hadn't needed to use in years.

"Slide over to the passenger side. I think we'll keep your blocker on for now. I don't know who else might be looking for you."

I moved to the next seat and pressed myself into the corner made by the back of the seat and the door. "You can keep the money."

Quincy laughed and sat in the seat beside me. "Yeah," he said. "I can. But that's not really what I want from you, is it?"

He pulled the gun out of his pocket and laid it on his lap, the barrel pointing right at my gut. His left hand stayed on it as he pulled out from the parking stall and drove out of the garage. Once on the road, he steered with his knee, pulling out a comm unit and placing a call.

"It's Quincy . . . Yeah, I got the girl . . . You'll meet us there? Okay, fifteen minutes." He closed the link and looked at me. "Looks like you're not taking a trip after all. The boss is on his way down already." He drove around the outskirts of the shuttle port, almost retracing the route I had taken earlier.

As he drove, the only illumination came from the streetlights placed at regular intervals beside the road. Pools of darkness gathered in between the pinpoints of light. It was darker than I was used to, with no Ambients spreading an even light across the landscape. Still, the canopy of black helped to calm me a bit, more like the ceilings of the lower levels.

We were back into warehouses spreading out from the airport like bums in Chinatown. Quincy pulled into a dark parking lot and backed into a spot by loading dock doors. He killed the car lights and waited. Faint light from the street reflected off his face, giving him a ghostly appearance. I tried the door in the dark. It was locked.

"We got time, how about that offer?" he said.

"Fuck you." The darkness that calmed me earlier now made me feel braver. It helped that I couldn't see the gun, even though my brain told me it was there. I didn't see his hand until it was almost at my face. I jerked to the side, smashing my head into the closed window. Stars fluttered in front of my eyes and Quincy's hand hit the headrest.

"You'll be wanting to watch what you say to me." His voice had taken on a harder edge. "Now move your little ass over here."

Lights from a car coming into the parking lot lit up the inside of my cage. Quincy still had the gun in his left hand; his right had unzipped his pants and was reaching inside.

"Fuck." He zipped up his fly. "There'll be time later, don't you worry."

He opened the car door and motioned for me to follow him. As I moved over to the driver's side, I noticed the keys were still in the ignition.

For a brief moment I thought of starting the car and speeding away. I would only need a second or two before the car would be on the road and I'd be racing away as fast as I could. But the gun in Quincy's hand was only a meter from my head, pointed right at me. I couldn't outrace a bullet.

"Get out."

I got out and moved away from the door. Quincy slammed it shut and stood beside it, leaning his tall frame against the car, as if he didn't have a care in the world.

The other car was a limousine, black and polished, reflecting the light from the street in hot white spots. The driver got out and moved to the back door. As he opened it, Quincy stopped leaning and stood straighter.

The boss had arrived.

SEVENTEEN

LEVEL 7—THURSDAY, AUGUST 11, 2140 8:35 P.M.

TO ME, the man getting out of the limousine looked like any other old man I had seen, except he was wearing an expensive-looking suit. And when he moved, it was as if he commanded the world to notice him. Tall and proud and in control.

He walked over to Quincy, making sure he didn't come between the gun and me.

"Did anybody see you?"

"No, sir," Quincy answered.

"Good. Bring her inside. Nobody else needs to see this."

The man walked past, giving me a wide berth, and opened a small door beside the loading docks. Quincy motioned me to follow and in turn followed me, the gun still leveled at my back.

The door led into a large loading bay. Boxes sat on top of palettes, some piled over two meters high. A group of forklifts that used to be orange sat in a row along the far wall. Along the other wall sat a line of offices, their doors dark and gray with dirt from the hands of the people who worked in them.

The man walked to the door on the end and opened it. By the time I got there, the lights had flickered to life and a swivel office chair from the desk jammed into the corner had been moved into the middle of the room. Quincy pushed me into it. My momentum rolled the chair into the far wall.

"Tsk tsk. Quincy . . . show the lady some manners." He turned to me. "My name is Jeremy. I already know yours. Would you care for a glass of water?"

When I didn't answer, Jeremy walked to the desk, moved some papers out of the way, and perched on its edge.

"I'm going to ask you some questions, Kris. I expect your full cooperation. If I don't get it, I'll simply leave you to Quincy. I believe you've seen his handiwork up close. Most unpleasant."

I felt the too-familiar cold knot in my stomach tighten.

"Let's start with the package, shall we? I'm assuming Quincy didn't find it on you, so where is it?"

"I don't know." I spat the words out.

Quincy took a step forward and backhanded me across the face. My head twisted and I could taste blood in my mouth.

"Let's try this again. Where is the package?"

I spat some blood out of my mouth and, with a bravery I didn't feel, gave Quincy a look that told him to fuck off and die.

"I don't know. I don't have it."

"I see. Then when did you see it last?"

"At the safe house. I had it with me. Just before your asshole showed up." I gave a nod in Quincy's direction. "A couple of guys came by and took it with them."

I could see Quincy was starting to get riled. Good. The fuckhead had pissed me off. I knew I would pay for getting him mad, but mad people also got careless. And careless gave me a chance.

"A couple of guys. You'll need to be more specific."

"I can't."

Quincy swung again, splitting my swollen lip open.

"Apparently, Quincy, you have lost your charm. Perhaps there is another way to convince her we mean business."

Jeremy walked to the open door and looked into the empty loading bay. He spoke, his back still toward me. His voice echoed in the large open area.

"According to Quincy, your friend Miller was being quite . . . attentive to you in the hospital. Surprising for a man who just had shrapnel taken out of his shoulder." He turned back and looked me in the eye. "You may be interested to know I have Miller."

I gave a slight start, and tried to hide it by shifting my weight on the chair.

"Ahh, yes. I see the feelings are mutual. Very well then. Tell me what I need to know without playing any games, and I'll let him live. And you as well, of course." He took his comm unit out of his pocket and touched the screen, ready to make a connection.

"Who has the package?"

"The two guys were from ACE. They took it with them when they left," I said, the words tumbling from my mouth.

"And who else has seen the contents of the package?"

"No one."

Jeremy looked at Quincy and sighed, putting away his comm unit. My stomach dropped like I was in a fast-moving elevator.

"No. Wait. Nigel ... Nigel Wood opened it as well. He ... he read it before he was killed."

"Much better, Kris. Did he scan it in as well?"

"Not that I saw."

Jeremy looked at me as if judging the validity of my answer. His calm questions scared me almost as much as Quincy's knife.

"Very well. ACE has the package, SoCal has a copy, as does Kadokawa. Not quite what I planned, but manageable."

Jeremy turned to Quincy and smiled, a small turn upward at the corners of his mouth.

"All of this effort over a silly courier, a little girl who is still too young to be away from her mother. A pity really. Don't make a mess in here, please." He turned and walked out the door, closing it silently behind him.

Quincy's grin was bigger than Jeremy's, much bigger. "Now, where were we when he came along? Yeah, I remember." He advanced on me.

LEVEL 7—THURSDAY, AUGUST 11, 2140 8:53 P.M.

My world turned inside out. I was back in my aunt's tiny apartment. Her husband, a bottle in his hand, had his pants already unbuckled and hanging down by his thighs. My fear disappeared, replaced by a burning rage and hatred that consumed me from head to toe.

The image swam out of focus, and it was Quincy approaching me again, a gun in his hand instead of a bottle.

It didn't matter. The intent was the same, and I wasn't going to be a fucking victim anymore.

I launched myself off the chair, aiming my head at Quincy's groin. He moved out of the way and lifted a knee into my chest. I slammed into the wall and the world went dark for a minute.

When I came to, Quincy had cleared the desk and thrown me on it. My jacket lay on the floor. He grabbed the front of my t-shirt, trying to tear it off me. The material held. I twisted, hoping to release his grip on me. Quincy reached behind his back, pulling a knife from its sheath.

I had seen the knife before.

He slid the blade along my stomach, pulling my shirt up to my rib cage, before twisting the blade and cutting through the material. It cut as though slicing through air. I held still, not daring to even breathe, as I felt the cold steel slide under my bra.

Quincy grabbed my face with his other hand, twisting it so I looked right at him.

"You like this, don't you? They all do, in the end. They always beg for more, before I watch the life drain from their eyes."

The knife twitched and I felt a burn. Quincy smiled, then jerked the blade toward him, cutting through the center band. He rubbed his finger between my breasts and raised it to his lips, licking off the blood.

He moved to the end of the desk, dragging the knife down over the tape holding on the black box to the button on my jeans. My stomach quivered. I pushed myself up to my elbows, my bra fell to the desk.

"No, please. I can do it for you."

I braced myself, trying to smile at Quincy through the tears. I reached a hand down, moving the knife blade out of the way, and undid the button.

Quincy paused, sizing me up before he put the knife

back in its sheath and began to unbutton his own shirt with one hand, the other still holding his gun. "Now that's more like it!" He moved as I sat up, reaching to push my jeans down.

I leaned back and swung my foot with all the strength I had, bracing my hands on the edge of the table, almost lifting myself right off the surface. I felt my foot make contact and drove it higher into his groin.

Quincy's face turned bright red and he stopped breathing. He fell to his knees and toppled sideways, his mouth opening and closing like a fish out of water.

I slid off the desk, picking the dropped gun off the floor, and stood over him. He didn't even notice.

"Never again," I said. I pulled the trigger. The gun kicked a little and made a soft "phhfft" sound. Quincy stopped squirming on the floor, a pool of blood forming under him.

I closed my eyes and pulled the trigger until the gun was empty before falling to my knees, drawing in deep ragged breaths.

I knelt there until I could feel blood soaking through to my knees. I forced myself back to my feet and looked at Quincy. There wasn't much left of his chest. It was my turn to smile.

I went through his pockets, not knowing what I was looking for. Nestled deep in the front pocket, I found my bike keys, the tiny golden Oscar still attached. A part of me felt more complete the second it was in my hand. I found my—Frank's—gun tucked beside the knife at his back.

I had to catch up with Jeremy, find out what he had done with Miller. Picking my jacket off the floor, I put it on, zipping it up while I raced toward the loading dock doors. Oscar went in the front pocket, where'd he'd always been, where he belonged.

By the time I reached the loading dock, Jeremy's car was already gone.

LEVEL 6—THURSDAY, AUGUST 11, 2140 6:50 P.M.

Devon left the service corridors on Level 7. The route he had chosen wasn't selected by the computer; it was one he had chosen by himself, years ago. As far as the computer knew, the route didn't even exist.

He was standing in the basement of Akorn Financial, and on his way to a new life. He'd had enough of this one, enough of ACE, enough of SoCal and Kadokawa and Meridian. Enough of all of it.

Before leaving the service corridor, he'd opened the package he had grabbed from under the catwalk, pulling out an identity he'd grown and nurtured throughout the years. A fully developed citizen of the world.

He had created Peter Martin when he moved into the special room, knowing that at some point he would be compromised. No matter what safety measures were taken, no matter how tight the security was, there was always a way to get the information. He should know.

But this was his. All his. No one knew about it, no one would miss Devon disappearing, and no one would notice that Peter Martin had actually started to walk the streets. Maybe his mom, but he'd left her comfortable enough to be happy without him. He wanted to make one last phone call to let her know he was all right, but he knew it would be a mistake. Everything was traceable.

Devon had wanted to create a superman, a full MIT scholarship and degree, a handful of the best schools before that. Instead he had settled for something more average, something that didn't stand out in a crowd so much. Peter had graduated from Caltech, tenth in his class. A good place to be, but not the best. He had gotten a good job, at Akorn Financial, developing investment modeling software.

Using his own knowledge of the markets, he'd invested wisely and managed to latch on to a company that IPO'd a few years back. His investments had skyrocketed and he sold his shares for a thousand times more than he'd paid for them. Two weeks later, the company took a nosedive, almost falling from the stock exchange tables.

He bought in again and rode the next wave up. It didn't go nearly as high as the initial IPO, but Peter had still turned it into millions. He had sold last week again, and the stock had started falling the next day.

The person who walked into the sub-basement was Peter Martin. Devon no longer existed as a real person. The first thing Peter would have to do was get a haircut; his long hair didn't match the slightly crumpled suit he now wore. He dumped his old clothes, stashing them under some hardware required for the city's infrastructure, probably an air recycling unit or something. Even if they found them, they wouldn't be able to connect them to Peter.

He had slid the computer into a small bag. This had turned out to be a bonus. He didn't need computers anymore, not with the money he had, but this one was special, unique. After working with it for the last year, he had grown to think of it as a family member, maybe even better than that. The fact that it couldn't be traced was just another bonus.

The basement of Akorn Financial had been turned into an underground mall, connecting several buildings in the financial district together. Employees could come down here for lunch or dinner if they were working late.

They could shop for Christmas gifts, get flowers for their wives. Pretty much anything they wanted without having to see actual sunshine. For a city whose main population lived without sunlight, he'd always found it strange.

Peter walked into a KwikCuts and asked for a simple cut.

"We can squeeze you in now, sir, if you'd like?"

"That would be great."

"Follow me, please. You can leave your bag behind the front desk if you like, and pick it up on the way out."

"No, thanks, I'll just hold on to it."

Twenty minutes later, the transformation to Peter was complete. His hair was short, no longer pulled back into a ponytail. A little bit of gel gave it some spikiness, adding two and half centimeters onto his height. When he walked out of the KwikCuts, even his step seemed to have changed.

He took the escalator to the main level and stepped into the sunshine, blinking in the sudden brightness. He flagged down a cab and sat quietly during the ride to the shuttle port.

When Peter walked into the terminal building, he didn't notice the chrome and the glass. The tiles on the floor didn't even catch his eye. He walked straight to the Qantas counter. They had a flight to Brisbane, Australia via Fiji leaving at eight in the morning.

At eleven in the morning a direct flight left. That would put him in Brisbane almost an hour ahead of the Fiji flight. It was worth the wait.

He purchased a first-class ticket and membership in the Qantas Club, Platinum Access. It was something Devon would never have been able to do. Peter decided if he was going to wait all night, he might as well do it in comfort. He walked to the second level and found the Qantas Lounge at the far end.

The lounge itself was like a tranquil bay in a sea of rolling people. Once the doors closed behind him, the regular shuttle port din was shut out. His feet sank into soft carpet. After showing his temporary membership card and ticket, he was let through into the inner sanctum.

It wasn't what he'd expected. The large open room was brightly lit and full of color, not like the old style gentleman's club atmosphere he'd imagined, with dark panel walls and the smell of cigar smoke hanging in the air.

Instead, the smell of a warm buffet wafted toward him. He skipped it and got a drink at the complimentary bar before moving to a small cubicle along one of the brightly painted walls.

He pulled the computer out of his bag and plugged it into the display and network before turning it on. The screen came to life, still showing his last running applications. He killed them without looking and started a simple search for Devon.

He'd be surprised if anyone was missing him yet, and even more so if the public databases he had access to would know about it. For a fleeting moment, he missed the flow of data his little office had provided.

LEVEL 7—THURSDAY, AUGUST 11, 2140 8:50 P.M.

I sat on the parking lot pavement, my head resting in my hands. What the hell was I supposed to do now?

The thought of Quincy lying dead in the office didn't give me any relief. Instead, it made me feel worse. The victory I'd felt earlier faded, not into remorse, but into a sense of loss. I knew it was either him or me, but did I have to kill him? I could have left while he was on the floor. I could have just walked away.

But then I would always be looking over my shoulder, wondering when he would be there, waiting for him to drag me back to hell.

The events of the last few minutes lodged themselves like a burr in my head; the only point that stood out clearly was the slight kick of the gun when I pulled the trigger.

It had all gone so terribly wrong. My flight to Las Vegas had left already, so I couldn't take that now. I knew I wouldn't anyway. Miller was supposed to be with the police, waiting for ACE to get their act together. Instead he was god knows where, with Jeremy.

What the hell was I supposed do now?

I lifted my head out of my hands and looked at the car. The keys were still in it, so at least I didn't have to go back in and search Quincy's body again. I didn't think I would have been able to do that. So, I had a car. Great. Where could I go? I could start looking for Miller, but where to start?

Jeremy had been right. I did have feelings for Miller. And why not? The fact that he had come like a knight in shining armor and rescued me helped, but I knew that wasn't it. He had made me feel safer in the last three days than, hell, since Mom and Dad had been killed. The safe house had felt almost like a home. And, for the first time I could remember, a man had cooked for me and washed my clothes. The thought of my clothes brought back another memory, of waking up in a soft, warm bed. He'd done that, too. He didn't even try to take advantage of me.

What was not to like?

I jumped to my feet. He had rescued me; the least I could do was try to rescue him back. I had to contact

ACE, or what was left of it. Quincy's comm unit wasn't the best choice for that. Besides, I didn't have a contact number.

Miller's comm unit was in his car, which was still where I'd left it at the shuttle port. I'd head there and try to contact ACE with it, if ACE was active enough. I hoped Miller's comm unit would have some way of contacting them. Maybe I could call the guy who had called us earlier, what was his name . . . David . . . no, Devon. I'd try to call back using the reply function. It might just work.

Without looking back at the warehouse, I got into the car and drove from the lot, turning toward the shuttle port.

The drive back was straightforward. I simply retraced the path that Quincy had taken earlier. Being a courier had given me some skills, at least.

I maneuvered down the twisty shuttle port roads to the parking garage where I'd left Miller's car. The "full" sign flashed as I tried to enter, and the bar didn't rise to let me in. I was forced to back out and drive around the terminal area to come around again. This time, I turned in to the outdoor short-term parking lot and walked back to the garage, avoiding the pools of light cast by the overhead lamps.

The car was where I'd left it only a little over an hour ago. I opened the unlocked driver's side door and stumbled back. The smell of blood on the seat had grown stronger and stale, almost pouring out of the open door. I took a breath and held it as I bent over and reached in.

The comm unit had some of Miller's blood on it. I wiped what I could off on the seat and slammed the door shut. I moved away from the car, distancing myself from the smell of the blood and the memories it brought back.

I powered on the unit. The batteries were running a

bit low, but I figured I'd be able to make a couple of calls on it at least. The status of the comm unit's batteries brought back thoughts of the black box still taped to my back. I had practically forgotten about it. It had become as much a part of me, of who I was, as my right hand. Something I didn't think I could live without.

I scrolled through the list of received calls. Nothing looked like it had come from ACE. I scrolled back to the top of the list, the last call that had come in. The list showed Diora's Restaurant, not Devon. Maybe he called from there.

I hit the recall button and waited. It took only a moment for the unit to give a faint beep. Damn it, no reception. I'd have to leave the garage to pick up a signal. I walked back to the stairwell and down the stairs.

EIGHTEEN

PETER FINISHED CHECKING the status of his stocks on the computer and downloaded the latest values into his own application. Devon was a man of modest means. It was one of ACE's requirements. Although they paid not too badly, their employees were not to show any extravagances. They were supposed to maintain a nice even keel and stay under the radar of the big three.

As Peter, he didn't really need to do that. Peter's wealth was not a sudden thing. It was a documented and monitored process that had occurred over the years. Maintaining an extravagant lifestyle was part of the cover.

He turned off the computer and unplugged it from

the network and display unit, placing it back in his bag. It was time to enjoy some of the free buffet, and maybe another drink or two from the open bar. He stood and turned, walking back to the buffet table with the cube hanging over his shoulder.

The buffet was more of an appetizer selection than anything that might form a full meal. Still, it would be enough to tide him over until the shuttle flight. There would be a full meal served on that.

"Perhaps you would like a more substantial meal?"

Peter looked up and took a step back in shock, bumping into another man.

"The Qantas Lounge is hardly the low profile ACE has asked you to keep, Devon. Or would you prefer Peter now?" William Clark stood beside Devon.

"Ummm, William, fancy meeting you here."

William motioned for the man Devon bumped into to grab his arm, and led the way from the lounge. The lady at the front counter smiled.

"Thank you for flying Qantas."

The door closed behind them and they were once again surrounded by the noise of the terminal. The three men moved through the thinning crowd and down to the lower level, exiting to the drop-off lane in front. Traffic was light this late in the evening, but it would pick up shortly as the night flights to the Sat Cities began. They marched across the street and headed toward the parking garage.

"So, how did you find me?"

"ACE is in the habit of protecting and monitoring its assets. The computer gave us its location the moment you went online."

"That's impossible, I've looked at every program on that thing, and rewritten most of them. There's no way it did that."

"You software guys are always so sure you've got the problem solved, aren't you? I don't think I said the software called home. I said the computer called home."

"The compu . . . Hardware! You bastards."

"Yes, and it's a good thing we set it up that way. When we approached your office earlier today, we weren't quite sure you were our leak. All we knew for sure was Meridian was getting its information very quickly, which meant somewhere close to where it came in to ACE.

"And you almost made it away safe. Nigel said you wouldn't be able to leave a system like that behind. He was right. Not that he would have been happy about it. He placed a lot of trust in you. Obviously too much."

"He wasn't supposed to die."

"When you set up operations like that, incidental casualties happen. When you gave Meridian the location of that meeting, you signed his death warrant."

Devon walked along quietly, calm and deep in thought. "I disagree. I think it was what it was, an accident. I'm not accepting the blame for it."

"You already have," William said.

They entered the parking garage stairwell and started walking up to the second floor. As they opened the door onto the parking area, Devon looked up the stairwell, hoping to use the person coming down as a distraction. "It's her, the courier."

William stopped and looked up as well, a smile starting to form on his face. Devon jerked his arm free of the second man and made a run for the parked cars. He only took two steps before his legs were knocked out from under him. He landed on the floor, a concrete rash blossoming on the side of his face.

As he looked back at the slowly closing door, he heard William start to talk.

"Kris! I'm glad to see you . . ."

LEVEL 7—THURSDAY, AUGUST 11, 2140 8:52 P.M.

I tucked the comm unit into my jacket pocket and started moving down the stairs, lost in thought. The jacket was uncomfortable without a shirt, and chafed under my arms and on my waist. I had just rounded the corner to the stairs when I heard a familiar voice call out.

"It's her, the courier."

My heart leaped into my throat. How had they found me so fast? I looked up and saw William Clark and two other men walking up the stairs, and relief flooded through me.

The one who had called out twisted away from the third guy and ran. I watched as he was taken down by a kick to the back of the knees.

William looked up and extended his hand. "Kris! I'm glad to see you alive. When Miller was taken, I feared the worst."

I kept looking at the man on the ground, one side of his face raw and bleeding from scraping against the concrete. His voice sounded familiar.

"That's Devon," I said, pointing at him.

William stopped, his hand returning to his side. "Yes, it is. And how do you know that?"

"He called Miller, telling him ACE was shutting down. That there was no one around who would be able to remove my tracker. Why is he on the floor?" William worked for ACE, but so did Devon. What was going on?

William reached for my shoulder and turned me so my back was to the other men. "I'm afraid Devon is our leak. He's the one that's been feeding information to Meridian. He's the reason Nigel is dead, and Miller is in a cell."

"Miller's in a cell? But I just saw Quincy and a guy named Jeremy, Quincy's boss. Jeremy said—"

"Jeremy? Jeremy Adams?" William interrupted. His voice had gone soft.

"I...I don't know. He never used his last name. Quincy phoned him and he showed up in a limousine."

"Describe him."

"Uh. Old...older than you. Gray hair. Expensive suit. Walked like he had a broom stuck up his ass."

William chuckled. "I don't think I've ever heard his posture described that way. But suitable, I think. Jeremy Adams is not only Quincy's boss, he's also in charge of security and defense for Meridian. A powerful man."

"Was."

"I beg your pardon?" William's face drained of color.

"He was Quincy's boss. Quincy is dead. I...I shot him when I got away." I closed my eyes, trying to shut out the image of Quincy on the floor. It didn't help.

William looked me over again, a critical look in his eye. "You've done some unexpected things, Kris. Very unexpected. The body is still there, I suppose?"

"Yeah."

"We'll have to send in a cleanup crew. No point in having the body found before it needs to be."

I described the location of the warehouse, using the turns and distances without knowing the names of the streets.

"I think we can find him. Now, what do we do about you?"

"I want to find Miller!"

"I already mentioned that Miller is in a holding cell. The police will let him go once our lawyers are done, and then he'll disappear, get a new identity."

"Jeremy said he had him. He said he was going to take care of him."

"Really?" William looked back at Devon still lying on the ground with a knee in his back. "We'll have to do something about that. We've already lost too many assets over this."

Assets? Is that all he was to them, all I would be? Right now, it didn't matter. "I want to help."

"Young lady, you are not trained. You don't have the skills the extraction would need."

I stood straighter and moved away from William. I might not be trained, but I had made it this far. "I didn't do too badly."

"True. A mixture of luck and spunk, I think." He looked back at me and stared quietly for a few moments, moving from my bloody knees to my bruised face. "Okay. You deserve to see this through to the end. If you survive, I think we at ACE will want to have another conversation with you. Do you have a comm unit?"

"Yes, I have Miller's," I said, pulling it out from my pocket.

"Good. Someone will call you on it."

"So I can help?"

"Possibly. You'll most certainly be there."

That was good. I deserved to be there. Needed to be there. Needed to know Miller was okay.

LEVEL 6—THURSDAY, AUGUST 11, 2140 9:00 P.M.

The back of the limousine was luxurious. A little above and beyond Jeremy's normal lifestyle, but if he was going to be in the city, he might as well make the best of it. In fact, this was the first time in years he actually looked forward to the trip.

The briefcase sitting in front of him was the sole

source of his pleasure. He cracked it open and stared at the contents. He hadn't used this in decades, but everything still shone like new. You had to take care of your equipment, or when you really needed it, it would fail you. Much like people. He ran his fingers over the small implements, some of them resembling dentist's tools, others eerily similar to various kitchen utensils. The cold metal seemed to come to life under his touch, stirring feelings buried deep in his soul.

Jeremy laughed. He was getting sentimental in his old age. No worries though, a small night's entertainment and he'd be back in the Sat City, sipping a twenty-five-year-old Bowmore Single Malt Scotch and reminiscing about tonight's events. Then he'd figure out a way to get rid of Yang. The president, nosy bastard though he was, could be handled. Yang could not, and therefore had to be eliminated.

He looked at his watch. Quincy should be done by now and on his way to the rendezvous point. Jeremy would have stayed and worked on the girl, but the thought actually revolted him. She was not worthy of what he brought to the table. But Miller. Miller was.

Anyone who could take out Abby had to be good, very good. He leaned back in the seat, staring at his tools and drinking some bottled water. It was interesting. The revenge aspect added a whole new sense of urgency to the job. It brought it down to a personal level that was entirely unexpected. Yes, this would be a good night.

The limousine pulled in front of the police station. First things first, he needed to get Miller out of there. His call to the Police Chief earlier in the day should have done that for him. A simple prisoner transfer from San Angeles to the Sat City's facilities. Nothing out of the ordinary, except that Jeremy himself was doing the pickup.

He strode into the building, looking for the elevators.

Miller was in a holding cell on the third floor. He rode the elevator, his excitement reaching almost physical proportions.

There was no receptionist on the third floor, not at this time of night anyway. He walked through an open door into a room filled with desks and stood there for a moment. No one appeared to notice him, so he walked over to the nearest desk and announced himself.

"Meridian Corporation. I'm here to pick up a prisoner."

The detective looked up from his paperwork, the look on his face a mixture between boredom and disinterest. "Name."

"Jeremy Adams."

The detective seemed to lose himself in his display for a minute, scrolling through the list of prisoners in the building. "*Prisoner's* name?"

"Oh ... Miller, Ian Miller."

After a few more seconds lost in the display, the detective looked back up and pointed a thumb over his shoulder. "Detective Stevens," and he went back to the paperwork on his desk.

How quaint, Jeremy thought as he headed over to the only other desk with a person at it, they still use paper.

"Detective Stevens?"

"I'm Stevens." The woman stood up and took Jeremy's proffered hand.

"I'm from Meridian, I'm here to pick up Miller."

She looked at him again, eying his suit. "You're a bit high on the evolutionary ladder to be picking up a prisoner, especially at this time of night."

"Meridian's interest in Miller is fairly high in the food chain, Detective. Can we get on with it?"

"Yes, of course." She indicated an empty chair by her desk. "Please sit. We'll get started right away."

By the time the paperwork was done, forty-five minutes had passed and Jeremy was starting to feel irritated. This was too much crap for a pre-approved transfer. When he finally got Miller, his tolerance for bullshit had reached an all-time low.

"Keep the restraints on him."

The restraint was a plastic zip tie around Miller's wrists. A simple piece of equipment that was extremely difficult for the prisoner to remove, though one of Jeremy's tools would be able to cut through it like butter. He grabbed Miller's elbow and walked him to the elevator banks. The detective kept watching from the doorway to her squad room, until the elevator doors had closed.

"You know who I am?"

"Jeremy Adams, Meridian Defense."

"Good. If you behave, you'll get through this just fine."

"Yeah, right."

Jeremy looked at him. "All I want is to find out what ACE knows about the package."

"Like I know."

"We'll find out."

When they got in the limousine, Jeremy made a show of closing his briefcase. He saw Miller's eyes widen, his nostrils flare.

A smile, brief and small, crossed Jeremy's lips. The session had begun.

———

LEVEL 6—THURSDAY, AUGUST 11, 2140 9:50 P.M.

The limousine pulled away from the curb and merged with traffic.

"I believe you know Abby?" Jeremy asked.

"Abby? No, I don't think so." It was obvious Miller was trying to look anywhere except the briefcase, and he was failing.

Irritation flashed in Jeremy's eyes. "You killed her in the hospital."

"Oh, her, yeah."

"Yes, well, she was a personal friend of mine. I'm going to miss her dearly."

"So this isn't about the package then, is it?" asked Miller, his gaze moving to meet Jeremy's.

Jeremy sat and thought about it for a while. Miller was right. It wasn't about the package anymore. "No. The package has done its job. The information in it is now 'in the wild,' so to speak."

Miller remained silent for the rest of the drive while Jeremy watched him.

The driver turned off the main road and into a small, quiet community. Most of the houses were dark, their owners safely ensconced and unaware. The limo turned into a driveway and pulled into a large garage.

"A safe house," Jeremy said at Miller's look. "One of ours, of course. Yours have all been . . . compromised." He lifted a gun and pointed it at Miller before pulling a set of small manacles out from a drawer under the seat and throwing them at Miller. "Put these on. I don't want you trying to run." As Miller bent down and snapped them around his ankles, he said, "Nice and tight, like a good boy."

The car door opened and light flooded in from overhead.

"Take the rest of the night off, Thomas. Come back to pick me up at eight a.m."

"Yes, sir."

Thomas helped Miller from the car and, as Miller and Jeremy entered the house, drove off down the street.

"I'm surprised Quincy isn't here yet. We'll have to start without him." He pushed Miller backward, forcing him onto the kitchen table. "Lie down. If you try anything, I'll shoot. Oh, not for a kill. That would be too quick. But I guarantee you won't enjoy it."

He tied Miller's hands first, bending them uncomfortably over the corner of the table and zip-tying them to the leg. He went around and did the same with Miller's feet. When Miller lay tied down, stretched from corner to corner, Jeremy put the gun down on the kitchen counter. "I'll leave it here, just in case."

He reached down and picked up the briefcase, laying it beside the gun. "Now, where will we start? Oh, and you can scream all you like, the house is soundproofed. I've had the opportunity to use it once or twice. Long ago, of course, back when I was in my prime." Another fleeting smile.

He turned back to his briefcase and pulled out the first tool before turning back to face Miller. "Is there anything you want to say before we start?"

"Fuck you."

"You'll change your tune before too long." He raised the first tool above the level of the kitchen table. "First, I'll need to clear the work area."

He had a pair of scissors in his hand. The look of terror, and then relief, that flooded through Miller's eyes made him chuckle. He still had it; even after all these years, he still had it.

He started at Miller's feet, slowly cutting through the pants and underwear before starting on the shirt. When he was done, Miller lay naked on the table. A fine sheen of sweat covered his torso. Jeremy could see the fear was really beginning to set in. Good. He tugged at the corner of the bandage covering Miller's gunshot wound and slowly peeled it off. Clotted blood pulled away with the bandage and Miller's shoulder twitched. Jeremy turned and placed the scissors back into their sleeve and returned them to the briefcase.

"I don't want to ruin my suit. Excuse me while I change." Jeremy left the kitchen.

And where the hell was Quincy? He was spending too much time on the girl. Usually, Quincy's tactics were quick and abrupt. He wasn't one for delaying the inevitable. Jeremy had tried to teach him, but it never seemed to work. The enjoyment, the raw pleasure, was before the kill. Before the soul left the weakened and mutilated body. He gave a shiver of delight and moved into one of the bedrooms. The closet already contained surgical gowns and gloves.

LEVEL 6—THURSDAY, AUGUST 11, 2140 9:00 P.M.

When I finished talking to William, I walked back to Quincy's car and plugged the comm unit in. I sure as hell didn't want the power to die on it.

I figured the best place to wait for the call would be near the hospital I'd left Miller at, one level down. I figured Jeremy would keep him down there. There was no security between Levels 6 and 7, but why transport someone farther that you had to? As long as they weren't in one of the gated communities, I was fine.

I started the car and drove out of the shuttle port, heading for the nearest main road. Once there, I turned on Quincy's map system and found the closest downramp. Slipping down to Level 6 felt like going home. The ceiling over top of my head and the dimmed Ambients brought back the feeling of familiarity and comfort.

Now I sat near the hospital, on a small residential street that seemed darker than the rest. I found some paper in the glove box and crumpled it until it felt softer, using it to wipe some of the blood off my face. It came off in small, dry flakes.

Every minute that passed felt like an hour. I had bitten my fingernails down to the quick, and still tried to tear off more. It was a habit I had gotten rid of two years ago. I forced my hands into my lap. They were shaking. Moments later, I had to do it again. The pattern repeated over the next hour.

Miller's comm unit rang, breaking the silence. I jumped in my seat, my heart racing like a shuttle leaving orbit. I reached out and touched the screen.

"Yes?"

"We found him." William gave me the address and added, "We have an extraction team on the way. They should be there in about twenty minutes. Do *not* do anything until they arrive. Do I make myself clear?"

"Yes."

I punched the address in the map system. Christ, the house was only a few blocks from where I was parked. I'd been here for over an hour, and all this time I had been walking distance away. I started the car and drove to the street, turning off the lights as I neared the address. The house looked dark.

Suddenly, the garage door opened and a limousine pulled out. It was too dark to see, but my guess was the only person in it was the driver.

The only problem was it was just a guess.

What if they were moving Miller? What if Devon wasn't the snitch, or mole, whatever they called him? Or what if there was more than one? If Jeremy had been notified of the extraction team's activation, then Miller would be in the car, being moved to a new location. Fuck! I had to find out. Did I follow the car, or check out the house?

As the limo drove past, I slouched down in my seat, keeping my head below the level of the windows. The tape slipped, and the black box shifted, cutting into my shoulder blades. I waited long enough for the limo to pass, and sat up again. The car was gone. My mind was made up. Check the house, and if Miller was gone, let William know. I opened the door, for the first time noticing the interior light didn't come on, and shut it with a soft click behind me.

The front of the house still looked dark. I cut through a neighbor's yard to get a look at the back, praying I had made the right choice, that Miller was still inside.

I could see a sliver of light escaping from the bottom of a curtain. Maybe the kitchen. The light blinked for a second and came back. Movement, someone was in there. But was it Miller and Jeremy?

The fence between the yards was a short one, just over a meter high, and I scrambled over it with no problem, adrenaline pushing away any pain I might have felt. I crept to the lit window and put my back against the rough exterior of the house, breathing hard even though I hadn't exerted myself.

I turned to face the wall, keeping my head below the band of light, and slowly straightened my legs. When my eyes reached the gap of light, it took them a few moments to focus on what was inside.

Miller was strapped to the kitchen table, and Jeremy was cutting away the last piece of his shirt. The rest of Miller lay exposed on the table, already stripped. Jeremy dropped the shirt on the floor and turned around, walking straight toward me. I dropped to my knees, scraping my forehead against the stucco.

The scene inside was eerily similar to what Quincy had tried to do to me. When Jeremy's shadow left the window, I raised myself up again.

Jeremy was gone. Only Miller remained in the kitchen, struggling against the straps holding him to the table legs. His wrists and ankles had started to bleed, slowly being cut by the zip ties. I looked around the rest of the kitchen as best I could. A doorway led to what looked like a hallway, and I could see the back door leading to the yard. I assumed it was locked. As my eyes scanned the room, I looked at the briefcase sitting open on the counter just to my left. I stood on my tiptoes, trying see into it.

I snapped back with a sharp intake of breath, falling backward against the next house. A dog started barking somewhere close by. I scurried over to a dark spot between two bushes and lay as still as I could.

There was no movement from the house.

LEVEL 6—THURSDAY, AUGUST 11, 2140 10:21 P.M.

The case contained the tools of a madman. When Jeremy started using them on Miller . . .

I couldn't let this happen. No one deserved what the briefcase promised. Especially Miller. I knew I had to move. The extraction team would be here in about ten minutes. A lifetime spent on the kitchen table. Jeremy's shadow fell over the window again and disappeared.

Waiting just wasn't an option.

I stood up and ran to the back door before I had too much time to think about it, and pointed the gun I'd gotten from Frank at the lock. I pulled the trigger, blowing the door open into the kitchen. By the time I ran through,

Jeremy was standing over Miller, holding a scalpel to Miller's neck. He had stuffed the remnants of the shirt into Miller's mouth.

Jeremy seemed to take it in stride.

"Kris. You never fail to surprise me. Quincy is . . . ?"

"Dead. And you will be as well if you don't move away from him." I pointed the gun at Jeremy, the tip of its barrel vibrating in my grip.

"Move? My dear girl, if you shoot, how do know my hand won't twitch and your boyfriend will be as dead as you want me to be."

I took a step forward, still aiming the gun at Jeremy's head. He was right, I didn't know.

"I would stop, if I were you." The scalpel pressed into Miller's neck, and a drop of blood oozed out from under the blade.

"You don't have a chance, Jeremy. More people are on the way."

"Then we'd best make this quick, wouldn't you say? If you let me go, Miller here lives. You prolong this, and he dies."

I looked at Miller lying on the table. His eyes were closed and his breathing was slow and shallow. It looked like he was holding his head as still as he could. What was I supposed to do now?

"What do you want?"

"I want you to put the gun down. Lay it on the floor and kick it behind you." Jeremy raised his voice. "Do it now."

On the table Miller had opened his eyes.

"If I drop the gun, what's stopping you from killing him anyway?"

"You have my word."

"I had your word at the warehouse. Do you really believe I think it's any good?" The tip of the gun wavered a small amount, feeling heavy in my hands. What the hell was I supposed to do? It seemed a litany I had repeated too many times. If I just stood here until the extraction team came, Miller would be dead. If I gave up the gun, chances are we would both be dead. What would Miller do?

"Okay," I said. "I drop the gun, and you move the scalpel away from Miller at the same time, drop it on the floor and kick it away." Exactly what he had asked me to do. If he agreed and then tried to make a move, I was pretty sure I could take on an old man. I might be small, but over the last few days, I realized I was tougher than I'd even pretended to be.

"It's a deal." Jeremy made a show of moving the scalpel away from Miller and lowering it to the floor as I did the same with the gun. Both weapons touched the floor at the same time and were kicked backward. Jeremy's ended up in the hallway. I heard the gun hit the doorframe and stop.

I walked toward Miller as Jeremy backed away. I made the last step and pulled the shirt out of his mouth.

"HE HAS A GUN!"

Cold realization hit me like a brick. We were both dead. Jeremy leaped toward the counter and reached behind his briefcase, emerging with the gun in his hand.

The moment he moved, I ran, willing my legs to move faster than they ever had. I collided with Jeremy before he could bring the gun to bear on me. It fell out of his hand and clattered across the floor, bouncing off the cupboards and ending up under the kitchen table.

I pushed off of Jeremy, diving for the weapon. Before I could reach it, a hand grabbed my ankle and pulled me back to the cabinets. I kicked my legs, breaking the surprisingly strong hold.

My foot made contact and Jeremy grunted. My hand

was close to the gun. I lunged forward. My fingers wrapped around the barrel.

My breath exploded from me and pain lanced through my lower back. Jeremy had jumped on me, driving his knees into my kidneys. The gun slipped from my fingers.

Jeremy scrambled on top of me and reached for the gun. I twisted around, driving him into the leg of the table. The leg snapped and the table collapsed. The gun slid from the impact, disappearing under the fridge.

Jeremy continued his roll, moving out from under the weight of the table with Miller still tied to it. He made a move for the fridge, changed his mind, and ran to the scalpel in the hallway.

I moved to the high end of the table, where Miller's head lay. I knew where Jeremy was going. I had to get to my gun first.

I stood and ran the few steps to the busted door.

"Nooooo." Miller's voice. I didn't have time to turn and see what was going on. One more step and I would have the gun.

I felt a pressure on my back, just below my shoulder blades. The pressure turned to heat, suddenly warm, and then hot and burning. The pain punched through my back to my chest as I ducked and retrieved the gun, spinning on one foot to face Jeremy and Miller again.

Jeremy no longer had the scalpel, instead he was running toward me. I pulled the trigger and the wall over Jeremy's shoulder exploded.

My world slowed to a crawl as Jeremy took another step closer. How the hell did I miss at this range? Another shot rang out from behind me, and a small red spot appeared on Jeremy's shoulder.

I spun again, facing the new gunman. He twisted the pistol from my grip and ran into the room, followed by four others. Three of them scanned the house, and I heard shouts of "clear" with every room they passed through. One pulled me out of the house to a black van with no lights sitting in the back lane. The others stayed behind, and I saw one of them approaching Miller with a knife in his hand before my view was cut off.

I screamed and struggled, kicking the man who held my arm, the shock of the last few seconds wearing off. They were after Miller.

"Hey, quit that. We're from ACE, we've got to get you and Miller out of here."

I stopped struggling as Miller ran out of the house toward us, a surgical gown wrapped around his waist. He was followed by one of the men.

I was pushed into the back of the van, followed almost immediately by Miller. One of them jumped in and slammed the door shut. The other got into the front seat.

"Move!"

The van took off like a rocket, its electrics almost squealing with the sudden input of power. We whipped out of the back lane and onto a quiet street, slowing down to legal speeds. The exterior lights came on, followed by reddish dim interior ones.

"Call Ops, tell them the mission was successful and we left two behind for cleanup." He turned and looked at me. "You got very lucky."

I just stared at him.

"Turn around."

"Why?"

"Do as he says Kris, they're on our side, remember?" Miller said.

I turned and the searing pain burned between my shoulder blades again. I turned back. The man held a scalpel in his hand; the tip and part of the shaft had blackened.

"You're a lucky girl. The black box stopped this from

severing your spine. A few centimeters lower or higher, and you might not have been here."

The black box. I had gotten so used to wearing it I forgot it was even there. "Can . . . can they track me now?"

"Nah, the van's shielded. You're okay in here."

"Do you have another one we can put on her?" asked Miller.

"Nope. Even if we did, I couldn't do it. The old one is melted into her back, and I don't want to move it."

I suddenly felt lightheaded. The pain in my back tripled now that I knew its source. I could almost feel the plastic drip down and burn more flesh.

"Doc Searls is the closest, if we can get him back," Miller said.

"He's already waiting for us."

Miller leaned into me, concern in his eyes, and rested his forehead against mine. "We'll be fine. Just a couple more minutes, okay?"

I nodded. I barely felt the needle slide into my arm.

nineteen

LEVEL 2—THURSDAY, AUGUST 25, 2140 6:00 P.M.

I KNELT DOWN AND unlocked my motorcycle. My
back still gave a twinge, even two weeks after the
doctor had operated on it. I would have a scar there for
the rest of my life. A reminder of what had happened,
and how my life had changed.

There was talk of plastic surgery and skin recoloring
to hide it, but I had pretty much thrown that idea out the
window. What was the point? I was who I was, and there
was no use in hiding it. My face had healed though, as
had the graze on my neck.

So they created new records for me. An unfortunate
accident when I was a kid. It would help me get past
Level 6 security when I needed to.

While I was in there, they modified my tracker, so now I could pretty much turn it on and off at will. They also changed the embedded ID. I kept my first name, but the last one was changed. I wasn't sure if I would get used to it, Kris Merrill.

The doctor had given me a clean bill of health, and after two weeks in a safe house, it was good to get out. I'd gone straight for my bike, with ACE's permission, of course. I was on probation, and everything needed permission. Tomorrow, I would be on my first shuttle flight. No place fancy, still on Earth and all, though they had promised me a trip up to the Sat Cities as part of my training.

Something was going on up there, though. The news vids were all over the recent takeover of Meridian by Kadokawa. There was no visible proof, but rumors were that the takeover was very hostile, and several people had lost their lives. Maybe the Sat Cities could wait.

I decided to keep to my agreement, and was going off to ACE's training facilities. Miller had called it boot camp and grinned his lopsided grin. He wouldn't tell me any more. I had a sinking feeling it wasn't going to be fun.

The bike had collected a couple weeks' worth of dust and Level 2 grime. I reached into my backpack and pulled out a cloth and some bottled water. Maybe a quick wipe-down before I got on, just for appearance's sake. I would have to give it a good wash before I went to the shuttle port, just to make it easier to get past the Level 6 security. When I was done, I pulled Oscar from my pocket, gave him a quick rub with my thumb, and put the key in the starter switch.

The sound of another motorcycle, gas powered, pulling up on the street beside me made me turn around. He had a helmet on his head, and a new one over his arm. It looked a lot like my old one, the one I had dropped in the elevator shaft a lifetime ago.

Miller took off his helmet and smiled. "Hey, good looking."

I smiled back. "Hi!"

He got off the bike and gave me a quick kiss on the cheek. "I got you this." He handed the new lid over to me. "Happy birthday."

Birthday. I had completely forgotten about it. Strange how seventeen felt just like sixteen, yet completely different from a few weeks ago.

"Thanks . . . Ian."

His eyes lit up and he smiled. A huge smile. "I like that."

"Yeah, me too. So what does it take for a girl to get a real birthday kiss?"

He laughed. "Another year?"

"If you think I'm waiting that long, you're crazier than I thought." I reached out and grabbed the front of his jacket, pulling him toward me. He didn't resist.

His lips were soft and warm, and he tasted like a bowl of warm, melted chocolate. I sank into the kiss, losing myself in the moment. His arms wrapped around my waist, pulling me into him. I never wanted the moment to end.

We slowly pulled away from each other.

"Not too bad, for an old guy," I said, getting my breath back.

"Hey, who are you calling old?"

I just laughed and pulled the helmet over my head. "Come on, I know a great place for Chinese food. The owner will be mad, though. He wanted me to marry his grandson."

"I can take him."

I laughed again. "The grandpa or the grandson?"

Miller shook his head and smiled the smile that touched his eyes. "Lead the way."

Now available in hardcover,
the thrilling sequel to *The Courier*,

THE OPERATIVE

Read on for a special preview.

WATCHED AS MILLER fell asleep, his features soft-
ening as the tension fell away. He'd always been
able to fall asleep quickly. It was a skill I'd never had. I
sat in my seat, listening to the general chatter from the
people behind me riding just under the buzz of the
thrusters. The medics and soldiers in front of me sat silent. Occasionally one of them would shift in their seat
or mumble a soft word to the people they were sitting
next to, but for the most part they stayed alert and quiet.

Pat sat curled in her seat, a thin blanket pulled over
her head. Every time the blanket twitched I stole a quick
glance, hoping she was coming out of it.

After a while, I ended up staring out the window on

the other side of Miller, not truly relaxed, but not as tense as I had been. The transport stayed low, following the contours of the land, keeping out of sight from the Canadians. We flew over tiny lakes of the purest blue and between mountain peaks that reached above the view from my window. Eventually the mountains gave way to foothills and the wilderness to farms. At one time, every square inch of fertile soil had been covered with cultivated land. Now, barren patches infiltrated around the edges. Of those left, the ones closest to the rivers and lakes were greener, more lush. The farther from the water, the more the land was wrapped in irrigation pipes. Some of the pipes terminated at the closest water source. Others, larger ones, ran to the Pacific Ocean's desalinization plants.

There were places like this all over the world. Greedy corporations had stripped the planet of most of its trees and natural coverings, and water had become scarcer. Once-fertile land became arid and dry. Places that used to generate more food than we knew what to do with now struggled to keep up with demand, sometimes trying to get three crops a year where there used to be only one.

By the time we reached the ocean, the view had given way to high-rise towers and fibercrete. It all fell away and water sparkled below us as far as I could see.

I turned to look out Pat's window. The coastline we passed alternated between massive desalinization plants and shanty towns that pushed themselves farther and farther into the water. We were racing too fast for me to make out any details, but from what I could see, it was as though someone had ripped the roof off of Level 1 and exposed all the filth and grime and poverty to the open sky.

A flat gray wall sprang up from the ground, and my view disappeared.

We were flying lower now, almost skimming the surface of the water. The grungy gray wall of the city reached into the sky, out of my line of sight. It passed by the window in a blur. That meant we'd reached San Francisco at least, where the city started. I knew from my classes that the wall wasn't as smooth as it looked. The years had taken their toll. The wall was laced with cracks and missing pieces caused by weather, age, and the earthquakes that occasionally shook everything. There were special teams of repair crews that went out and worked on the wall almost daily. SoCal couldn't— wouldn't—let the average citizen see the outside world. If the low level workers knew the outside was attainable, they wouldn't do the menial work required to keep San Angeles running. It was what had worked for generations.

When I was young, I think I was seven or eight, Mom and Dad took me to see the wall. Back then I didn't even think of it as the inside; it was just the wall. The fact that there was an outside was something I never really thought about until I'd stood on Level 7.

My parents and I had gone to watch them replace a section damaged by an earthquake. Repair crews had built a temporary structure to support the levels above, and knocked out a piece of the wall. Dad had talked about the new materials, the flexibility of the wall so it could stand up to some shaking. Mom talked about the sun, the water, how everything we knew needed both to survive. Including us. I was too young to understand.

The memory had stuck in my head. I don't know if it was because of the huge expanse of water I saw through the man-made hole, or the number of corporate soldiers standing there, each one with their back to the wall, their weapon ready, keeping the tourists—us—away.

It was one of the few outings we'd done as a family.

Maybe I remembered it because of that, because I had felt wondrously safe and happy. It bothered me that the thought had come second, after the soldiers with their guns.

The sound of the thrusters changed, pulling me back. The transport rose and more of the wall came into view, reaching almost two hundred meters high. Seven levels of city. Faded white letters flashed by, painted six meters high on the wall. *San Padres*.

Part of ACE training was remembering the world the way it used to be . . . before the corporations took over. San Padres used to be what they called a national forest. Families camped and hiked under the canopy of trees, the green-speckled light warm on their skin. All that was left of it now was faded white letters painted on an immense wall of fibercrete. Fibercrete. Another word I'm sure I learned at school, and relearned at ACE. It's what had started the cities moving up and out, until the multi-leveled structure almost covered the entire west coast of the continental United States, and the individual cities became wards instead of separate entities. Even the forests disappeared, replaced by cheap housing, city supporting infrastructure, and corporate run factories.

They had built the first three levels quickly, starting in the city cores of San Francisco, San Jose, and Los Angeles. Building until nothing was left. Level 2 was flat, hiding the irregularities of the ground, taking away anything that made a place unique. In downtown Los Angeles, they chopped off anything over five stories tall to create Level 2. In San Francisco, the buildings were taller, but had received the same humiliation.

Everyone who could afford it moved up, following the sun, until even that was denied to them. Now only the elite could live on Level 7, the ceiling of the entire structure. Up there, the grass still grew, manmade lakes held water. And the shit settled on the lower levels. Over four generations had lived since the walls went up, never knowing how the sun felt on their skin.

Eventually Level 1 became a "hive of scum and villainy," as one of the old vids we watched described a fictional city on a fictional world. Only here it wasn't fiction. It was true. Most of Level 1 became a refuge for those who didn't fit, or want to fit, in with society. Drug dealers, murderers. Rapists.

Those who lived there still needed money, and strangely enough still wanted a roof over their heads. More than what the Level's ceiling provided. So the corporations had built sewage and water treatment plants, taking up a lot of Level 1 real estate to keep those on the higher Levels happy.

That had been my world from when I was thirteen, when my parents were killed, until I was sixteen, when I managed to scramble my way out of the dirt. I became a courier, riding my motorcycle between Level 2 and Level 5, delivering whatever was given to me.

Ian had a small place on Level 5, right at the cutoff of the third build. When they'd built the last two Levels, they'd segregated the population. No one was allowed into Level 6 without permission. It took a lot to get that.

I'd been up there, watching a real sunset for the first time, the open air making me feel exposed and small. Back then, the black box taped to my back had given me access, blocking my ID tag from transmitting its location. The box had also given me my scar.

Now I was part of ACE, and I had access without the box. The tracker ID's were a SoCal invention. A way for the corporations to track the population without their knowledge. A way to keep us in our place.

That first sunset felt like a lifetime ago, but was less than a year. A year spent under the open sky in the

Canadian mountains, but that first sunset still sends a thrill through me when I think about it.

More faded letters flashed past the window. All I caught was *Barbara*. We were really moving.

The transport suddenly wallowed, nosing closer to the water before righting itself again. The pitch of the thrusters changed. The soldiers, most of whom had been sleeping, jumped to their feet and started gathering their gear. Beside me, Ian had woken up. He reached across my body, grabbed the seatbelt, and buckled me in, cinching the belt snug. I turned to face him, my stomach tightening into a knot.

Ian's head blocked the window as he stared out across the Pacific Ocean. I looked out the wedge of window behind the seats in front of us. All I could make out was the gray water and the waves, closer now, rolling over each other in a rush to make it to shore. Ian jerked his head back, and I caught a quick glimpse of a smoke trail. I couldn't tell which way it was heading, but I was smart enough to hazard a guess.

The smoke trail got closer, disappearing under the window out of my view. The transport shook like a dog getting out of water. There were no explosions or smoke or fire. The knot in my gut loosened. A dud. Someone was firing at us, and it seemed like they couldn't afford real equipment. I noticed that Ian hadn't relaxed yet. Instead he was reaching for his own seatbelt and muttering under his breath.

The lights went out and the world went quiet.

I lost all feeling of forward motion. My stomach reached up, nestling at the bottom of my throat. We were plummeting. People started screaming. Over the noise I heard orders being barked to the soldiers. The transport twisted, leaning to the left. Ian fell against me still struggling to get his seatbelt on. I stared out the windows behind him. The ocean tilted at a dangerous angle.

This thing wasn't even close to being a glider. I figured the only thing keeping us in the air was our forward momentum, and without thrusters we were losing that. The sliver of window I had looked out before darkened, turning a dull matte gray. The wall. And we were heading straight for it.

The gray was replaced with white, and the transport pulled nose up. We hit the top of a sandy cliff, bouncing back into the sky. I felt my stomach dig its claws into my throat before everything went really wrong. The seats in front of us tore from their moorings, launching upward. I grabbed onto Ian's arm, but it wasn't there anymore. He floated above his seat, his head near the ceiling.

He was smiling at me.

The side of the transport disappeared in a rush of screaming air and fibercrete, leaving sharp chunks of composite pointing into the cabin. A hungry mouth with jagged teeth. I screamed and grabbed for Ian again, hoping to pull him back down. His seat was gone. So was he.

I didn't have time to think, to scream, to cry. The transport slammed to a stop and my head cracked against the seat in front of me.

Margaret Fortune

—NOVA—

978-0-7564-1081-0

And don't miss the thrilling sequel

ARCHANGEL

coming in 2017

To Order Call: 1-800-788-6262
www.dawbooks.com

DAW 216

Julie E. Czerneda
Species Imperative

"This novel bears the hallmarks of Czerneda's earlier books: strong, complex, and appealing characters and a thoughtful, intricate plot. Czerneda creates an original and terrific alien species...and the plot is packed with vivid images and events. Czerneda is a masterful storyteller and one of the best of the recent voices in science fiction."   —*Voya*

SURVIVAL
MIGRATION
REGENERATION

The entire trilogy, now available in a single volume for the first time!

ISBN: 978-0-7564-1014-8

"A creative voice and a distinctive vision."
—*C. J. Cherryh*

To Order Call: 1-800-788-6262
www.dawbooks.com

Jacey Bedford
The Psi-Tech Novels

"Space opera isn't dead; instead, delightfully, it has grown up."　　—Jaine Fenn,
author of *Principles of Angels*

"A well-defined and intriguing tale set in the not-too-distant future.... Everything is undeniably creative and colorful, from the technology to foreign planets to the human (and humanoid) characters."
—*RT Book Reviews*

"Bedford mixes romance and intrigue in this promising debut.... Readers who crave high adventure and tense plots will enjoy this voyage into the future."
—*Publishers Weekly*

Empire of Dust
978-0-7564-1016-2

Crossways
978-0-7564-1017-9

To Order Call: 1-800-788-6262
www.dawbooks.com

Tanya Huff

The *Confederation* Novels

"As a heroine, Kerr shines. She is cut from the same mold
as Ellen Ripley of the Aliens films. Like her heroine,
Huff delivers the goods." —*SF Weekly*

A CONFEDERATION OF VALOR
Omnibus Edition
(*Valor's Choice, The Better Part of Valor*)
978-0-7564-1041-4

THE HEART OF VALOR
978-0-7564-0481-9

VALOR'S TRIAL
978-0-7564-0557-1

THE TRUTH OF VALOR
978-0-7564-0684-4

To Order Call: 1-800-788-6262
www.dawbooks.com